Love

Blooms in Providence

By
Jaycee Anderson

PublishAmerica
Baltimore

First printing

ISBN: 1-4241-0848-9
PUBLISHED BY PUBLISHAMERICA, LLLP
www.publishamerica.com
Baltimore

Printed in the United States of America

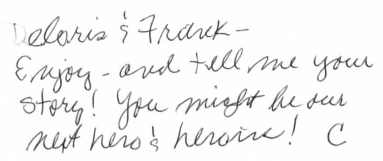

Deloris & Frank –
Enjoy – and tell me your
story! You might be our
next hero & heroine! C

Dedication

For my husband, David, who has been my most staunch supporter, pushing me to keep writing when I was ready to give up, and encouraging me when the going got tough.
Jody Blosser

and

For Faye Bowen, who has been my devoted fan since I first put words to paper many years ago. Carole Dickey

Love makes the world go round!
Welcome to the world of Providence.
Enjoy!
Carole Dickey ♡ Jody Blosser

Acknowledgments

We'd like to offer a special thanks to Charles J. Ochipa, co-editor of the book *An Introduction to Orchids: A Guide to the Growing and Breeding of Orchids,* published by The South Florida Orchid Society, for all the wonderful knowledge on orchids he shared with us for use in our story. We'd also like to thank Sarah Starr of Starr Editing (starrediting@hotmail.com) for her comprehensive editing. Thank you, Sarah for cleaning up our act!

CHAPTER ONE

"This—is—the—worst—day—of—my—life," Jenna Kincaid muttered between clenched teeth.

She was lying on the ground, limbs tangled with a man she'd never seen before while an insanely cheerful dog the size of a freight train was lapping her face with a wet tongue. The man's five o'clock shadow was waging a winning war with the tender skin of her face, while his hard body pressing against her awakened feelings she'd thought extinct. Her tee shirt had crawled halfway to her neck, her hair was full of twigs, her elbows caked in dirt, and her face fogged with doggie breath powerful enough to suffocate a dinosaur. She wouldn't be surprised to learn the black devil dog that had leaped joyfully into the tangle of arms and legs *was* part dinosaur.

Jake Corbin shoved at the dog, but kept his gaze fastened on the woman's tanned face just inches below his own, taking in the flashing sparks in her emerald green eyes, a tumble of auburn curls framing high cheekbones, a stubborn chin, and a neck so long and smooth it begged to be kissed.

"Get off, Buster!" As Jake twisted around to get a better grasp on Buster, the woman's soft curves beneath him awakened a hot response in his own body.

His voice was deep, Jenna noticed, with a velvet edge, a slight drawl reminiscent of Charlestonians. Jenna thought she detected amusement as well, in both his voice and his electric blue eyes fastened on her face with frank appraisal. Paul Newman eyes. Eyes that could sizzle a woman's skin, melt her bones. Eyes she wanted about 100 miles away from her. *Right now.*

The dog ignored the man's command, and burrowed himself further into the tangle, bestowing on his master and Jenna a bucketful of slurpy kisses.

"Get your dog off me!" Jenna sputtered, carefully timing each word so she wouldn't have her mouth open when Buster lapped her face. "I'm going to cut out that tongue and send it to Texas for drought relief."

The man's chuckle was low and throaty and, to Jenna's surprise, brought a smile to her own face, which quickly disappeared as a dog paw plowed through her hair.

The man, having finally managed to untangle himself, gripped the dog by the collar and wrestled him off Jenna. Inches from her eyes, his biceps flexed with the effort. His cotton shirt, pulled taut as he struggled with his Cerberean playmate, hinted at broad shoulders and tantalizing pecs before he spun away from Jenna to struggle with the dog.

The afternoon had started so well, too, Jenna thought, swiping at angry tears as she sat up, catching her breath and gingerly moving her arms and legs, making sure they were all in one piece and still working before she tried to rise. She'd been working with her orchids in the greenhouse, paying special attention to three of the plants she planned to enter in the orchid show. Her favorite, a *Cattleya* hybrid, was shaping up so beautifully Jenna just knew in her heart it would win a first class certificate. By the time the show began in three weeks all those tiny new buds would be in bloom, and the large number of buds in and of themselves made the plant a showpiece. If the blooms were as exceptional as the buds, the certificate was a foregone conclusion.

She hoped.

Yes, the afternoon had started so well. She had walked out of the greenhouse, all smiles, her thoughts on the upcoming show and the hoped-for certificate that would guarantee her fledgling orchid business a giant boost, when she'd seen it.

The trash. The holes. The dog!

The dog had been plaguing her property for a week. He always managed to time his visits when everyone was busy in the house, leaving a calling card that was hard to miss—trash scattered over the yard and a hole or two by the bushes. This was his third visit. The first two times, Jenna had caught fleeting glimpses of him running past her office window after he'd finished his destruction. But today she had caught him in the act and was determined to put a stop to his destructive behavior. Payback time. She'd grabbed a rake and gone after the creature, venting her fury in unladylike shouts.

The dog had given her a reproachful look, as though she had broken a major rule in a Little League game, then playfully avoided her lunges by romping beneath a table holding several pots of young orchid plants. The table had lifted, tilted, and twenty small pots had gone sliding to the ground, some smashing, some spilling out their contents. Then the Neanderthal's exuberantly wagging tail had wiped out the few survivors.

Those were plants Jenna had planned to use in her orchid exhibit, background display for her orchid entries. Thank goodness her orchid entries themselves were still in the greenhouse, along with the vast majority of her orchid plants.

But the monster from hell hadn't been through. He'd barely started. As Jenna raged after him with the rake, he had bounded into her hanging plants. Jumping around with superabundant energy, he'd caused the pots to swing haphazardly against each other, reminding her that all of her orchid entries *hadn't* been in the greenhouse after all. In horror, she'd watched her large *Phalaenopsis* which had been hanging from a low tree branch crash down to mix with the rest of the broken pottery.

With fury burning in her breast, Jenna had turned cunning. "Nice hairy Big Foot," she had crooned, taking a step toward him. "Nice demon from Pet Sematary," she had murmured softly, taking another step.

The dog had stood his ground and watched her approach, his mouth stretched in what looked like a grin, his body shivering with gleeful anticipation, his wagging tail sounding a drumbeat against an overturned garbage can.

"I'm going to wrap that stupid tail around your stupid neck," she'd cooed. Another step. "I'm going to cage you up and send you to animal research," she'd whispered seductively. Another step.

When she reached him, she would strangle him with her bare hands.

A man's voice yelling "Buster!" had brought her up short. Turning toward the woods that stretched behind her border of six-foot hibiscus bushes, Jenna had sought the voice's owner, but a sudden wild barking jerked her attention back to the dog. She saw him barreling in her direction with all the enthusiasm of a wide receiver running the ball toward the goal line. With a strangled yelp she had tried to leap out of the path of the furry cannonball, slamming instead with full force into a man emerging from behind the red hibiscus. Her startled shriek had mingled with oaths and excited barks as man, woman and dog went down in a tangle of arms, legs and lethal tail.

"The worst day of my life," she repeated now, eyeing the stranger who seemed to be using brute strength to win the struggle between man and beast. He still had his back to her and was bent at the waist, forcing the dog to sit. *Nice butt* registered on a subconscious level as Jenna brushed pebbles from a scraped knee.

The man turned to her, his eyes raking over her. He looked concerned. He looked amused. He looked interested. She hastily jerked her tee shirt into place.

"Are you okay?" he asked, taking her hand and pulling her to her feet. His eyes traveled from her head to her toes and back again.

Jenna felt her skin tingle under the lengthy inspection. He wasn't just assuring himself that she wasn't hurt. The impertinent louse was ogling her. This was no "are you okay" look. He was looking at her like a man looks at a woman. A look she felt in the pit of her stomach, a look that reached inside her and whooshed her breath away.

Angry and more than a little flustered at feelings she didn't even want to acknowledge, she concentrated on brushing the dirt and leaves from her body and carefully plucking a caterpillar from her shoulder. (Monarch, she noted automatically, placing it on a nearby leaf.)

Well, if there was one thing she'd learned from her five-year, destructive marriage to Ned, it was to never let a man think he had the upper hand. So with a deliberate, insolent look belying her fluttery stomach and quickened pulse, she gave him back stare for stare. Her narrowed eyes traveled slowly from his head with its thick mane of brown locks needing a trim down his heaving chest, over the embattled casual slacks and shoes whose polish was now hopelessly scuffed, then slowly back up again to stop when her eyes met his. Then she quickly lowered her lashes, afraid he might read in her eyes the grudging admiration her brief scrutiny had elicited.

His eyes were an arresting shade of blue. Deep, deep blue. Magnetic. Amused. It was the amusement that fueled her irritation.

"I'm all right," she said, turning from him to survey the damage his pet had wrought. "But—" She waved her hand angrily to indicate the wreckage. Broken pottery, smashed orchids, trash scattered hither and yon, two new holes.

Jake reluctantly tore his gaze from her trim figure and flushed face to look around. "Buster did all that?" He sounded contrite but not surprised.

"For the third time this week," she said, her clipped tones heavy with accusation. "The other times he just upset the trash and dug holes, but this time—" She stopped, swallowed back an angry sob, collected herself, and went on. "This time he got my orchids. I wheeled them out for some sun and air. They have to have that exposure, you see, to—to live," she finished bleakly.

She turned quickly away from any inadequate apology he could offer and walked over to the broken pots and plants that were piled on the ground beside the table. Kneeling, she carefully brushed the broken pieces away from the purple *Phalaenopsis* that had somehow survived the canine onslaught. There were one or two others that might still make it, she figured, but as for all the rest—

She sighed and gently picked up the purple orchid, discovering damage on its large lip. "Sorry, sweetheart," she murmured softly. "I'm afraid that sexy orchid lip isn't going to attract any bees now."

As though understanding her words, the blossom hung for a moment, then softly, silently, gave up the ghost and plopped to the ground. With a small cry Jenna scooped up the flower and cradled it in her palm, then raised it to her nose and sniffed the sweet fragrance.

"You were one of my favorites," she whispered. She'd had high hopes for the flower. Its vibrant, unusual shade of lavender, the large size and perfect shape, the proud posture, all had promised that the orchid would be a serious contender in the orchid show. The plant's genealogy stretched back eight generations, all carefully entered in her computer records that contained the description, natural habitat, and genealogical history of all seventy species of orchids she owned.

If this orchid had earned the top rating, a first class certificate, it would have brought $5,000, maybe more, at the orchid show, depending on how avid the buyers were. Buyers paid good prices for top-rated orchids because they used them to cultivate thousands, millions, of seeds, which they then sold to the orchid market worldwide.

"You would have had some beautiful offspring," Jenna said, carefully laying the orchid back among its ruined siblings. Maybe she could salvage some of the pollen, use it to cultivate another plant worthy of competition in some future show.

Damn it, she was counting on the upcoming orchid show. She needed a winner. She needed the money and she needed the recognition to build her orchid business. For the last several years cultivating orchids had been little more than a hobby, but with her divorce behind her and a child to raise, she was determined to turn her hobby into a viable enterprise.

And now—now—to see the ground strewn with broken orchid parts, like a bad omen of things to come, she felt despair poking at her dreams. Now she knew what Gaul must have looked like after Caesar's troops swept over it. All because of that mangy, lop-eared, sorry excuse for a member of the canine persuasion.

She turned to glare at the object of her fury and found herself instead nose to nose with his master. He was crouched beside her, sympathetically surveying the destruction. She was so startled she nearly toppled into the pile of broken pots. The man caught her arm in a firm grip and rose effortlessly to his feet, pulling her with him.

"I'm sorry about all this," he said, concern troubling those blue eyes that still gleamed with interest. "By the way, I'm Corbin. Jake Corbin."

Bond. James Bond, she thought. Sean Connery's sex appeal. Roger Moore's good looks, except a little more rugged with that small scar along his lower jaw. Pierce Brosnan's charm. Definitely James Bond. A man who could slip past a woman's defenses in a heartbeat, if she dropped her guard.

"Your neighbor," he said, tilting his head to indicate a direction beyond the hibiscus border.

So this is my neighbor, she realized, the one in the white ranch-style house about a quarter mile up the road, the one with the weedy yard she drove past on her way to town. She'd never seen him outside, but she'd been so busy in the six months since she'd moved here, transferring plants from her mom's house in Ohio to this one, and had been so immersed in getting her orchid nursery going, that she hadn't had time for socializing or even thinking about being neighborly.

She tried now to think of something neighborly to say, but nothing seemed appropriate in view of the destruction scattered about her yard. As she struggled for something, anything to say, her eyes met his.

They were the bluest eyes she had ever seen. And they were piercing her with a gleam she would have to be in a coma not to recognize as desire. Her body was telling her that she was definitely not in a coma. His hand still holding her elbow had a lot to do with her uncharacteristic tongue-tied confusion.

After waiting a moment for her response and realizing he wasn't going to get one, Jake continued, "I'm sorry about not stopping by sooner to welcome you to the neighborhood." He smiled, white teeth flashing in a tanned face. "If I'd had any idea how beautiful my new neighbor is, I'm sure I would have been over long before this to borrow a cup of sugar."

Jenna knew her clothes were muddy, her fingernails grimy, her knee scraped. She knew without touching her hair, though she had an almost uncontrollable urge to reach up and smooth it, that it was straggling in disheveled clumps. And she could feel dirt caked on her cheek. Apparently, her neighbor's intense blue eyes were not very observant, or else his mouth housed a silvery tongue. She suspected the latter, since it was doubtful those eyes missed anything.

"Sugar is no problem," she said, choosing to ignore the flirtation. "But this…" and she waved her arm around the destruction, "…is unacceptable." She was relieved that she managed a stern tone of voice, since the hand holding her elbow—still holding her elbow—was sending hot tingles up and down her arm.

He winced. "Look, I'm really sorry about all this." He waved his free hand, taking in the flowers, the trash, "Miss—er—"

"Jenna Kincaid," she supplied grudgingly.

"Well, Jenna," he said slowly, as though he were testing the sound of her name, "I'll clean up the mess and of course pay for any damage. But I think you should know, it couldn't have been Buster that messed up your yard those other times you mentioned. I keep him fenced in."

"Like you kept him fenced in today? How can you stand there and say that? Do you think you're talking to an idiot?" She wasn't normally so sarcastic; in fact, she prided herself on her self-control, but today's events would have had the angel Gabriel whacking old ladies with his horn. She pulled her arm away, instantly feeling a chill replace the warmth where his hand had rested.

"Today was an anomaly," he said, a frown furrowing his forehead in a way that only added to his masculine appeal. "He must have slipped out of the yard this morning before I locked the gate. But I do know he was fenced in all the other days, because he was in the yard every night when I came home."

"Oh, sure. And that black behemoth I saw galloping away from my yard was just my imagination, I suppose!"

He studied her for a second, as though wondering if it actually had been her imagination. As though wondering what other things she might imagine. Jenna clenched her fists so she wouldn't wrap them around his neck and squeeze that speculative expression off his face.

He finally spoke, the corners of his mouth twitching. "I can't imagine what you imagined," he said softly. "I doubt that it was a behemoth. And I know it wasn't Buster." He glanced around curiously. "Perhaps you have something in your yard that attracts all the neighborhood dogs." He quirked an eyebrow at her.

Jenna hated people who quirked eyebrows. She'd never mastered the art.

"And you know," he continued in a reasonable, almost patronizing tone, "raccoons are pretty bad about this kind of thing."

"Ha! Maybe I'm new to Florida, but I know darn well you don't grow 'coons big enough to swallow a turkey whole. Palmetto roaches, yes. 'Coons, no. It was Buster, buster!"

In her agitation she was stabbing him in the chest with a grimy index finger, furious that he could have the audacity to try and talk his way out of such an obviously guilty situation. Silver tongue, she reminded herself. "It would be pretty darn hard to mistake any other dog for that devil's disciple."

His shirt must have popped a couple of buttons during their foray on the ground for now it gaped open, exposing dark curling hair crawling toward his stomach. Embarrassed that she found the sight so intriguing, Jenna jerked her finger back and looked quickly away, but not before she saw a gleam darken Jake's eyes.

She had an enchanting habit, Jake noticed, of shoving her lower lip out slightly when she was angry. He felt a nearly irresistible urge to nibble it, despite her presumptuous accusations.

"Where is that walking time bomb, anyway?" Jenna asked in sudden panic, glancing quickly around her yard. Knocking over oak trees? Chewing the foundation out from under the house? Terrorizing widows and orphans?

"I tied him up with my belt," Jake said.

Her eyes slid to his waistline, where pants clung tenuously to slim hips. She felt, with alarm, a response arc through her body. A sharp yearning that caught her totally off guard, took her breath away. She hadn't felt desire—for that was the only word for it—for a man since the early days of her marriage to Ned. Before his true, cruel nature showed itself. That disastrous period in her life had taught her a valuable lesson. She was obviously not a good judge of men, and fear of making another horrible mistake had kept her gun shy ever since their divorce a year ago.

She quickly forced her eyes from the sight of Jake's taut body, angry with herself and a little mystified that she was so vulnerable to this man's blatant sexuality.

"Wears it like a sword," she muttered, turning away.

"Beg pardon?" Jake said.

"Just get your dog out of my yard and keep him out." Her tone sounded sharp, even to her own ears. The sharpness it always took on when she was frightened. But of course she wasn't frightened, not of this man or his dog. *Not of the man, not of his dog. Of myself. Of the attraction that makes me vulnerable.*

Jake stared at her back for a second, at the unyielding set of her slender shoulders. Then, with a physical and mental shrug, he strode purposely over to the scattered garbage and started scooping it up and tossing it back in the can.

Jenna grabbed the rake and applied herself to the task.

"Don't feel obligated to help," he protested stiffly. "I said I'd do it."

She ignored him and kept raking, the steady dig and pull of the rake a yard task she happened to enjoy. The earthy smell of fresh-turned soil and the warm sun on her back gradually soothed her ruffled feathers.

Jenna was not one to hold a grudge and besides she possessed an ability—one she frequently considered a handicap—to see both sides of an argument. Jake apparently hadn't realized his dog had been causing problems, so she couldn't really blame him. And if she hadn't tried to attack the dog with a rake, he probably never would have tipped over the table. So in a way, the destruction was partly her fault. And while the orchids would be a loss, she still had her major inventory in the greenhouses.

She sighed, glancing around. Maybe she could salvage something from the orchid blossoms. She hated throwing so much work away.

Jake stole covert glances at Jenna as he worked, admiring her lithe body. Her movements were graceful even while wielding a rake. Her mass of red hair, tangled with leaves and twigs into an untidy halo about her head, caught the sun and sparkled like copper. The splotches of dirt on her face did nothing to conceal a delicate bone structure under smooth tanned skin. When she bent to her task, working the rake with quick sure strokes and no wasted movements, her shorts rode up slightly in the back, barely covering her firm little butt and exposing a long smear of dirt that traveled up her thigh to end somewhere under the blue denim material.

What would it feel like to put his hand on that smear of dirt and follow its path?

He forced his attention back to the overripe tomato he'd just picked up. Buster, you worthless mongrel, he thought indulgently, look what you've done. Look what you've got me into. He smiled ruefully, remembering the anxiety he'd felt when he'd arrived home and there was no Buster waiting inside the gate to leap all over him, to greet him with sloppy kisses and muddy paws. It still astonished him how attached he'd become to the lovable black-haired mutt in the short week since he'd adopted him. A mixed breed, the vet said, a lot of collie and Saint Bernard with some setter and "a few others" thrown in. Yeah, Jake thought, like Sherman tank and cement mixer.

At first, when he'd arrived home and discovered the dog gone, he'd worried maybe Buster was lying in a corner somewhere sick, but a frantic search had proved that false. Then he'd toyed with the idea that somebody had stolen him, a notion he'd quickly ruled out as improbable.

After checking for holes along the base of the four-foot high chain link fence and finding none, he'd finally decided the dog must have gone through the gate. He'd probably not latched it securely in the morning when he left.

There was just enough of an incline in that part of his back yard that if the gate were left standing open, it swung closed by itself, sometimes hard enough to latch. If Jake hadn't latched it properly in the morning, Buster could have nudged it open and made his escape. Then the gate could have swung to behind him, latching itself.

And the dog, celebrating his freedom, had torn over to his nearest neighbor and had a little fun.

Jake's eyes strayed back to his neighbor, to the slender tanned legs a few feet from his face—and the smear of dirt traveling up under her shorts.

He tore his eyes from the sight as Jenna turned to face him, but he knew by the narrowing of her gaze that she'd caught him staring.

"I just got Buster last week," he confided, scooping up an empty soup can and tossing it into the trashcan. "Rescued him from the animal shelter. His time had run out. They were going to—you know…"

"Much as I commend your noble rescue, I'd be more impressed if you kept him on your own property." Attack, she thought. Attack is the best defense. And she knew she had to keep her defenses up around this man.

He glared at her with a steely glint in his eyes that sent thrilling little shivers coursing up and down her spine. "I've already apologized about today," he said in measured tones, "and as I explained, the other days he was fenced in. There are no holes under the fence either, so don't even suggest he dug his way out."

"Too bad he wasn't that considerate about my property." She pointed to the two new holes. "Those foxholes could conceal a regiment."

Before Jake could argue, she continued. "Obviously, he jumped the fence."

Like the dog that had jumped the fence when she was ten. It had chased her for two blocks, nipping at her ankles with its sharp little teeth. If she hadn't been wearing heavy socks and long pants, who knows what the outcome might have been. She shuddered at the memory. Dogs were not her favorite people.

"Sort of like macho men climbing a mountain just because it's there, you know?" she continued. "It's the same with a dog. You fence him in, he's going to jump the fence. It's a dog thing."

"Oh, sure, and then he looks at his little doggy watch and jumps back into the yard in time to greet me when I get home." He grinned. He knew he had her.

She rolled her eyes to express how ridiculous she found his sarcasm. Without commenting, she returned to her task. Jake stooped and picked up another handful of trash. Studiously ignoring each other, they worked side by side cleaning up Buster's mess.

Jake turned so he wasn't facing in her direction, so his eyes couldn't stray to her derriere, so he couldn't see the sweat beading behind her knees, glistening in the sun. It made him think of ocean waves lapping over golden sand. It made him imagine what it would be like to be lying with her on that sand with the water washing over them.

He tried to focus on the woods that started at her property line and extended for several miles. His woods. Normally at this time of day, an hour before dusk, he would be doing his three-mile run through those woods. The woods he vowed would never be sacrificed to real estate development as so much of Florida's natural beauty already had been. As most of Providence, his hometown since birth, already had been.

He breathed deeply, trying to capture the scent of live oak, saw pine and red maple. There wasn't enough breeze. Their fragrance couldn't carry past Jenna Kincaid's hibiscus plants.

The fresh, flowery scent Jenna Kincaid was wearing couldn't compete with the hibiscus either, but that didn't stop it from tantalizing his senses. All he had to do was close his eyes to remember the fragrance of her skin and hair as he'd lain tangled with her beneath the red hibiscus.

He glanced around, wanting one more look at that streak of dirt. A man could lose himself in that streak of dirt.

"They were really going to—you know?" she asked, breaking into his thoughts.

"Yeah," Jake said, dragging his eyes back to the eggshells he was picking up, keeping his lashes lowered until he could subdue any sign of lust. "He was a stray. Well, not always. He used to belong to Old Man Logan—that's what everyone called him. Logan lived in a shack a few miles from here, on the other side of the woods. He was a loner, kept to himself, just the old man and his dog, driving his truck into Providence every Saturday for supplies. Then one day the grocer realized he hadn't seen Logan for a while. He asked the cops to check up on him. They had to break into the house, found him in his bed. Figured he'd been dead for a couple of weeks."

"And Buster was sitting faithfully by his side?" Jenna could envision the scene, but not with Buster playing the role of faithful companion, and the slightly acerbic tone of voice when she asked the question betrayed her aversion to the dog.

"No." Jake stared at her bemusedly for a second, realizing she was not a dog lover, or at least not a Buster-lover. "He would have starved. Buster's a survivor. He was in the woods foraging for himself, stealing eggs from a farmer, chasing chickens, fighting other dogs, probably a coyote or two. You know we have coyotes in the woods? They're not native to Florida. They've migrated down from Texas and the plains."

"Yes, sometimes I hear them at night." Actually, she liked their mournful cry. It was so cowboy, kind of romantic.

"When the pound finally caught up with Buster he was in pretty bad shape. Part of his tail was missing. His ear was torn—you probably noticed that?"

She nodded absently, noticing what fine ears Jake had. Not too big, not too small. Just right.

"So anyway, they couldn't find a home for him."

"Hmmm. I wonder why," she said innocently.

They both laughed, the tension between them easing.

"Do you think I should change his name to something more appropriate, something like Digger or Trasher?" He thought for a minute. "Or Dozer or—"

"How about Streetcar Named Destruction," she suggested sweetly. They laughed some more.

His eyes intrigued Jenna. They gleamed with interest, they twinkled with mirth, they glinted with anger, yet beneath all those emotions she thought she saw something deeper. A fleeting impression of pain, there, then as quickly gone.

He was watching her watch him, his thick lashes hooding his eyes, his expression unreadable. She looked away, deliberately breaking the connection with this man who could slip past a woman's defenses if she blinked.

When the last eggshell had been deposited in the trashcan, he stood and gave her a rueful look. "I'm not much good with flowers and stuff," he admitted, wagging a hand at the broken orchids.

His fingers were long and slender, his hands graceful, Jenna noticed. They looked strong, but gentle, his gesture self-possessed, confident, even as he admitted his failing. Hands that would please a lover, she thought, tearing her eyes away from them. She cemented the crack in her defensive wall with a casual smile, a shrug.

"It's okay. I can say, with no modesty intended, I'm very good with flowers and such. I'll take care of it."

Potpourri, she decided, focusing on the subject of orchids. Not even this man with his mystery eyes, intriguing smile and sensual hands could compete with her love of orchids. She had to believe that.

Lots of potpourri. She could make up sachets, tie a little tag on them with her company name and logo, and sell them to gift shops as orchid potpourri. Give them a name like Orchid Bag or Sun Scents or something. Yes, a pretty little ribbon, and a tiny folded card that named the species and briefly described the history of the plant. Her mom could create a small orchid design to print on the cards. And little Carlee could help with drying, crushing and bagging the orchids. She would get a kick out of that. It would be a family operation. For the first time since Buster had bulldozed her yard, she felt excitement stirring.

Jake watched her, a smile tugging at the corners of his mouth, and Jenna realized her inner excitement was showing. She knew she was cursed with a face that concealed nothing. Worse, she felt an urge to talk about her plans, bounce them off a listener, test their validity.

She even opened her mouth to say something, but closed it quickly, irritated with herself for even thinking about making friends with this man and his dog. For a moment he'd done it, this man with his poignant smile and bold eyes, his seductive voice and subtle humor, for just a moment he'd slipped past her defenses. For just a moment she'd let him in.

They strolled over to Buster, who was determinedly chewing his way to freedom. Luckily for Jenna he was chewing on Jake's belt, not the porch railing. From the looks of the belt—a fine grade of leather, she noted—one more chomp and Buster would have busted his way out of the slammer.

The martyred sigh of a long-suffering parent escaped Jake's lips as he retrieved the remains of his belt and took Buster firmly by the collar.

"Well," he began, smiling at Jenna, "since we're neighbors and all, maybe we can—"

"Mama." Carlee's piping voice interrupted whatever Jake was going to say, and Jenna turned to smile fondly at her soon-to-be four-year-old. "Gramma says dinner will be ready in a few minutes."

Carlee inched up to Jenna, carefully keeping her mom between her and the man. When she spoke again, her words were very low, almost a whisper, and uttered very reluctantly. "Gramma says you can invite that man to dinner."

Carlee's hand clutched Jenna's in a death grip, her eyes riveted on Jake.

Jenna stooped to place an arm around Carlee's shoulders, and Carlee shifted her gaze from Jake to Jenna.

"Oh," she said softly, studying Jenna critically.

For the second time in twenty minutes, Jenna was getting a head-to-toe appraisal. Carlee's large brown eyes—way too somber for her young age—widened at the sight of Jenna's dirty arms and legs. Her rosebud lips pursed in contemplation. "Gramma told me to wash for dinner. P'raps," she suggested delicately, "you should too."

"P'raps I should," Jenna said, laughing and kissing Carlee's freckled nose and ruffling her carrot top.

She turned to Jake and the laughter died in her throat. Jake's face was white, his features like stone, and the expression in his eyes unreadable. Without a word he turned and strode rapidly away, Buster loping at his side.

Puzzled, Jenna looked about her, searching for a clue to Jake's strange behavior. She didn't see anything. Did Carlee's suggestion that she invite him to dinner scare him off? *I had no intention of inviting him anyway,* she thought with a huff.

"That man doesn't like me," Carlee said with childish perception and frankness.

"Don't be silly, darling," Jenna said, squeezing her hand gently and walking toward the door. "He doesn't even know you."

She paused and glanced around again. *Something* had certainly turned

Jake Corbin to stone. And there wasn't any Medusa lurking behind a bush, no sirens beckoning from the birdbath, no basilisk curled on a rock. There was nothing to cause Jake's abrupt transformation. Nothing at all.

Except Carlee.

CHAPTER TWO

"Gramma cooked chicken," announced Carlee, skipping ahead of Jenna into the house.

Jenna didn't need Carlee's input to recognize the tantalizing aroma of her mom's special basil chicken and rice pilaf. Probably with steamed vegetables and applesauce or some other fruit for dessert, she guessed, knowing her mom's anti-cholesterol campaign.

She sniffed appreciatively, suddenly aware of gnawing hunger pangs. Tumbling around on the ground with a weird neighbor and his mammoth dog must be good for the appetite.

"Sorry I stuck you with the cooking, Claire," she said as she walked through the kitchen on her way to wash up. "I know it was my turn."

She'd moved in with her mother when she'd divorced Ned, and to avoid daily arguments about kitchen duty, each wanting to spare the other the work, they had agreed to take turns. She and Claire got along together very well, their relationship based on mutual respect, love and consideration. And the ability to laugh at themselves. They both doted on Carlee. So the three-generation family of females had turned out to be a good arrangement.

She still felt odd calling her mom by her first name, but Claire insisted. It was part of her new image, conceived after she was widowed a few years back.

The new image was still in its larval stage, evolving bit by alarming bit. She'd gone through a spell of classical music, loading the 10-disk CD changer with Pavarotti, Domingo, Carreras, Jussi Bjorling, Leontyne Price, and Maria Callas. From morning 'til night, the house was filled with Puccini's love songs, Rossini's comic opera, Donizetti's merry music, all wonderfully and passionately sung—in Italian, in German, sometimes in French or Spanish. Claire finally admitted that while she loved the music, she really enjoyed songs more when she could understand the words. She still listened to her opera tapes when the mood struck her, but for the most part it was back to popular recording artists, movie themes, and an occasional country music station.

After music she'd switched to sports, joining a baseball team, a bowling league and a senior hiking program. A bruised hip from a poorly pitched ball, a sprained thumb in the bowling alley, and ugly hiking boots put a mercifully swift end to that phase.

For the last two months Jenna could only describe Claire's image as flamboyant. Bright clothes, wild hairdos, gaudy jewelry. That was okay with Jenna. She knew—boy did she know—how restricted Claire's life had been for the 23 years she was married to Jenna's domineering, overbearing, self-absorbed father before he died of cancer. If she wanted to kick up her heels a little now, all Jenna could say was, "Go for it!"

Claire turned from the stove, where she was dishing up the food, and grinned at Jenna's dirt-streaked face and disheveled clothes. "I saw you out there rolling around with that gorgeous hunk. Is that some new mating game or something? I just can't keep up with you kids nowadays. At the risk of sounding ancient, I can remember when I was a teen, sitting on the sofa with a boyfriend. If he so much as laid his arm across the sofa back, my mother would give him "that look" that warned him he'd better move his arm or lose it. Times sure have changed." She grinned again, looking at Jenna. "Nowadays kids have more fun. Who was he, by the way? And at what point do you bring him in to meet your parent? I don't care how contemporary you think you are, I still insist on that."

Jenna gave Claire a playful punch on the arm, keeping a neutral expression about Claire's neon orange shirt, green toreador pants and purple belt. "Good try, Claire, but you know that was no romantic entanglement you witnessed."

But Jenna felt her face redden. She was remembering the way Jake had looked at her, his eyes raking slowly down her body and back up as though she were standing naked in front of him. Worse, she remembered her instant treacherous arousal. Just remembering it now sent a tremor of arousal skipping through her body.

She had been too long without a man, she thought, trying to dismiss the incident. It was the physical contact that did it, his hard body pressed against hers. That physical contact had awakened sexual instinct, that's all. The sleeping giant. And not just awakened it, but shoved her starving, neglected hormones into overdrive.

A sigh escaped Claire's scarlet-rouged lips. A loud exaggerated sigh. "I keep hoping," she said.

But the look she gave Jenna was discerning, much too discerning, and Jenna escaped upstairs to wash.

* * *

Jake was halfway home, striding along the path that skirted the trees, when he came to the main trail leading into the woods. He turned onto it and began to run, taking in gulps of air like a man setting foot on his native soil after a long separation.

He ran faster and faster, oblivious to the street shoes he wore, oblivious to the dog loping beside him, oblivious to the trees stretching their leafy arms out, plucking at his clothes. He ran until the sun was low in the west, until his chest heaved and legs ached, and his mouth felt parched. He ran on until the only sensation he felt was the wind blowing through his clothes, cooling his sweat, soothing his trembling body, blowing away the image of the little girl with the big eyes. He ran until his memories had once again receded to that spot deep within him, locked safely away.

Only then did he stop, collapsing against a tree to catch his breath. He stayed that way for several minutes, his back braced against the trunk of a live oak, his face turned up, breathing in the earthy scent of the woods, the musky odor of the lacy Spanish moss, the faint piquant scent of mint plants.

Finally his heart stopped hammering. Buster looked up at him and whined, whether in sympathy or to remind Jake it was dinnertime, it was hard to tell.

Jake reached down and scratched behind the dog's ears, then turned toward home. He jogged at a comfortable pace, picking his way along the trail in the fading light.

* * *

"So tell me about your handsome stranger," Claire said. They were finishing their meal in the dinette, where the three normally ate. They moved to the larger dining room when they had company, but preferred the cozier and more convenient dinette for everyday meals.

"He doesn't like me," Carlee said, her sharp little mind knowing instantly who the handsome stranger was. She spoke in a hushed voice, as though she were speaking of the devil himself, who might be crouched behind a piece of furniture, hiding and listening.

"But, darling, that's quite impossible," Claire protested firmly. "How could he *not* like you? On the I-like-you scale of one to ten, you are definitely a ten!"

"I don't know," Jenna said thoughtfully. "He did act kind of weird when he saw Carlee. It was just—just—weird. One minute he was talking about us maybe—er—about how we are neighbors, then Carlee came out and he clammed up like a losing bidder at an auction and took off without so much as a by your leave. Very, very weird."

"Hmmm. Well. Maybe he remembered he'd left the soup pot on the burner. One thing's for sure," and Claire turned to Carlee, tapping her playfully on the tip of her nose, "his sudden departure had nothing to do with a certain little freckle-faced monkey. And the next time we see him, we'll *demand* an explanation."

"It's okay," Carlee mumbled with a worried look clouding her brown eyes.

"So," Claire added, turning back to Jenna. "Tell me about him." And she propped her elbow on the table and rested her chin on her hand. "I'm all ears."

"Since you obviously had your nose pressed against the window, you know what he looks like."

"Don't be snide. Besides, he was too far away to see the color of his eyes. Are they brown? Blue? Green?"

"Blue. In fact, remarkably close to that royal blue streak you put in your hair." Jenna leaned toward her mother for a closer look. "Is it an inch or so wider today than it was yesterday?"

Claire patted her hair with undisguised pride. "I touched it up a little this morning."

"It's quite—interesting. Adds a sort of, um—excitement—to your ash blond. Do you plan to keep it that way long?"

"As long as it suits me. Now stop trying to change the subject. How about his teeth? Are they white, straight, healthy?"

"All of the above, Dr. Colgate."

"And his name? Surely you caught that somewhere between the tumble in the grass and the nose-to-nose by the flowerbed?"

Ye gods, the woman *had* had her nose pressed against the window. "His name's Jake. Jake Corbin." Bond. James Bond. "He's our neighbor. Lives down the road, I think in that ranch style with the weedy yard."

"A man in need of a woman who has a way with yards," Claire murmured.

Jenna grunted. "Probably married with a dozen kids." The thought displeased her.

"Jake," Claire mused, ignoring Jenna's negativity. "The name has a solid comfortable sound to it. Don't you think so, dear?"

It was time to bring this matchmaking inquisition to a screeching halt. Jenna looked pointedly at her watch. "Will you look at the time," she exclaimed with mock alarm. Jumping up, she started to make her way across the kitchen. "Sorry, Claire, I'd love to stay and chat, but my orchids are calling to me. They desperately need some attention before it gets too late." Jenna glanced out the window. The sun was already setting; she'd have to work by porch light.

"Gramma and I made some cookies today," Carlee piped up. "Do you want one?"

"We experimented with a new fat-free recipe," Claire said. "If you like them, I thought I'd cook up a batch for the auction next week. Phil Averies suggested it."

Jenna glanced at Claire, wishing she could quirk an eyebrow. Phil Averies was attracted to Claire, and Jenna suspected it went deeper than that. She'd more than once caught the man looking at Claire with an expression in his eyes that seemed—caressing, adoring, something.

"Phil Averies, hmmm?" she said, teasing.

"Yes. He stopped by and sampled my cookies."

Jenna laughed out loud at the gaffe, and Claire used her fingers to snap Jenna on the head. "Behave yourself. He swore he'd stop at no price to buy them at the auction. Even though he knows I'd be happy to make him a batch for nothing. What a dear old man."

It was funny to hear Claire speak of Phil as old, when he was just a year or two older than Claire herself. Jenna suspected she did it to deliberately distance herself from the handsome, white-haired lawyer, determined not to allow a man to get too close and destroy her newfound and much-cherished freedom.

Jenna could understand. She certainly appreciated her own freedom, out from under the suffocating authority and menace Ned had brought to their marriage. She had suffered often under his heavy and domineering thumb, back in the days when she was young and foolish. She was still foolish, she admitted to herself. She had hated—really, really hated—the idea of divorce and would probably still be married to Ned if it weren't for Carlee. For better or for worse, she had vowed. Vowed.

But Ned's strict, domineering attitude, his obvious dislike of children and his severe punishments had resulted in Carlee's withdrawal into herself and her growing terror of men. That was what had pushed Jenna to take that hated, ultimate step, to remove herself and Carlee from the destructive environment.

And, on the positive side, it gave her the incentive to turn her hobby of collecting orchids into a business.

She turned back to the window, appreciatively eyeing the two greenhouses. When Claire, who was itching for a change of scenery to complement her change of lifestyle, found out about the rural property north of Tampa, she'd snatched it up. The three acres, complete with greenhouses and a home, were perfect for Jenna's planned orchid business.

And here we are, as snug as three bugs in a rug, Jenna thought.

Except that a short distance down the road from their rug dwelled a man who had, with one shake of that rug, turned her world upside down.

Not to worry. She would right her world in a hurry. Because despite the obvious attraction she felt for Jake Corbin, she had no intention of letting him into her life. She would keep her defenses up. She never again wanted to have her life dictated by a man, and even more important, there was Carlee to think about. She would never, never again put the child in a situation where she would be the helpless victim of a man's cruel behavior.

Jake had awakened her long-slumbering sexual desire, that was true. Boy, was that true. But in those last few seconds, before he'd turned and bolted, she'd seen Jake's face when he'd looked at Carlee. She couldn't even interpret the look. Aversion? Horror? Fear? Whatever it was, it was not Disney World or Hallmark cards.

Instinct told Jenna she needed to be careful. Very careful.

No, Jake Corbin would not slip through her defenses a second time.

"Mama, do you want a cookie?" Carlee's impatient voice interrupted her thoughts.

She turned from the window and smiled at Carlee's expectant face. "Of course, precious. Where are they?" She stepped toward her collection of whimsical animal-shaped cookie jars lining the shelves of her large corner china cabinet.

"You have to guess," Carlee said, clapping her hands with delight. This was one of her favorite games.

"The frog on the log," Jenna guessed, playing along. She loved to see Carlee laugh. The first three years of her life hadn't been very happy. More than once Ned had sent her to bed without supper because she had made too much noise while playing. If she accidentally spilled or broke something, punishment was swift and brutal, usually a ruler across the palms of her hands. The time Jenna came home from the grocery store and found Carlee cowering in a corner while Ned sat in a chair holding the ruler and taunting her to step across an imaginary line had been the final push that sent Jenna to a divorce lawyer.

None of Ned's punishments had left scars on the child, not on the outside. Carlee's scars were all on the inside. Jenna recalled how the little girl had cringed earlier when she'd seen Jake standing outside with Buster. Would her scars ever heal, Jenna wondered.

"Nope," Carlee squealed, shaking her head, her eyes shining. "Guess again. Guess again."

"The cat and the bat," Jenna guessed, pointing to the orange and black Halloween cookie jar.

"No, no, guess again!" Carlee bounced up and down on her chair.

"Hmmm." Jenna slowly ran her finger along the rows. She had seventeen jars in her collection now, but like Midas and his gold, she could never have enough. She cherished every jar, probably to an extreme degree. But it could be worse, she rationalized. She could be collecting space hogs, like those waist-high oriental decorator pots, or cars for pete's sake like that lady back in Ohio who had twelve at last count, or budget busters like diamonds. Every time she introduced a new cookie jar into her collection Claire tactfully suggested switching to thimbles, or made chirping remarks about spoon collections, or wove fanciful tales about old buttons, but—nah—too boring.

Guessing which jar held the cookies could be quite a feat—if it weren't for the cookie crumbs clinging to the rim of the bunny jar.

"This might take some magic," Jenna said, closing her eyes and waving her index finger like a wand. "Abracadabra, near and far, point my finger to the jar." She opened her eyes. "The sunny bunny jar!" she shouted.

"Yes, yes!" Carlee jumped up and down before taking the cookie jar off the shelf and carefully removing the lid.

"How about sending a little of that magic my way," Claire said. "I'd like colored contact lenses. I'm thinking along the lines of Elizabeth Taylor violet."

"Why would you mess with perfection?" Jenna quipped, only half kidding. Claire had beautiful greenish hazel eyes, wide-spaced, exotic, long lashes, naturally arched brows. No amount of magic could improve that look.

But why not? Jenna closed her eyes and waved her finger in front of Claire. "Abracadabra, do or die, give this woman a blind eye, to every man who happens by, so she won't play matchmaker *all the time!*"

She opened her eyes and smirked at Claire, whose scowl was too comical to take seriously. "Oh, gee, I'm sorry," Jenna said in exaggeratedly innocent tones. "Did I say the wrong spell?"

She grabbed a cookie and headed out to the back yard. She needed to deal with the orchids Buster had mangled.

As Carlee tagged along beside her, her nimble little fingers helping gather the broken flowers, Jenna tried to keep focused on the task at hand.

It was impossible.

Her thoughts continually returned to Jake Corbin. It had been a year since she'd divorced Ned. Since then she'd led a celibate life, avoiding the complications that seemed to come with a man. Apparently her libido had decided enough was enough, and when a body like Jake Corbin's was entwined limb to limb with hers, the physical contact had sent desire skyrocketing.

Any kind of friendship between the two of them would be a double disaster, she told herself. He has that dog, and I have Carlee. But the voice of reason was no match against her vivid memories of Jake's dangerous blue eyes raking her body.

From head to toe. From toe to head. Like she was naked.

The voice of reason was no match for the arousal she felt when she thought of his soft, firm lips and imagined what his kisses would be like.

The voice of reason didn't even try to compete with the memory of Jake's hands, the remembered hot touch on her elbow, the certainty of what those hands would feel like on her body.

"Enough!" she vowed, rocking back on her heels and looking around for something, anything, that would keep her mind off her neighbor.

Everything she saw reminded her of Jake. The broken plants reminded her of the few moments when they were nose to nose, he kneeling beside her, catching her elbow when she started to fall, and the heat that danced up and down her arm when he'd touched her. The rake propped against the stone wall reminded her of their shared efforts to clean up the trash, of his humorous suggestions for new names for Buster, and the moments they had laughed together. When was the last time she had actually laughed with a man? Years. A caterpillar crawling over a leaf reminded her of the one on her shoulder when she, Jake and Buster had tumbled on the ground, and the feel of his hard body against hers.

He was hard all over, she remembered. His muscles, his stomach, his thighs. Everything.

She woke from that reminiscence with a start, and glanced quickly at the kitchen window, hoping Claire hadn't spotted her sitting on her heels with a besotted expression on her face. That's all the encouragement Claire would need to hatch several dozen matchmaking schemes.

Claire waved gaily from the window.

"Damn," Jenna muttered.

She looked at Carlee, carrying a bag of crushed orchids to the greenhouse. Carlee, her precious gift, the one thing that made her five long years with Ned worth every hurt and indignation she'd suffered. Carlee, with her little hand clutching Jenna's in a death grip, her somber brown eyes dark with apprehension as she'd looked at Jake Corbin standing in her yard. Carlee. That's the only memory she needed to dwell on. That was her first line of defense.

Back in the house Jenna showered, then began to pack a suitcase. In the morning she was leaving on a whirlwind business trip that would have her visiting several orchid wholesalers, garden shops and other flower businesses over the next four days. Her first destination was Tallahassee, where she had a whole list of calls to make, then Jacksonville, Orlando, and finally Tampa, where she planned to check out her competition at a local orchid show before heading home. This was her first official business trip since starting her nursery, and she was as excited as a kid in a toyshop.

"And I'll be too busy to waste any thoughts on That Man," she kept telling herself. She figured that referring to Jake Corbin as "that man" instead of by name would help keep him relegated to a low level, not worth thinking about. And I won't think about him, she promised resolutely. And what's there to think about, anyway, she argued with herself.

Okay, he's a hunk. Okay, we tumbled around on the ground in positions you won't find in any book. Okay, the way he looks at me turns my bones to jelly and his touch could start a forest fire. Okay, he's got a hard body and a tender smile and his eyes, when they're not undressing me, laugh despite those glimpses of pain. Okay, his eyes undress me. Okay, I'm thinking about him again.

Making a sound of disgust, she snatched up her list and checked off the items, making sure she had everything packed.

"Tallahassee, here I come," she sang with determined gaiety. "Where my plants will knock 'em—numb. Open up those order books. Tallahassee, here I come."

* * *

Jake paced his office, throwing Buster a fierce scowl each time he faced in the dog's direction. He hadn't forgiven the dog for his part in the dilemma Jake now found himself in. Buster, delighted with any kind of eye contact from his beloved master, thumped his tail on the rag rug each time Jake scowled at him.

Jake pounded his right fist into his left palm, then with each turn, switched and pounded his left fist into his right palm. Each whack kept time with his steps. It was his way of trying to find answers when no answers would come. Finally, admitting defeat, he sank into the nearest chair and buried his face in his hands.

He didn't know how long he sat there. The chirp of crickets and the song of cicadas drifting in through the open window and the occasional soft snores from Buster as he dreamed his dog dreams were the only sounds breaking the silence. When he finally raised his head, a cloud had drifted across the moon, obscuring its glow. The small lamp on his desk, turned to a low wattage, filled the room with a soft light he found unexpectedly comforting.

For the most part, Jake was a doer, facing his problems head-on and resolving them. But his take-charge attitude had failed him when his wife and child had been killed in a car accident, and since then every day had been a meaningless struggle to survive.

He couldn't write, at least not the children's books that had brought so much joy to himself and little Lizzy and countless other readers. He had written the books for Lizzy, always for Lizzy. With her gone, he couldn't face the memories the stories evoked, couldn't call up a single word to put on paper.

His writing now was limited to objective journalism, newspaper stories that were safe, that didn't touch his personal life, that didn't scrape across that ceaseless pain lurking just below the surface. It was so important that he not feel, because when he did, the pain destroyed him.

Today he had felt the pain.

Today he had suffered two shocks in rapid succession. First that encounter with Jenna Kincaid. When they were tangled on the ground, when he'd felt her heart pounding against his chest, when those slender legs had wrapped around his—his body had responded like a sex-starved maniac.

Granted, he *was* sex-starved. It had been over two years since Barb's death and he had not, as the Bible quaintly put it, known woman since; grief and guilt had effectively nullified any desire for the opposite sex.

He was thankful at least that Jenna hadn't noticed his reaction. He'd disentangled himself and jumped up, keeping his back to her while he struggled to get Buster—and himself—under control. Remembering that moment now, he realized that he had never in his life wanted a woman more than when Jenna had been struggling under him, her breasts heaving, her eyes flashing, her lips so damnably, unbelievably kissable.

Jake straightened in his chair, facing his dilemma head on though he still didn't have any answers. "I want her," he said with a groan. He couldn't deny the ache that throbbed in his body even now, just thinking about her. A hungry ache that gained in intensity until it settled between his legs with all the pent-up ferocity of a volcano ready to explode.

The second, more jolting shock, had been the sight of the little girl with the red hair and big brown eyes. She looked about the same age as Lizzy had been when she'd died.

Lizzy. Even thinking the name brought a familiar stab to his heart. Lizzy, Lizzy. Every day he missed her. "God, god, will it never stop," he groaned.

Buster emitted a soft questioning woof and looked at Jake anxiously.

Jake drew a deep, steadying breath and rose from the chair. "It's okay, fella," he said gruffly, walking over and stooping to scratch the dog's ears. "It's okay."

But it wasn't okay, because he knew the pain twisting through his heart would never go away. Jake remembered the well-meaning mourner at the funeral who had patted his arm and promised him that time heals all wounds. Now he laughed bitterly. Maybe, he thought, time heals some wounds. But not the death of your child. Never the death of your child.

Without being conscious of his actions, he walked to the credenza and picked up the dusty, incomplete manuscript shoved to one corner. "Wendy the Wood Nymph Saves the Day" was the working title. It was the fourth in a series of Wendy books. He had written one for Lizzy's birthday every year of her young life. He had been struggling to complete this one in time for her fourth birthday when the accident had made a mockery of the effort.

Jake blew the dust off the cover sheet, then hesitantly flipped to the beginning of the story. Taking a deep breath, he began to read the first few sentences out loud, the way he always did when editing one of his children's books. He only stumbled on a word or two as memories of the story he hadn't worked on in over two years came flooding back.

```
Wendy looked down from her comfortable
perch in the crook of the big old live oak and
gasped in alarm. Brushing aside the hanging
moss for a better view, she looked and gasped
again in even greater alarm. Far below her,
three large men, wearing rough clothes over
bulging muscles, were striding down the path
leading to the forest—her forest. They were
laughing with loud, coarse noises and
pointing at the trees.
One of the men carried a big, wicked-
looking axe that glinted in blinding silver
streaks where the sun struck it. The other two
men carried chain saws whose rows of sharp,
jagged teeth lined the saw edges like
horrible mouths.
The trees, as though sensing impending
destruction, whimpered in the cool breeze.
```

Jake dropped the manuscript back on the credenza, unable to read any more. The book was almost finished, telling how Wendy had gathered the woodland creatures to help outwit the woodcutters, the dangers they'd overcome and the triumphs they'd shared. Just a few pages short of a happy ending.

But Jake had not been able to write a word in his Wendy series since Lizzy's death. Without her to share it with, there was no point.

Lizzy, Lizzy, Lizzy. Every day he missed her.

Even in his intense grief, Jake couldn't ignore a totally different feeling. One he hadn't felt in a long, long time. The one he'd experienced today tangled with Jenna under the hibiscus bush. Desire. So insistent, so demanding, that it relentlessly shoved its way to the forefront, nudging his pain back, just a little. He could almost hear his desire's seductive promise. She will help you live. She will help you stop hurting.

"I want her," Jake admitted again, aloud.

Buster, who was disappointed when Jake had stopped reading, woofed encouragingly.

The dog's response caused Jake to look at him and smile. Then, remembering Buster's socially unacceptable behavior earlier that day, he scowled at the dog.

Buster thumped his tail.

Thinking of Buster's behavior brought his thoughts back to Jenna. His neighbor. So close, just down the road. A quarter mile.

He walked to the window and looked out, as though he could see through the dense growth of trees, see around the curve, see her standing by her orchids. But it was dark, she would be thinking about bed, maybe taking a shower. It wasn't hard to imagine her standing under the stream of water, her head back as the clear water sliced through her thick tangle of red hair, to imagine her hands sliding across her breasts, soaping and sliding all over her naked body.

His own hands clenched into fists to subdue the arousal that lingered on the edge of every thought since that bodily encounter they'd had. But he didn't really want to subdue it. He wanted to act on it. He wanted to bolt out the door, race madly down the path, burst into her bedroom, sweep her into his arms, and make her his in every possible way a man could take a woman.

That physical contact had been his undoing. Those soft curves yielding beneath his body, those kissable lips inches from his mouth, her heart beating a tattoo as compelling as a war dance, an irresistible call to action. Every male urge he'd ever had and a few he'd never known about answered that call. Emotion coursed through his veins like a warrior scenting blood and primed for battle. The urge to ravage her there on the spot, that unknown woman, that beautiful, delectable, kissable stranger, was so primitive and immediate that the very shock of what he wanted to do, the unbelievable intensity of his desire, was the only thing that saved them.

It had shocked him to his senses.

Oh, the wanting didn't go away. Every minute that he was with her, every look, every word, was skirting the edge of that urge to take her, take her right there under that red hibiscus that had played host to their tangled encounter.

For the first time in over two years, he had felt like a man instead of a zombie.

And he liked it. He *liked* it. He liked the feel of her body against his, the scent of her, the taste of her where his lips had grazed against her cheek in their crazy tumble. He liked that jolting reminder that he was still alive. He liked the sensation of his blood pumping, the hot excitement when he touched her, the throb between his legs.

Jake dragged a hand over his face, a choked laugh coming from somewhere inside him. "Hell, I more than like it," he said to the window, to the woods beyond, to the redhead in the wood frame house. "I love it."

For too long he'd been walking in a fog. Now, suddenly, he was acutely aware of his surroundings, of all things bright and beautiful. Of Jenna Kincaid. And he knew he didn't want to lose this feeling. He didn't want to go back to his zombie-like existence, plodding through each day with his emotions carefully corralled and locked away. He wanted to live again. He wanted to *live!*

Life with a woman like Jenna—

For several minutes, standing at the window and gazing out, he let his imagination stray to those few minutes on the ground, Jenna's body entangled with his. He let his imagination carry her slim, long-legged body from the hard, twiggy ground to a soft bed, replace her denim shorts with nothing but soft fragrant skin, tanned like honey and tasting sweeter. He let his imagination pull her softness against him while he breathed in her scent and covered that sweet soft body with kisses. Her face, that graceful neck, her breasts, that flat stomach. As his imagination trailed his trembling lips lower, he forced his thoughts back to reality.

"That's the trouble with being a writer," he muttered. "Too damned much imagination."

He wanted her.

But there was a problem. A problem that had kept him pacing his office for two hours. A problem he hadn't found a solution to. The little girl with the red hair and big brown eyes.

It was painful for Jake to look at kids, any kids, since Lizzy's death. He went to great lengths to avoid them because their shining eyes, their active bodies, their childish laughter—all were devastating reminders of Lizzy, torturous, crippling reminders. Sometimes contact with children was unavoidable and he'd learned to look past them, turn off his emotions, focus on something else. Usually it worked, got him through the ordeal, kept him sane.

But today, when he'd seen that little girl with the red hair and big brown eyes, it was so unexpected, he hadn't had time to prepare, to steel himself. And his emotions were so raw at that moment, so unguarded, his senses so enhanced.

That small hand reaching toward her mother.

It had hit him like a grenade, shattering every defense he had. In that instant he didn't see a little girl with red hair and brown eyes. He saw his little Lizzy with her soft cornflower blond hair, her big blue eyes, her little hand reaching for his hand, reaching—

And he'd fled the image, knowing it wasn't real, could never be real again. He'd had to run. Run until the image faded and he was sane again.

So how could he stand here at the window fantasizing about Jenna Kincaid when he knew it wasn't just Jenna Kincaid he would be letting into his life? He would have to accept the little girl too.

I can't, he thought, turning his back to the window. I can't do it. I'm not ready for that. I'll never be ready for that.

He took two steps and stopped. He felt like a man who's just had his first breath of freedom after a long confinement and was now rejecting that freedom, walking back into prison. Slowly he turned back to the window, leaned his hands on the sill, and stared into the night.

For several minutes he didn't think any thoughts, just stared at the woods he loved and let the peace and strength and wisdom of centuries wash over him. Finally his confused thoughts and emotions were still, and in that stillness he was able to think clearly. A glimpse of the old Jake, the doer who tackled his problems head on, broke through the blanket of despair he'd wrapped round himself.

Two thoughts took shape and solidified into resolution.

He would not go back to his zombie-like existence. He would not give up this new lease on life. That was synonymous with saying he would not give up Jenna Kincaid. She was the one who had unlocked his cell door, while ironically trapping him securely in her allure. From now on he would celebrate life to its fullest, and he would celebrate it with her.

His second resolution was more difficult. He would allow the little red-haired, brown-eyed girl into his life. He knew intuitively that was the only way he would stand a chance with Jenna Kincaid. To do that he would have to master his grief. For two years it had mastered him, that hopeless lifeline he'd clung to like a drowning man, his only link to Lizzy. He would never stop loving Lizzy, he would never forget her, but he had to master his grief. The little girl was the key to that. Just as Jenna Kincaid was the key to his new lease on life, so Jenna's daughter was the key to mastering his grief. He would let her into his life.

This would be one of the most difficult things he had ever done, he knew that. He thought about her little body, the childish face topped with unruly red curls, those big, solemn brown eyes.

The little hand reaching out.

How could he reach out to that little girl without seeing Lizzy, remembering the way she'd put her little hand in his whenever she was afraid?

Jake had never run away from a fight in his life, none but one, and he was still fleeing that one. Would this little girl help him face his demons, or would she give him the final push to that blackness where only demons roamed? Would Jenna Kincaid's little girl be his salvation? Or his destruction?

He clenched his teeth and clenched his fists. There were very few times in Jake Corbin's life when he'd felt fear. This was one of those times.

He began to pace again. Now that he knew what he was going to do, he had to plan how he'd accomplish it. He could hardly march over there with open arms and say, "Welcome to my world." After several minutes of pacing and thinking without conceiving the remotest idea how to proceed, he realized with dawning enlightenment just how dominant a crutch his grief had become.

How do I get on with my life, he thought, more a demand than a question. How?

The telephone rang, its shrill bell insistent, demanding. Annoyed, Jake walked to his desk and waited for the answering machine to kick in. He wasn't in the mood to deal with a sales pitch about changing his long distance service, buying insurance, subscribing to the newspaper, or donating to this week's charity.

The upbeat tones of his agent's voice filtered through the machine, the Boston accent pronounced. "Jake! I know it's late, but I've got to talk to you. This is really important. If you're there, please pick up the phone."

A long pause followed the words. Mentally, Jake balked, knowing Caulder just wanted to nag him into finishing his next Wendy book. Then remembering his resolve to get on with his life, and wondering if this was fate throwing the challenge in his teeth, he picked up the phone.

"Hey, Caulder, what's up?"

"Jake," Caulder said, his relief evident, "so glad I caught you at home. You ready for a change of scenery, buddy?"

"That depends," Jake said cautiously.

"Well you know Brooks and Dunning are pushing a fantasy theme this month in their bookstores across Florida and they're featuring your Wendy books in their children's section. I know, I know, you've already told them you won't do the book signings, but hear me out. One of the author's who's due at a book signing tomorrow came down with the flu and the bookstore will be caught with egg on its face. Publicity's already gone out, that kind of thing. They wanted me to ask you once again—hell, to plead with you—to do the book signing, cover for the author till she gets well enough to come back. It should only be for one, two days at most."

Jake felt a heavy dread descend on him, thick, suffocating. Autograph his Wendy books to crowds of strangers, all with little kids in tow? A task that would have been all in a day's work two years ago was now a crushingly painful reminder of Lizzy, of his loss. He'd rather face a 12-foot alligator.

"You know Brooks and Dunning sell more of your books than any other chain," Caulder reminded him. "Those royalty checks you get are 60% due to them."

"Yes," Jake said, his voice strained. I can't do this, I can't do this, he thought.

"Caulder," he began, the tone of his voice already conveying his refusal, but then he stopped.

Not two minutes ago he was pacing the floor, trying to figure out how to get on with his life. The answer had just been handed to him.

I can't, he thought again. All those kids, their laughter, the big eyes looking at me, their little hands reaching out for the book.

Reaching out.

I can't.

But then an image of Jenna taunted him, the feel of her body, those lips so close to his mouth, her fragrant skin. That streak of dirt. Did he want that fantasy to become real? Or was he just blowing smoke? What did he want?

I want her.

"It might be fun to get away for awhile," Caulder coaxed.

Jake swallowed a lump in his throat and managed to croak, "You might be right. I'll—I'll do it. When did you say it was? Tomorrow?"

Caulder actually laughed with relief. "Right. Can you be ready to leave that soon?"

"Yes, okay," Jake said, talking slowly and thinking fast. He had just finished his deadlines for the paper, so he should be all right in that department for a few days. "Where's my first stop?"

"That big Brooks and Dunning store in Tallahassee. You were there when your first book came out."

"Tallahassee. Okay." Memories of his last book signing there were vivid. It had been a madhouse. And the kids, so many kids. Laughing, shouting, reaching out. So many. He drew a long, shuddering breath and stared the demons down. He'd taken a step forward and he wasn't going to let despair knock him two steps back.

I'll check out what's new in the bookstore, he thought, determined now to go through with it. Mixed with his dread was the enjoyment of making the first decision of his new life, accepting the first challenge, feeling the adrenalin start to pump. I'll see what's happening in children's literature, I'll visit that men's clothing store next door. I can do this. I will do this. And maybe I'll even stop fantasizing about Jenna Kincaid.

Although, what man would want to stop fantasizing about Jenna Kincaid?

"Thanks, Jake," Caulder said, breaking into his thoughts. "I know how hard this must be for you. I—and Brooks and Dunning—really appreciate this. And Jake," he added before hanging up, "welcome back."

Jake slowly replaced the receiver, hoping he hadn't made a big mistake.

But all other considerations aside, it probably was a wise move to get out of Dodge for a few days, put some distance between himself and his alluring neighbor, give his hormones a chance to cool off so he could approach her like the civilized man he was supposed to be.

The way he was feeling right now, he'd jump her bones if he caught her alone out weeding the garden. Women found things like that a little offputting. He could see the headlines. "Children's book author ravages orchid lady. Passionate lovemaking blamed for explosions in Hallelujah Firecracker Factory three miles away."

And before his imagination could grab that ball and run with it, he forced his thoughts to more practical matters.

What would he do about Buster? He could ask Jenna to come and feed him, he thought with a chuckle. Yeah, she'd love trotting over here a couple times a day to give TLC to her favorite animal in the whole world. He laughed, recalling her remarks about the dog. "Send his tongue to Texas for drought relief." He shook his head, still laughing.

That was another thing that had made a sudden reappearance in his life. Laughter. He could thank Jenna Kincaid for that, too.

He should run over there right now and thank her. She'd probably be in bed. He'd throw pebbles at her window until she appeared, looking down at him with sleepy eyes and tousled hair, the moonlight playing peek-a-boo with her lace gown. Or bare skin.

If she slept naked.

"Yes, Buster," he said, scratching the dog's ears, "It's time to get out of Dodge. Tallahassee is just where I need to be."

CHAPTER THREE

Tallahassee. A thrill of anticipation swept over Jenna as she passed the city's welcome sign. She was actually here! Doing something positive to push her business in the right direction. She drove around looking for a place to eat breakfast. It didn't take her long to find a cozy little restaurant advertising home-style cooking. She parked and went inside. The tantalizing scents that greeted her entry made her realize how hungry she was. Over a hearty breakfast, she considered her options for the day.

Her first order of business would be finding a motel. Then she'd get a map of the city and plot her course. There were four businesses on her list she had appointments with. Others she would cold call. She hoped to meet with the owners, show them her portfolio and convince them she was exactly what they'd been looking for. She'd also encourage them to visit her display at the upcoming Memorial Day Orchid Show or even her greenhouses at home.

Once she had her business out of the way, she had some personal shopping to do. She wanted to get Claire something special, a thank you for her help with Carlee while she was away on this business trip. Then there was Carlee's birthday, just ten days away. Hopefully, she'd be able to find a gift or two for that. It was hard to believe that Carlee would be four in just a few short days.

Tomorrow she'd head for Jacksonville and repeat her agenda, then on to Orlando Thursday for more of the same. She'd reserved all of Friday for the orchid show in Tampa where she planned on walking around, checking out the displays, talking to people, and showing her portfolio of orchids to anyone who showed an interest. She also hoped to pick up some ideas that would help her with her own display for the Memorial Day Orchid Show.

"Whew, I've got a lot to do over the next few days!" Jenna mused as she shoveled the last of her hash browns into her mouth.

Many hours later a weary but very pleased Jenna drove toward her motel. The day had gone exceptionally well. She'd impressed several people with her portfolio and they'd shown genuine interest in her price lists and brochures. After looking at inventories, listening to individual needs, and eliciting promises from many of them to visit her display sometime over the Memorial Day weekend, she felt instinctively that she had made at least one or two new customers.

Overall, it had been an exhilarating day, one which she'd topped off by dining at a lovely little restaurant where the tablecloths were not plastic and the dishes were china.

She was almost to her motel when she spotted the mall. Impulsively, she pulled into the parking lot. This would be the perfect place to find a gift for Claire.

She strolled through the mall slowly, going from one store to another, picking out a gift for Claire here, buying a birthday present for Carlee there, in no hurry to head for her motel room and television.

She wished she'd remembered to pack a book. She loved to read, especially in bed when Carlee was down for the night and the house was quiet. It was an enjoyment she particularly relished because it was one she could never indulge in when married to Ned, who had demanded lights out immediately upon going to bed.

When she passed a bookstore, she didn't have to think twice about entering. It was a large bookstore with rows of well-ordered books stretching down several long columns. She noticed a small crowd near the back. There were several children milling about and a line of people circling around behind a shelf. Some author signing books, she thought, grateful the mayhem was in the children's section, not in the main part of the store where she was.

She headed first to the romance section and began browsing through books. Big mistake. It seemed that every cover featured a hard-bodied man. If she took something like that back to the motel room with her, she wouldn't be reading or sleeping. She'd be thinking about Jake Corbin. Thinking about those blue eyes, the desire darkening the blue to midnight. Thinking about those soft firm lips trailing kisses across her face. Thinking about those sensuous hands scorching a trail over her skin. She'd be remembering that hard body tangled with hers, his mouth inches away, his eyes dark and hungry. And remembering her own hungry arousal.

She used a book to fan her face while she headed for the mysteries. They really should up the air conditioning in the romance section.

It was tough choosing something to read from the wide selection on the shelves, and she picked up and put down about twenty books without coming to a decision. Finally, ready to take anything just to get out of there, she spotted a book that caught her interest and she couldn't resist picking it up. She knew if she bought it she would probably regret it, but couldn't force herself to put it back on the shelf.

With her selection in hand, she began making her way toward the cashier. She was almost at the front when the crowd at the back of the store drew her attention to the children's section once more. It wasn't very often that she made it into a bookstore, so while she was here, maybe she should get a book for Carlee.

"I'd like to purchase a book for my daughter," she told the clerk. "Could you recommend one?"

"Sure. How old is she?"

"She's almost four."

"I bet she'd like a Wendy book," the young clerk said with a flashing smile.

"A Wendy book?"

"Yes, the Wendy series are fantasy books popular with kids as young as three and as old as ten."

"That's quite an age range."

"True, but the text is written at a level for older kids while the pictures illustrate the story for the younger audience. They're especially popular with kids your daughter's age. And as luck would have it, the author is here right now doing a book signing."

Jenna glanced dubiously at the crowd near the back. The line hadn't thinned out at all. Standing in line didn't appeal to her. She was coming down from her exciting day, feeling a little dragged, looking forward to a hot shower, cool sheets and a good book. "I'm not sure," she said. "I'm sort of in a hurry."

"Well, you don't have to get it signed. We have plenty on the shelf. Just pick one out and bring it up here. The first one in the series is called *Wendy the Wood Nymph*. It was a best seller when it first came out and it's still a hot item. I think your little girl will like it."

"Thanks," Jenna said, giving the young man a smile. Skirting the crowds of milling people, she made a beeline for the shelf prominently identified with a Wendy series headboard. Within moments she'd found the book the clerk recommended. She was about to pick it up when a different title caught her attention. *Wendy and the Butterfly Queen.* Carlee loved butterflies. She even had her own butterfly garden.

Jenna picked the book up and started toward the checkout, casually leafing through the pages. Yes, she thought, seeing the pretty wood nymph and colorful illustrations of various butterflies, Carlee would definitely like it.

When her turn came to check out, she closed the book and slid it across the counter. That's when she noticed the author's name. Jake Corbin. *Jake Corbin?!* She snatched the book back and read it again, as though somehow she could have read the name incorrectly.

Her eyes slid from the name on the cover to the crowd at the back of the room. She couldn't see the author, he was behind a shelf of books. But she knew by the fluttery feeling in her stomach that the man doing the signing was not just any Jake Corbin. He was the Jake Corbin who had wreaked havoc on her libido, who had been on the edge of her thoughts, and frequently in the center of her thoughts, since that electric moment when fate had literally thrown them together.

She should drop the book like a hot potato, turn on her fashionable navy pumps, and flee as fast as her tight thigh-high suit skirt would let her. Flee!

Instead, she paid for her books, willing her hands not to tremble. Then, clutching *Wendy and the Butterfly Queen* to her breast, she walked toward the crowd surrounding Jake. She took her place at the end of the line and waited. As she progressed slowly closer to Jake, an anonymous voice announced the closing of the bookstore in twenty minutes.

When she rounded the corner, she saw Jake for the first time since their tumble in her yard. He looks tired, Jenna thought, hungrily devouring his features as she waited her turn. He looks exhausted. He looks, he looks—anguished.

"My daughter just loves your books, Mr. Corbin," a woman was gushing. "I've read all three of them to her at least ten times each. When are you coming out with number four?"

"I'm not sure," Jake said, smiling at the woman. "When I work through my writer's block, I guess."

Jenna noted the way Jake wiped his hand across his eyes. Was he trying to erase the pain that seemed more pronounced tonight than it had yesterday? She noted how he avoided looking directly at the children who accompanied their parents to the book signing. And she thought she understood. It's the kids, she thought, remembering the way he had reacted to Carlee. Jake Corbin just doesn't like kids. That's the plain truth of the matter.

And then she was at the table. Silently she laid the book down and slid it across the table. Without looking up, Jake reached for the book, his movement slow, lethargic.

"You look tired," Jenna said, forcing her voice to sound light and teasing. "You and that dog been wrestling unsuspecting females to the ground again?"

Jake's eyes flew up to her face and the transformation was amazing. The fatigue disappeared and a smile crept from his mouth to his eyes.

"Jenna," he breathed, his voice almost reverent.

"Jake," she breathed back jokingly, but she couldn't quite pull it off. The word came out with a catch to her voice, a voice every bit as charged with emotion as Jake's had been.

Then he seemed to get control of himself. "You following me, lady?" he teased with that quirked eyebrow.

"Hmph. Does a rattlesnake do the cha-cha?" she asked, tapping the book to remind him of his duty. On a sigh, she thought. He could slip past a woman's defenses on a sigh.

"Is this for your little girl?"

"Yes, it's for Carlee." She spelled it for him.

Jake signed the book with a flourish, then handed it back to her.

"Will you wait for me?" He glanced behind her at the few remaining people. "I should be finished in about ten minutes or so."

No, no, a thousand times no her logical mind warned. "Sure," her treacherous mouth blurted.

Jenna found a bench and sat down, her books on her lap, her eyes on Jake. He'd been so friendly with her just moments before, but now, once again, he looked strained. As Jenna watched, a little girl approached him, holding out her book for him to sign. She heard Jake's murmured question asking the girl for her name. When the little girl answered, her piping voice rang crystal clear in the rapidly diminishing crowd.

"Elizabeth. With a zee."

At the words, the color drained from Jake's face. Even from her distance of several feet Jenna could see Jake's agitation, see his hand shake as he signed the book. When the child took the book from him, smiling, he looked over her shoulder, acknowledging her thanks with a curt nod.

Jenna was puzzled. Jake was obviously a successful children's book author, yet he seemed to have this strong aversion to kids. Why? Maybe she should ask him before spending too much time in his company. Hopefully it was something he was willing to talk about because it was definitely something she needed to find out about.

It took about 15 minutes for Jake to finish up, but eventually the last book was signed, and he and Jenna left the store together.

"How about a soda or something to eat," Jake asked. "There's a place right around the corner. It's kind of noisy, they play disco, but the sandwiches are good."

"I'm not hungry, but a Coke would definitely hit the spot," Jenna said.

As they walked the short distance from the bookstore to the mall's disco, Jenna silently chastised herself. Why am I doing this? If I am going to go ga-ga over a man, this has got to be the worst choice in the world. He's got some weird aversion to kids, which I really need to find out about, Carlee's scared of him, and, bottom line, he's too potent. I can't even think straight when I'm within hailing distance of him. Talk about a recipe for disaster.

Jake's thoughts were a little less complicated. I'm going to celebrate life to the fullest. And I'm going to celebrate it with Jenna Kincaid.

They spotted an empty booth in the discotheque and slid in, Jenna on one side, Jake on the other.

"I couldn't believe it when I saw you standing in front of me at the bookstore," Jake said, toying with the saltshaker. Jenna tore her gaze away from the sight of those slender, competent fingers gliding across the shaker as he turned it in his hands.

"I'm here on business," she said, and launched into a lengthy explanation of her trip.

As she talked about orchids, Jake watched her, fascinated by her animated expression and sparkling eyes. He interrupted occasionally to ask a question, and it didn't take long for him to arrive at the conclusion that behind that feminine allure was an astute businesswoman.

She was relating an amusing episode with a wholesaler who'd mistaken her for a fast food delivery person when a live band stepped onto the stage. Within minutes, the noise level in the small discothèque was so loud that they couldn't hear each other without shouting. After repeating herself several times with increasing volume, Jenna shook her head and gave up.

Jake moved to her side of the table and squeezed in beside her. He laid an arm across the back of the booth, leaned his face close to hers and spoke in her ear. "Much better," he said.

Jenna continued her story, trying hard to ignore his breath wafting through her hair, causing individual strands to flutter about, tickling her face and neck. Was he aware of the sensations he was creating in her? Like the heat radiating from her thigh because his was pressed against it? Or the electricity racing through her veins at the touch of his broad chest brushing against her shoulder when he leaned her way?

Of course he was. Nobody could have that much potent charm and not know it. He probably left a bevy of fainting females in his wake wherever he went. She should stop this nonsense. End it. Now.

But she couldn't. His touch felt so good, and the electric currents shooting through her body were so addictive. A tune danced through her thoughts and she reworded it to match her mood. I've grown addicted to your touch, addicted oh so much, addicted to your touch.

She looked up at him then, and knew with certainty that he was feeling the same things she was. He wanted her. The hooded eyes did nothing to hide the desire darkening the blue as he devoured every inch of her face. As his hands continually touched her, on her hand, her arm, her shoulder.

She finally did find the willpower to pull away, turning slightly so her back was to the corner of the booth, leaning into the corner and holding her drink between them like a cold, wet, chaperone. Immediately she missed his touch.

She set her glass on the table and straightened in the booth so they were once again shoulder-to-shoulder, thigh-to-thigh. Just for a few minutes, she thought, no defenses. Just for a few minutes, I'll let him in. And she leaned toward him, hopelessly lost in the warm breath stirring her hair, in the slender fingers that made seduction an art.

I want her.

Jake knew he was behaving like a lovesick teenager, but he couldn't seem to stop himself. He deliberately shifted his weight just to feel his body move against hers. He placed his hand over hers while talking to her. He even reached up and tucked her flyaway red hair behind her ear. But it wasn't enough, not nearly enough. Those fleeting touches were like mosquito bites that had to be scratched or he'd go mad. He wanted her in his arms, wanted to feel her body against his.

"Care to dance?" he asked.

Yes, yes, hold me in your arms. "Better not. I haven't danced in years," she said.

"Like riding a bike," he said, taking her hand, ignoring her feeble protests, and leading her onto the small dance floor.

Then she was in his arms, being held much too close, her breasts pulled against his hard chest, and her arms entwined around his neck.

The music was fast, but Jake and Jenna weren't dancing to the music. Their world was confined to the space of their arms, and they were making their own music. It coursed through their veins in a melody old as time.

Jake loved the scent of her, her hair, her skin, so flowery, so subtle, pulling him closer, tempting him to bury his face in her hair, in the curve where that beautiful neck met her shoulder, between her breasts.

"What is it?" he asked. "That fragrance you're wearing, designed to drive a man crazy?"

She hesitated, knowing the name was a blatant invitation, then finally told him. "It's called Kiss Me Quick."

His intake of breath was proof enough that it was aptly named.

Jake slid his fingers up Jenna's back and entwined them in the silky strands of her hair. Her head tilted back so it rested in the palm of his hand, and she looked at him from under lids grown heavy with desire. Her green eyes smoldered. And her lips, those unbelievably kissable lips, were slightly parted.

"You're driving me mad," Jake whispered in her ear. His lips trailed from her ear across her cheek to her mouth.

But Jenna, though her body was clamoring for that kiss, found the resolve to turn her face before Jake's lips claimed hers.

"Jake," she pleaded in a whisper, looking around. "Not here."

Jake stopped, his body protesting, but his heart singing. She didn't say no. She'd said not here. He could feel the blood coursing through his body, his nerves tuned to a fine edge, his flesh and bone and muscle primed for action. He felt like lifting his face to the stars and shouting. "Vincero! Vincero!" like Calaf in *Turandot*. "I shall win! I shall win!" He had never felt more alive in his life. And he had never wanted a woman more.

He moved away from her a half step and lifted his face, but he kept his arms around her. He couldn't break that contact.

Jenna didn't move away from him, and she kept her arms around his neck. Their eyes met. Their desire hung in the air between them, alive, palpable.

"Let's get out of here," Jake said.

Jenna nodded without speaking, knowing her voice would come out shaky.

Jake took her hand and led her off the dance floor. They held hands as they walked through the mall and out to the parking lot. When they reached Jenna's car, Jake leaned against it and pulled Jenna into his arms, between his legs.

She felt so good. His blood seemed to be singing, and the music was as fast as the disco beat had been.

"I don't want to say good night, Jenna," he said, putting a hand on each side of her face and gently hooking her willful hair behind her ears. "I don't want to let go of you."

"We—we can hardly go through life joined at the elbow," she said, trying to lighten the intensity. Her voice betrayed her, coming out strangely deep and throaty.

Jake smiled in appreciation of her attempt. Even Billy Crystal and Robin Williams standing in front of them having an ad lib tournament couldn't distract him from Jenna or tamp his desire, he thought. He traced his finger across her cheek to her mouth, outlining the delicious curve of her lips.

"I think I could go through life with you joined at the lips," he said softly. "But first I'd like to explore that hypothesis."

Jenna swallowed, overwhelmingly conscious of those sensuous fingers seducing her mouth. "Yes," she whispered, "a hypothesis of that magnitude should be tested."

Jake kissed her then, a tender kiss, tentative at first as though giving her an opportunity to stop. When she responded with a hungry ferocity that alarmed her, he plunged into her mouth, plundering it with savage joy, a mad contagion that swept her into its dizzying whirlpool. She moaned, little sounds of pleasure, need, and greed, and Jake gave her what she craved, his kisses reaching deep inside her to draw her very essence to mingle with his.

Then he kissed her gently, playfully, small exploratory kisses that nibbled at her lips, her earlobes, her neck, her eyelids, the tip of her nose, and back to her lips again, where another hungry kiss sought the velvety recesses of her mouth and brought her to the brink of fainting.

Jenna floated on the edge of the swoon, feeling more completely seduced, more completely melded, more completely loved by Jake's kisses than she had ever felt in five years of marriage to Ned. Jake's kisses seduced her, aroused her, awakened responses that thrilled and enchanted her. She met his hungry kisses with a raw appetite as ravaging as his own; she responded to his tender kisses with kisses so beautiful, so soft that tears sprang to her eyes.

As he explored every inch of her face with gentle, exciting nibbles, she playfully nipped his wonderful lips and ears and neck. She was floating in an unreal world made up of Jake's lips and hands and hard body, floating in sensations that burst in her and around her, and finally, were her.

"I never knew—I never knew," she whispered, wonder lighting her face.

Jake laughed softly, burying his face in her sweet-scented hair. Kiss Me Quick hair. The knowledge that he was going to bed this intoxicating woman rushed through his blood like Niagara Falls. A celebration of life.

He threw back his head and laughed in exultation. Jenna looked at him, puzzled, his contagious laughter bringing a smile to her own lips. He couldn't explain. How could he tell her what she'd done for him, given him? Tonight he could only speak with kisses.

Her responses humbled and thrilled him at the same time. Her trembling body, her hungry kisses. Her woman's hands, so hesitant yet so adept as they stroked his face, his neck, his mouth. Each seeking touch was an arrow tipped with Cupid's magic, a shaft carrying desire that tore through his flesh.

There was so much woman inside her waiting to be awakened. I didn't know, she'd said. Jake both cursed and thanked the lazy lout of a husband who had never taken the time to pleasure her, explore her, seduce her. He would gladly be her tutor. He pulled her against him, reveling in the feel of her, the flat stomach, the soft breasts, the trembling thighs. He pushed his hardness between her legs and gasped as her sudden tightening legs nearly undid him. The throbbing demand, the burning desire, raced through his body, consumed him.

He wanted her now, here, this minute.

And he laughed again, a soft laugh colored with exquisite anticipation.

Her trembling thighs were his undoing. He had to touch her, had to feel her flesh against his. He wrapped his hands around her derrière, that firm, soft, delightful piece of anatomy, and slid his hands down her thighs under that short skirt. Kiss Me Quick skirt. Then his hands were between her thighs, caressing the soft flesh as they slid up to her womanhood.

His blood was pounding, fast. She was moist, ready, and he had to have her.

"Jake," Jenna's whisper was ragged with emotion. She was looking around. "We're—we're in a parking lot, for pete's sake." She tried to laugh, but it was too shaky to be convincing.

Jake had to physically shake himself to bring his senses back to the mundane world of parking lots and onlookers.

"You're right," he said when he could speak above a husky croak. He took her face in both his hands, brushed a kiss across her lips, trailed the kiss up to her ear, and whispered, his breath a warm caress, "At the risk of sounding very, very, trite, your place or mine?"

They decided on her motel room, since it was only a short distance away. Jenna drove Jake to where his Land Rover was parked and Jake followed her to her motel.

They got out of their cars and walked toward each other a little self-consciously. The short drive had given them a few minutes to cool down, to question the wisdom of taking this next step, and had the drive been three or four weeks longer, they may have talked themselves out of the tryst.

But their blood had barely ceased boiling, and the minute they reached each other and joined hands, desire swept through them with the force of a hurricane.

Jake pulled Jenna into his arms, unwilling to wait the minute it would take to walk to the motel door, unlock it, and step inside. She was trembling.

"Are you cold?" he whispered, running his hands up and down her arms. In the still night, whispering seemed the natural thing to do.

"No," she whispered back. "I—I don't know why I'm shaking."

"Are you scared?" He fervently hoped not. He stroked her hair.

"No." The thought made her laugh softly. "No. I guess I'm just nervous. I—this—" She motioned toward the motel. "It's been a long time. I might not be too good at this. You might be disappointed." She was babbling. "Just nervous."

Disappointed?! A wave of emotion swept over him, an urge to protect her, to shield her from every kind of hurt, physical and emotional. He wanted to say something, do something, that would reassure her, that would make the trembling stop.

"You wonderful, desirable, beautiful, silly little goose," he said, kissing her face between words. "You could never disappoint me. Fate threw us together, you know. Yesterday and today. We were meant for each other." He voice dropped to a seductive growl. "Let me prove it to you."

The trembling stopped beneath the ardor of his kiss. There was no room for doubts when kisses fused their lips and their bodies melded into one.

"Let me prove it to you," he whispered again. "Out here, or in there." In that moment he didn't care where they made love. In the gravel parking lot, in the motel room, atop the flagpole.

They didn't break apart as they moved the few steps to the motel door. Jenna fumbled in her purse for the key as Jake stroked his hand down her back, his fingers leaving a trail of promises her body acknowledged with tremors of need.

She finally found the key, finally fitted it in the lock, finally opened the door.

Jake was already cautioning himself to go slow, go slow. He wanted to make it good for Jenna. He wanted this to be a night she would never forget, hours of sensual pleasure while they explored erotic zones and shared their bodies' secrets. The thought of Jenna beneath him, her eyes smoldering, her body writhing, the soft little cries she made, her passionate responses bringing them both to the brink of ecstasy—he'd prolong the sweet torture until he'd awakened every pore in her body and each and every one was begging for release. Then, only then, together they'd make that dizzying flight to heaven.

Go slow, go slow, he cautioned himself. He knew he would, for Jenna's sake, for Jenna's pleasure, but keeping his own body in check was going to be a tough struggle.

Once inside the hotel room, Jenna turned to Jake with that fascinating contradiction of brazen innocence that pumped his excitement up a couple more notches.

He reached for her, and as he did his eyes slid across the bed and lit on the picture frame on the nightstand. It was one of those folding stand-up frames that hold three separate pictures. In each of the three frames was a picture of a little girl. Jenna's little girl. Carlee with the red curls and big brown eyes. In one picture she looked about a year old, holding a teddy bear, in the middle picture about two with an ice cream cone dripping down her hand, and in the third about three, swinging in a tire swing, her hair blowing in the wind.

And all he could see was Lizzy. With a crippling blow that struck like lightning, he felt the pain of his loss, a pain so sharp it stabbed through his heart, staggering him.

Jenna felt Jake jerk away from her, gasping, his face twisted with anguish.

"Jenna," he said, his voice choked with emotion, his eyes burning with pain and despair. "Jenna, I'm sorry. I'm so sorry. Forgive me. I can't do this. I'm sorry."

As she stared at him in shocked silence, he stepped back from her, turned and fled.

In his car, Jake gripped the steering wheel till his knuckles were white, banging his head against the back of the seat. His heart was pounding, his blood racing, yet he felt drained, empty.

Those pictures, those damned pictures. In the fleeting minute his eyes had focused on them, Lizzy was back. Lizzy, one year old, toddling about the house, reaching for everything her alert blue eyes could see. Lizzy, two years old, climbing into his lap for her good night story, her Wendy story, she always insisted on a Wendy story. Lizzy, three years old, chasing butterflies, trying to hold a fishing pole, begging for just one more push in the swing.

He hadn't expected to see those pictures, he wasn't ready, he hadn't steeled himself. And the pain had been so instantaneous, so sharp and so intense it had overpowered all other thoughts and feelings. Instinct took over and he had fled.

He laughed a short, bitter laugh. How ironic to think that Jenna had been worried that *she* would disappoint *him*.

As the pain subsided, he tried to rationalize what had happened. Maybe subconsciously he knew that it wouldn't be fair to Jenna to start something with her before he'd resolved the issue of Carlee. Or maybe he thought Carlee was a threat, that she'd replace Lizzy. He couldn't betray Lizzy, couldn't let any little girl take her place. He knew the logic was flawed, but it was the best he could come up with.

And right or wrong, no logic could change the fact that he had had the most desirable woman he'd ever known in his arms and one look at the pictures had made him powerless to finish what he'd started.

How could he ever put Jenna or himself through that again?

He couldn't.

Jenna was still in a state of disbelief as she heard Jake drive away. What had caused his sudden transformation? A feeling of déjà vu swept over her. It was just like yesterday when Carlee had walked out on the porch and Jake had turned and fled.

Jenna glanced around and her eyes rested on the pictures of Carlee. That's what had caused Jake to turn cold and leave, she was convinced of it. Jake had seen the pictures of Carlee and torn off like a fox running from the hounds.

"Damn," she said quietly. She felt humiliated, let down, confused. And hungry for Jake, wanting nothing so much as she wanted to finish the journey his hands and lips had promised.

Finally, she stripped off her clothes and took a shower, a very long and very cold shower. Then she climbed into bed.

And thought about the book she'd purchased on impulse earlier that night.

"I'm not going to read," she muttered. "No way am I going to read." She reached over and grabbed the TV remote. Flipping through the channels, she found only one clear enough to watch. The featured program was a talk show. She hated talk shows.

With a heavy sigh she punched the off button. Her eyes strayed to the book she'd purchased. Not gonna happen! She fluffed her pillow, switched off the light and tried to go to sleep.

After fifteen minutes of tossing and turning, she gave up. With another heavy sigh she snapped her light back on and retrieved the treacherous book.

Opening the book, she settled down and began to read.

"My name's Bond. James Bond."

CHAPTER FOUR

"I'm home!" Jenna called cheerfully as she walked through the door, then followed the mouth-watering aroma of baking cookies. She found Claire in the kitchen taking a batch of macaroons from the oven to add to several piles of chocolate chip, sugar, and windmill cookies stacked on the table.

"Oh, good," Claire said. "I was starting to worry that you might not make it back in time for the auction."

"I cut my visit to the orchid show short so I'd get back in time."

"So how'd it go?"

"Better than my highest expectations. It seemed like nothing could go wrong." If she overlooked those few hours of insanity with Jake. She busied herself placing cookies on a tray so Claire wouldn't read in her eyes the confusion she still was feeling. For three nights and three days she had tried to rationalize Jake's behavior, but nothing she could think of explained his actions. Even his dislike of kids didn't seem to be a strong enough motive to cause that swift and complete reversal of feelings. So ironic, she thought, that a man who disliked kids as much as he did should be such a successful children's book author.

When she spoke she made her voice upbeat. "I'm positive that every dollar I spent on this trip will return big dividends. Umm, Claire, don't you think you've got enough cookies?"

"It's all for a good cause," Claire reminded her. "Those dear little tykes. If this small effort on my part can put some joy in their lives—" Claire shook her head as her words trailed off.

The auction was a fundraiser to send the Elmwood House kids to camp. Elmwood House kids were abused, neglected, or abandoned kids that the state of Florida had placed in state care. Their ages ranged from birth to 16, and some of them reached the haven of Elmwood House in near dead condition, with broken bones or starved bodies, many with physical and mental scars. Ever since Elmwood House had opened its doors four years ago, the community had rallied behind it. Just about every organization in Providence and neighboring towns had Elmwood House at the top of its list of charitable causes.

The auction, Jenna had learned from Millie, her hairdresser, was a big annual event, promoted and backed by a couple hundred businesses, civic groups, and charities. There would be a lot of media coverage, from the smallest newspaper to regional magazines and TV stations.

Jenna was going, not only to support such a worthy cause, although that was certainly reason enough, and not only to represent her business, which, too, was reason enough and had prompted her to donate a large orchid arrangement to the effort, but also for a more selfish reason. Millie had told her the last time Jenna had a haircut that one of her customers was donating a cookie jar. So Jenna was feeling good on three levels. She was doing a good deed, she was promoting her business, and if she were lucky, she could add a neat cookie jar to her collection.

"Where's Carlee?" Jenna asked, wondering why she hadn't poked her inquisitive little nose into the kitchen yet.

"Out in back with her butterfly garden," Claire said in a voice indulgent and full of pride. She thought her granddaughter a genius with an aptitude for plants well beyond her years. "Our little Mozart of horticulture," she called Carlee.

"I'll just go say hi to her before I take a shower," Jenna said, heading for the back door and dropping a kiss on Claire's cheek as she passed her. "I love you, Mom," she said.

The impulsive action surprised both of them. Jenna hurried outside while Claire touched a hand to her cheek and stared after her daughter with a quizzical look.

In the yard she found Carlee was in a sunny corner they had officially designated her butterfly garden. It contained milkweed, sage, fennel and other herb plants to feed the caterpillars after they hatched from their pin-sized eggs, as well as brightly blossomed plants to attract butterflies desiring a taste of nectar. Framing the garden on two sides were shelter shrubs and trees where butterflies could sleep in comparative safety from predators. Many of the plants were native to Florida and native to their yard. They'd only had to make one or two additions to satisfy Carlee's critical appraisal and turn the spot into a one-stop butterfly Eden.

To a lesser degree, Jenna agreed with Claire's opinion of Carlee. She definitely did have an aptitude for horticulture. She knew the common names of the plants in her butterfly garden, and even some of the scientific names. She'd been talking in complete sentences since the age of two, and had picked up the names of plants when she accompanied Jenna to plant nurseries. While Jenna walked around picking up seedlings or other things for the yard, Carlee would engage the astonished clerks in intelligent dialogue. She never remembered to put her dirty clothes in the laundry basket when she took a shower, but when it came to plant talk, her memory was phenomenal and she'd always come home quoting new gems of knowledge to Claire and Jenna.

But she looked very much like a little girl, not a horticultural prodigy, as she struggled with an oversize watering can, sprinkling a few drops of water into a shallow dish.

"Mommy! You're home!" Carlee set the watering can down and ran to meet Jenna, throwing arms around Jenna in a big hug. Then she scrambled free and took Jenna's hand, tugging her toward the butterfly garden.

"Look, Mommy," Carlee pointed to a large flat rock sitting in a dish. "This rock is perfect for the monarch. See how flat it is, and big. I found it over there by the woods. The monarch likes rocks like that. It can rest there while it unrolls its probsis and drinks the water."

Jenna grinned. Carlee might know the terms, but it would be a while before she could roll her tongue around words like "proboscis."

"And hello to you too," Jenna said. "It looks like you kept yourself busy while I was away."

"Uh huh," Carlee said, pulling Jenna to the other end of her garden.

"Look." Her voice dropped to a reverent hush. She pointed to a curling leaf. "Willy's starting to make his chryslis."

"Wow, that's a very nice chrysalis," Jenna said.

"Pretty soon he'll be a butterfly," Carlee announced as though she were a teacher addressing a student. "In seven to ten days."

"Should we have a coming out party for it?" Jenna joked.

"Could we? Could we?" Carlee squealed, her eyes sparkling with excitement.

Oh-oh. Jenna had been joking but she realized she'd gotten herself into something. She found it almost impossible to say no to Carlee if it meant dashing the child's joy.

"Well," Jenna said, "I'm pretty busy with my show coming up and everything, so you'll have to make all the plans. Okay?"

Carlee nodded, her face suffused with happiness.

"Look," she said, pointing to a large trash bag stuffed half full. "I pulled all those weeds out of my garden."

"Hmm," Jenna said. "Are you sure they're all weeds?"

Carlee gave her mother a scornful look.

"Okay, okay," Jenna said, laughing and backing away, holding her hands out as though to ward off a blow. "Forget I said that."

Her laugh was drowned out by a sudden clap of thunder. They both jumped. "I guess that's Mother Nature telling me to get inside and take my shower," Jenna said. "But before I do, I bought something for you. Want to come inside and see what it is?"

She took Carlee's hand and they ran toward the house.

Once inside, Jenna unzipped her suitcase and handed Carlee the bag from the bookstore.

Carlee quickly tore the book from the bag. "Oh Mommy, Look! Butterflies! Read it to me."

"I wish I could, munchkin, but I won't have time tonight." Jenna said, rummaging through her bag for the box with Claire's gift in it.

"I'll read it to you tonight when you're tucked in bed," Claire promised.

"And this is for you, Claire," Jenna said, handing her the box. "Thanks for taking such good care of Carlee while I was away."

"You didn't need to get me anything," Claire said, but a smile curved her lips as she removed the lid from the box. "Oh, I love it," she said, holding the navy blue vest splashed with wild colors to her chest and doing a comical strut across the room.

"It's reversible," Jenna said. "The blue side is for your wild and crazy moments. The blue even matches that streak in your hair. The other side…" She paused as Claire reversed the vest. It was a conservative cream color. "If you ever decide you'd like a more sedate look," Jenna finished.

Claire wrinkled her nose. "Sedate? Not in this lifetime."

Jenna laughed and headed upstairs to get ready for the auction.

"I laid out a dress for you to wear while you were outside with Carlee," Claire called up after her. "I figured that would save you a bit of time, since it's getting so late."

When she stepped into her bedroom Jenna noticed a newspaper lying on the bed, folded to highlight a story. Curiously she glanced at it. Good grief, it was written by Jake Corbin. Was there some plot afoot to torment her with that name? Everywhere she looked, there it was, blazoned across a book, blazoned across a newspaper. She picked the paper up and read the story, curious despite herself about anything he had written. It was a succinct account of a ribbon cutting ceremony at a new hardware store, which held little interest for Jenna. She was more intrigued by the thought that Jake wrote for the paper. Would he be covering the auction tonight?

Jenna's gaze slid to the dress Claire had laid neatly across her pillows. It was her emerald green sheath, a short clingy number that she seldom wore. It was cool, it was comfortable, and it made her look terrific, but despite its simple cut it usually came off looking too dressy for the places an orchid grower went.

Jenna sighed at Claire's blatant machinations—the newspaper story placed where she couldn't miss it hinting that Jake might show up at the auction, and the sexiest dress she had in her wardrobe waiting for her to step into. You would think that Claire, who was so wary of a romantic entanglement herself, would stop trying to nudge Jenna into one, especially after her disastrous experience with Ned. But as Claire often remarked when the subject came up, Ned had been a bad mistake and it shouldn't deprive Jenna of happiness or Carlee of a father.

"Claire, Claire, Claire," she murmured, heading for the bathroom.

Several minutes later, fresh from the shower and wearing nothing but a towel wrapped around her wet hair, Jenna padded across the bedroom, carefully skirting the queen-size bed protruding into the middle of the small room. Why do architects always skimp on bedroom space when everyone knows that's where all the biggest furniture goes, she wondered rhetorically. She had enough bruises from her wrestling match on the ground with Jake and Buster; she didn't need to add any more by banging her thigh into the bed's footboard. Been there, done that.

She paused in front of the closet door's full-length mirror to judge the extent of her bruises. The night was hot and humid, sticky, the way it always got before a thunderstorm, and the auction was liable to be crowded, a lot of body heat to contend with. The cool sheath was sounding better by the minute, but it was short and it was sleeveless. Would her bruises show? And if so, would people speculate about their cause? Think she was a battered wife perhaps? She turned slowly before the mirror, examining her arms and legs.

When Jenna was fifteen, she'd fantasized about being a model, wearing beautiful, sexy clothes, appearing on the cover of *Cosmopolitan* in some impossibly seductive pose. She'd don her bikini and buckets of makeup, then spend hours in front of the mirror, her lips puckered, a lock of hair brushed over one eye, perfecting the pose that would best show off her budding cleavage.

Luckily, by the time she was sixteen, she'd discovered the joys of horticulture, thanks to a part-time job in a local nursery, and modeling lost out to hybridizing. Luckily, because her height peaked at five feet five, far short of the requisite inches that got you past the receptionist's desk at modeling agencies. Creating a hybrid plant, she'd discovered, was so awesome and emotionally rewarding that she'd gone on to major in horticulture at Ohio State.

During those years she'd discovered orchids and from the time her first plant had burst into glorious lavender bloom, she'd been lost to the charms of the beautiful, big-lipped plants. She joined orchid groups, read orchid books, attended orchid shows, started collecting, growing and cataloguing orchids. She was obsessed, a willing captive in that exotic world.

Immediately after graduation she'd married Ned.

It had been a lot of years since she'd practiced sexy poses in front of a mirror.

Jenna blinked in surprise. What in heaven's name had triggered those memories?

A quick scrutiny reassured her that her bruises had faded to near invisibility. Great. She pulled open the dresser drawer that held her panties and bras. Her favorite white cotton ones lay on top and she reached for them automatically. But as she started to pick them up, she hesitated, then reached toward the back of the drawer.

It only took a moment for her fingers to encounter the silky objects she'd stuffed way back there when she and Claire had first moved in. She pulled the matching panty and bra set out for inspection. The pieces were scarlet red, a gift from Claire the first Christmas after her divorce. She had never worn them. They were too sexy, too suggestive. After five years of marriage to Ned, sex was something she wanted to escape, not wrap around her. Without giving herself time to question her motive, she snatched her nail clipper and snipped off the tags.

As she dressed, she watched her movements in the closet mirror—one foot in the panties, then the other, the silky red fabric sliding up her legs smooth as Jell-o. The bra caressed her breasts like a lover, its thin spaghetti straps whispering against her skin. She stepped to the mirror, tugged the towel off her head and shook her hair so it fell in wild tangles about her face and spilled over her shoulders, its dark auburn color sparkling under the overhead light. She finger-combed a lock over her eye, puckered her lips seductively and struck the pose she had perfected when she was fifteen. Yep. It still made her cleavage look pretty darn good.

Only it wasn't *Cosmopolitan* she was posing for this time.

Straightening abruptly, Jenna finished dressing quickly with no more absurdities. Jake was not an option, she reminded herself as she slipped into panty hose, pulled the dress over her head, and dug her white slings—the only shoes she had that went with the dress—out of the closet. One, her life was too complicated right now to throw a man into the mix. Two, that transformation Jake had gone through in Tallahassee was pretty scary. And whether Carlee was at the root of the problem or not, Jenna couldn't say, but she was positive that Carlee fit into the mix somehow. If Jake had a problem with kids in general, or worse yet, Carlee in particular, then he definitely wasn't welcome in her life. Especially now, with Carlee finally coming out of her shell, finally daring to laugh and play and make noise without being scared that she would get punished or shouted at or—damn the man—stuck in a corner and terrorized.

But she wasn't going to harp on that tack again. Ned was history.

And she was not going to make another stupid mistake with a man. No, Jake was not an option. Why was she even having this internal argument? There was absolutely nothing to argue about!

Still, she reflected, as she passed the blow dryer back and forth over her hair, even though she would never be a model, it would be kind of fun to have sultry eyes, pouty lips, and legs to the moon. She had no illusions about her looks. She knew she wasn't ugly, but she also believed she didn't have the bone structure for a classical look or the features for a seductive look. And yet. And yet. She remembered the way Jake had looked at her, his eyes frankly admiring, at times almost adoring, and always, always, dark with desire.

She sank down on the bed and for a rapturous minute allowed herself the indulgence of reliving Jake's touch, his magic hands, and those hungry, consuming kisses.

"Oh, Jake," she whispered. "What happened? What happened?"

* * *

It wasn't yet raining when Jenna pulled her van into the hotel's crowded parking lot, but the thunder was getting closer, the lightning more frequent. Another bright flash split the black sky and Jenna automatically counted the seconds between that and the thunderclap that followed, a childhood game that had carried over into adulthood.

After driving around the parking lot twice looking for an empty space close to the hotel entrance, Jenna resigned herself to parking in the farthest corner, a sparsely lit section that gave her the willies. There were no people milling about, and a feeling of isolation swept over her as she swung her van into one of the few remaining spaces.

The emotional roller coaster she'd been on all week still buffeted her feelings, leaving her one minute depressed about her destroyed flowers, then the next excited about her potpourri sachets, new customers, and a possible winner at the upcoming orchid show. One minute she was strung out, frustrated, humiliated, confused about Jake Corbin, the next minute absolutely tingling with desire, aching for his touch.

It was going to be a battle getting Jake Corbin out of her system. It's just an immature, egocentric craving to have what she couldn't have, she told herself, trying Psychology 101 to make sense of her feelings. How could she harbor any feelings for a man as unpredictable, as downright rude, as Jake Corbin? And he had given her a very clear signal in Tallahassee that he didn't want a relationship with her. Mixed signals, she amended, but the bottom line was the same. When she got home she'd half-expected—half-hoped, to be honest—there would be a message for her from Jake, an apology, an explanation, something. But there wasn't, and that was certainly signal enough.

Before getting out of her van and heading in to the auction, Jenna gave herself a few seconds to relax, to gather her thoughts and feelings and expel Jake from her system. Or at the least, push him way back.

And to try to figure out how far away the storm was. She really hoped it would hold off till after the auction and she was back home, snug in bed. She didn't like driving in the rain. She hated driving in a storm. She cocked her head to get a better view of the sky through the windshield. At the next flash of lightning, she began counting the seconds until the thunder cracked.

Thunderstorms always triggered her imagination; they so frequently played such a pivotal role in the mystery novels she loved to read. Authors of murder and mayhem loved storms. And dark corners of parking lots. And a woman alone in a car in a dark corner of a parking lot in a thunderstorm. It was really dark and isolated and eerie, the right side of her brain noted, while the left side of her brain methodically counted 16—17—18—

The loud thunderclap, accompanied by a sharp tap on the window close to her head, was so sudden that she emitted a frightened squeak and jumped convulsively.

The face leering in the window belonged to Ryan Nichols, the founder of Elmwood House. Though he was a young man about her age, he had enough money to start his own bank should he want to. But Ryan Nichols' passion, when it wasn't focused on Elmwood House, ran to horticulture, not banking. He had a green thumb and a genius imagination, which led to his establishing a landscaping business that featured fantastic designs. He was very popular with many of the homeowners moving into the planned community developments that were springing up in Providence. Jenna occasionally ran into him at a nursery they both frequented. Ryan was always, in a half-humorous, half-serious sort of way, trying to seduce her, but he'd never intrigued her interest or aroused her hormones like a certain children's book author.

"My lucky day," he said as she opened the door. "Sorry I startled you."

"Eighteen miles," she said, climbing out of the van. "That's how far away the lightning is." She circled to the back of her van and opened the hatch. Inside, next to her own donation of an orchid arrangement, were two large tins filled with the cookies Claire had baked for the auction. "I sure hope it waits until I get home before it rains." She handed the cookie tins to Ryan before reaching back inside for the orchids.

"Me too. I'd like to get my car in the garage first. I just had it washed today."

"I hate driving in the rain," Jenna said, as she fell into step beside him. "But I love sleeping in the rain."

They reached the revolving doors leading into the hotel and pushed through. "I mean," Jenna said, relishing the blast of cold air that hit them as they stepped into the hotel lobby, "listening to the rain while I'm falling asleep, not really sleeping *in* the rain."

"Yeah, I guess sleeping *in* the rain gives a whole new meaning to wet dreams," Ryan said with a laugh. Jenna's groan was accompanied by her own laugh. They were both still chuckling as they entered the banquet room where the charity auction was being held. The hotel had donated the space as well as the refreshments in support of Elmwood House, prompted by good PR as much as good will, Jenna guessed.

As they turned the cookies and floral arrangement over to a volunteer, Ryan mentioned something about drinks and headed for the bar at the other end of the hall.

"Very nice," Jenna murmured, scarcely noticing what Ryan had said as she looked around. At least a dozen linen-draped tables, covered with auction items, lined the east and west walls. A dais, centered at the front of the room, held the auctioneer's stand, and about a hundred and fifty chairs filled the area directly in front of it. Several small groups of people milled about, their soft murmurs floating around the room.

Jenna noticed several people she knew. There were Polly and her grandmother; they owned a popular inn on the outskirts of Providence that catered to the rich and famous, people from Miami and other busy cities that wanted to escape the rat race for a few days. Jenna had recently received an order for several floral arrangements from Polly. She hoped it was the beginning of a long and lasting business relationship. Phil Averies, Claire's almost-boyfriend, grinned at her and headed for the home-baked goods table to check out Claire's donations, and of course, Seth Elmwood, the owner of Elmwood house, was here. Across the room, Jenna spotted Millie, her hairdresser. She waved and headed in that direction.

While she walked, her eyes moved past Millie and lit on one more person she knew. Jake Corbin. He was watching her with an unreadable expression in his eyes. Was it wariness? Remorse? Whatever it was, it was eclipsed by the desire that seemed to inevitably dominate every meeting they had. He took a step toward her. Was he coming to apologize for Tallahassee, for building her expectations to a fever pitch with his silver tongue, then walking out? She felt a tug of anticipation. Or would he pretend that nothing had happened? Or, like her, was he, too, consumed with this incomprehensible, fatal attraction? Was he planning to drag her into one of the rooms in this hotel and finish what they had started at the motel?

Whatever. He looked so good. So, so good. Thick dark hair falling over a tanned face. Blue bedroom eyes. Hard body. Weak idiot that she was, she hoped his intentions were the third choice.

Obviously he was here to cover the story for the paper, but he still seemed somewhat out of place in these surroundings. Glitter and glitz didn't seem quite his cup of tea. He seemed more the casual type, outdoorsy, swinging from trees, maybe. Although with that dog of his, he was more George of the Jungle than Tarzan. Yes, there was definitely an outdoorsy look about him, despite his profession as a writer.

How did he stay in shape, she wondered idly. It was hard to picture him in a gym, huffing and puffing under a barbell. No, he'd be outdoors, jogging or swimming or macho-mastering some physically demanding sport like mountain climbing or racquetball.

"Here's to a successful auction." Ryan interrupted the moment, handing her a chilled glass of wine, then clicking his glass against hers.

"What? Oh, sure." Jenna would have preferred water, but she accepted the glass and took the requisite sip Ryan's toast demanded.

"This place is packed and they're still coming. It should be a *very* successful night," she agreed with a smile.

Over the rim of her glass, her eyes slid back to Jake. He was standing still, watching her with cold eyes before he deliberately turned and walked away. Baffled, she lowered her glass slowly and stared after him. A second before, he had been heading her way with a predatory look in his eye that brought those Tallahassee kisses vividly to mind, and then, in a heartbeat, that all-too-familiar transformation into the abominable snowman. There was no Carlee in the room to blame it on this time. *What was his problem?*

CHAPTER FIVE

"Jenna! You made it!" Millie grabbed Jenna's arm and pulled her close enough to whisper in her ear, "Lucky you. Every woman at this auction would like to be in your shoes. Be a buddy and introduce me so I can at least say I actually know him."

"I'll be your real buddy and *not* introduce you," Jenna said. "Believe me; you don't want to know him. He's the weirdest neighbor I've ever had. Has this dog the size of an elephant. Keeps tearing up my yard."

Millie stared at Jenna with an expression bordering on awe. "Ryan Nichols is your neighbor?"

"Oh! You mean Ryan! I thought you were talking about—well, never mind." Jenna felt her face turning red and tried to laugh it off.

"So how come you've never told me about you and Ryan Nichols?"

"Because there's nothing to tell. Honest," she added in answer to Millie's skeptical look. "He's just a friend, an acquaintance."

Millie looked again at Ryan with a stare that went way beyond casual interest and when she spoke, her voice was wistful. "I've seen him around town, but I've never actually met him."

"Okay, okay." Jenna said with a grin. Turning, she beckoned to Ryan, who had wandered a few steps away to look at some leather goods on a table.

"I want you to meet my good friend and wonderful hairdresser, Millie Givens."

Millie offered her hand to Ryan. He took it, and with a courtly bow, raised it to his lips. "Ryan Nichols at your service, dear lady."

"Millie's been my lifeline since I moved here," Jenna explained. "Gave me a tour of Providence, introduced me to all the good restaurants and shopping places…" Her voice trailed off. Ryan and Millie were smiling at each other, oblivious to her chatter. Three's a crowd. She sighed and backed away. Time to look for that cookie jar.

She looks so good tonight. Despite his better judgment, Jake couldn't keep his eyes off Jenna Kincaid.

She must hate him. After that disastrous mess he'd made of things in Tallahassee, how could he ever face her? Yet, despite his resolve to spare her and himself any chance of a repeat performance, all his good resolutions had flown out the window when she'd walked through that door tonight. Looking so damned good.

And why was Ryan Nichols panting after her? Didn't she know Nichols had a reputation for being fast and loose with the ladies? A fierce desire to walk over and slug Nichols silly burned in him. Stupid, he thought. Get real, he thought. But he couldn't ignore the way the muscles in his gut had tightened when he'd seen them enter the banquet hall, laughing together. And again when Nichols' fingers brushed Jenna's as he'd handed her the drink.

The drink. That's what he needed to focus on. Sure she had an eager smile that lit up her face, lips that fascinated him. And that body, so seductively enhanced by the dress she was wearing. He knew what was under that dress—a firm butt, soft thighs, and heat between her legs. His hands had explored that body, begun to, anyway, and now he wanted desperately to finish that exploration.

He wanted her. God help him, and God help her, he wanted her. He wanted to love her, he wanted to make her his, he wanted to make the Tallahassee trip a bad dream they could laugh about as they grew old together. He wanted to make love to her.

But even if he could, and he wondered if he could after what had happened in Tallahassee—she was a drinker. She hadn't been there two minutes before she was guzzling a glass of wine. Well, maybe not guzzling, but guzzling, imbibing, sipping—they all added up to the same thing. She was a drinker. Nothing could induce him to walk that path again. Not even Jenna Kincaid.

He forced his gaze back to his notebook. Work. That's why he was here.

Who else did he need to interview? Ah, Sam Lindquist, a friend as well as the mayor, he was a big sponsor of the charity auction each year. He cornered Lindquist and began to take notes.

She looks so good tonight.

"I declare, Jake, you seem a little distracted."

"Sorry, Sam. You were talking about, um—" a quick glance at his notes, "the plans for remodeling City Hall."

"About five minutes ago. And you were *thinking* about a certain pretty redhead. No, don't deny it. I've got eyes; I'm not blind."

Jake smiled and tried not to let his inner torment show in his eyes. "You're right. I'm sorry, Sam, I confess I just can't seem to keep my eyes off her—"

Mayor Lindquist clapped a large paw on Jake's shoulder. "Don't apologize, son. If you ignored that pretty little filly, now *that* is something to apologize for." He squeezed Jake's shoulder. "I've known you since you were a colt, Jake. Was good friends with your daddy. I know what tragedy you've had to endure. I've suffered with you, you know that. Maybe not outwardly, but here." He placed a hand over his heart. "You've gone through hell, Jake. You deserve some happiness. So don't go apologizing to me because you've got your eye on the prettiest little woman here. Just be sure—" he pointed at Jake's notebook, "—you spell my name right." He winked and headed for the bar.

Jake laughed, as was expected of him, but he looked around, embarrassed. He knew he'd been watching Jenna, but he didn't realize he'd been so obvious. Suddenly he felt like everybody in the place must know he had the hots for her. He resolved to keep his eyes off Jenna and his mind on his job.

She looks so good tonight.

He should talk to her, apologize for Tallahassee. Try to find the words to explain what had happened. But what *had* happened, his sudden inability to perform was something he wasn't, and probably never would be, ready to discuss with Jenna or anybody else. And how could he tell her about Lizzy, make her see what a beautiful treasure she had been, still so much a part of his heart, his life, his soul. How could he talk about her death without breaking down? Oh, that would really cheer up the charity auction!

Most of the time he could contain his pain at some level below the surface, but one glance at Jenna's little girl had reawakened every memory. The good, the bad, the ugly. Lizzy's happy, active little life; Barb's resentful, pathetic, alcoholic existence. If only he'd divorced Barb, or at least separated from her, and taken custody of Lizzy, they would both be alive today. But he'd hung in there, hoping for the best. He'd finally convinced Barb to join AA and she had started to attend meetings. For all their sakes he wanted to keep the family together and had convinced himself that things would work out.

Then came that fateful night. A night like tonight, he realized as a loud clap of thunder reverberated through the banquet hall.

He'd gone to the library to do a little research on armadillos in order to write the final few pages in his Wendy book. Lizzy had been running a low-grade fever, and he'd debated canceling his trip into town, but he knew if he didn't get the research out of the way that night, he wouldn't be able to finish the book in time for Lizzy's fourth birthday, just two days away. He needed to write the ending, then format, print, and bind a special copy for her.

He had always read the newest story to her on her birthday, and she had been expecting it. Wendy the wood nymph had been Lizzy's favorite story character. He'd read the first three stories to her probably fifty times each, and she was looking forward to the new one. As her birthday approached, that's just about all she had talked about.

He had a bike in the garage, red ribbon wrapped around it, and he'd been sure she would get lots of enjoyment out of it, but Lizzy hadn't even asked for any birthday gifts other than the Wendy book. Despite her begging, he wouldn't give her any sneak peeks at the story, so after making her wait, he certainly had not wanted to disappoint her by not having it finished.

Barb had been home and sober, and other than her low-grade fever, Lizzy seemed okay.

So he had left for the library.

Barb had always resented his leaving, especially if the cause was in any way related to his writing. She had resented his writing, jealous of the time and attention it demanded and the accolades he received. As she had frequently pointed out, he had all the fun while she was stuck at home with the kid.

He took responsibility for Lizzy as often as he could so Barb could get out with her friends and do things she wanted to do. He loved to spend time with his beautiful little girl, watching her grow from an infant to a toddler to a bright, happy, preschooler. And he used his influence to get Barb a freelance job with the newspaper. But she was undependable; she forgot interviews and missed deadlines. Her stay in the world of journalism was brief.

She preferred to drown her unhappiness in drink rather than take positive steps to pursue an interest. In the whiskey bottle she found escape from her failures—and Jake's successes. In her worst moments she would scream obscenities at him and deny him her bed. Toward the end, her bed was the last thing Jake wanted, and all his love was lavished on little, beautiful, smart Lizzy.

He probably could have done things differently, spent more time with Barb, taken her on a cruise where she could feel pampered all day, taken her out to dinner more, sent her flowers. He could have, should have, done more, he admitted, burdening his conscious with another layer of guilt.

So that night, over Barb's objections, he had gone to the library, and spent a couple hours immersed in the life of an armadillo so he would know what he was talking about when he wrote the armadillo episode. When he had finished and was leaving the library, the storm broke in all its fury. His cell phone rang, but he waited until he got into his car, out of the rain, before answering it. It was Barb, her voice slurred with drink. Getting drunk was her favorite way of punishing him, and she must have felt the need to punish him for not staying home with her that night. She'd called to tell him that Lizzy's fever had risen and she was taking her to the emergency room.

"Stay right there," he'd ordered. "I'm on my way. I'll drive you."

"Don't bother," she'd slurred, her voice bitter. "I wouldn't want a family emergency to interfere with your *important* work!" And then—Was she laughing or crying? He couldn't be sure—she'd slammed the phone down.

Jake had tried calling back as he'd started the car and begun the frantic trip home, hardly able to see through heavy rain pounding against the windshield. There was no answer, but he prayed she was sitting by the phone, gloating because she'd gotten his attention.

He wasn't that lucky. Neither were Barb and Lizzy.

He'd been the first one on the scene of the accident. Barb's smashed

Corvair was on the side of the road, upside down, its headlights cutting two eerie paths of light through the downpour.

He'd learned from the police report the sequence of events. She'd been driving too fast for conditions, way too fast. She'd lost control of the car, skidded about fifty feet before leaving the road, smashed against a tree and somehow tipped upside down. Barb and Lizzy were both dead.

If only he'd stayed home that night. If only he'd left the library twenty minutes sooner. If only, if only—

Another loud clap of thunder jerked him out of his reverie. He was standing stock still in the middle of the banquet room, gripping his notebook way too hard, dripping with sweat. He forced himself to relax and glanced casually around. People were too busy looking at auction items and talking among themselves to notice his lapse into the past.

Everybody but one.

Across the room Jenna Kincaid was looking at him, her expression puzzled to say the least. As he looked her way, she quickly turned back to the items on the table, giving them her full attention.

He had enough information for his story. He should leave. Now. Jenna wasn't meant to be, not for him. Not now, at least, he thought, with the hope that springs eternal. Perhaps some way, somehow, he could beat this grief that robbed him of a normal life and normal emotions. Maybe some day. And maybe Jenna would give up drinking. Yeah, right. No, Jenna would have to remain an unfulfilled fantasy.

He looked over his shoulder at the door. Yes, he should leave. He started to walk, but not toward the door. He started slowly toward Jenna.

Does a moth know, he wondered, when it flies toward a flame, that its ecstasy is also its doom?

Jenna was feeling like the proverbial moth also, drawn to Jake by some basic instinct that overrode caution and common sense. She wished she could talk to Millie about the auction items. That might help keep her wayward thoughts on the straight and narrow. But Millie and Ryan had hit it off with their first eye contact and seemed less than intrigued by the auction items. She would have felt like an intruder tagging along after them if she thought they were even aware of her. But to be fair, she wouldn't be the best of company anyway. She was too preoccupied with Jake, too aware of his presence in the room.

Let it go, she commanded herself, but this consuming fascination she felt for him was stronger than her common sense.

She was just a sucker for a stray. The thought seemed to spring from nowhere, catching her by surprise. A stray? She'd never thought of Jake as a stray. Not consciously at least. Yet now, thinking about it, she realized he did have that sort of lost, hurt look submerged in the depths of his eyes that surfaced briefly and disappeared before it could be named. Of course, that's it, she thought with relief. She was just responding to his pain. It was ye olde mother instinct, alive and well. It had absolutely nothing to do with desire or sexual attraction or—

To her embarrassment she suddenly realized she'd been staring at Jake, who was standing motionless, as though suddenly paralyzed, in the middle of the room.

At that moment he looked up, straight at her, and their eyes locked. Even from a distance she saw the pain, *felt* the pain he was trying, in his macho way, to conceal. She turned quickly back to the table, blindly touching the auction items, trying to focus. Her hand trembled, splashing a few drops of wine from the glass she still carried onto her hand and the white tablecloth.

She didn't even notice the spill, her emotions were in such a turmoil. She willed herself to move on legs gone rubbery, stepping alongside the table, forcing her attention on the collectible dolls, vintage jewelry, old clocks and depression era glassware.

"Check out table three," Millie had told her, so she knew that's where she'd find the cookie jar. She refused to let herself rush madly toward that table, opting instead to start at table one and work her way down the line. Now she was barely aware of what she was seeing, because Jake Corbin was dominating her thoughts. As she touched a particularly beautiful German-made cuckoo clock, she started to hum, a habit she had when trying to collect her wits, but stopped abruptly when she realized the tune she was humming: Some enchanted evening, you will see a stranger, across a crowded room—

"I love old clocks, don't you?"

Startled, Jenna spun to face Jake, who'd materialized at her side. Unfortunately, when she stopped moving, the wine in her glass didn't. In the second or two that seemed to stretch into hours, Jenna watched it slosh violently, then continue its vengeful journey over the rim of the glass. A rather large amount landed with noisy satisfaction on Jake's right, superbly polished black shoe.

Oh, damn. "Jake, I—I'm sorry." Her thoughts were jumbled, her cheeks flushed, her words nearly incoherent. If only he hadn't sneaked up on her like that, caught her off guard, just when she was thinking about him. Ridiculously, she felt as though she'd been caught out in a guilty secret.

"Let me—just—just—clean your—your shoe—" She placed her glass on the table and groped hopelessly through her cluttered shoulder bag. Where was the darn tissue? This was fate punishing her for not cleaning her purse. A year's worth of clutter—okay, okay, five year's worth—did not lend itself to instant access.

As she searched for the tissue, she surreptitiously watched Jake. She couldn't help but notice his slight drawing away from her, his suddenly grim mouth, the look of distaste flitting across his face. All because she'd spilled a few drops of wine on his shoe? His dog had completely destroyed dozens of her orchids, and all she'd done was spill a shot of wine. Come on, man, loosen up. It's only a shoe for pete's sake!

If he'd just stop staring at her like that, so—so—judgmental. He was the one with the terrorizing dog. He was the one who'd walked out on her in the motel. She should be the one giving judgmental looks.

"I know I've got a tissue in here somewhere!"

"It's okay," Jake said, pulling a handkerchief from his pocket and stooping to wipe his shoe. She'd definitely had too much wine, he decided. Every time he looked at Nichols it seemed the idiot was heading to the bar for refills. Jake jabbed angrily at his shoe. Ply her with wine, then seduce her. What a lame scenario. But Jenna obviously fell for it. He remembered the feel of Jenna's legs entangled with his own while his imagination pictured Nichols and Jenna tangled together. He scrubbed more vigorously at the shoe, unaware of the soggy handkerchief or his clenched fist.

Jenna watched Jake with mixed feelings.

Guilt, because she had caused the damage. And he certainly did seem fond of those shoes, the way he was scrubbing that one.

Relief, because his attention was focused on something other than her, giving her a chance to regain her wits.

Desire, because his shirt was pulled taut across his shoulders and back, reminding her of their tumble in the yard and their near tumble into bed.

Now through no command of her own, her gaze slid to his crotch. She had felt him pressing between her thighs, his excitement, his need, when they were standing by her car in Tallahassee. She didn't have to look to know he was more than adequately endowed. She suspected he would have no problem luring women to his bed, a ship passing in the night leaving a wake of sated females. Certainly she had been a pushover.

When Jake finally straightened, Jenna didn't jerk her gaze away fast enough and knew he'd caught her staring. She couldn't meet his eyes and felt her cheeks burning. She tried but couldn't think of anything to say.

Jake finally broke the spell, his voice sounding a little strained. "Did you see anything? I mean," he said, a flush creeping up his neck, "anything you'd like to bid on?" Why, he wondered, was he standing here trying to strike up a conversation with a woman rapidly getting drunk who'd just dumped wine on his shoe? He really was a masochist. But when he'd caught her eyes glued to his crotch, it instantly brought back those minutes in Tallahassee when she was in his arms, molded to his body. And he couldn't walk away.

Avoiding her look, he tossed the soggy handkerchief into a nearby wastebasket. She looked like she felt as awkward as he did, and realizing that gave him the courage to speak. Clearing his throat, not quite meeting her eyes, he said, "Jenna, about Tallahassee, about what happened—"

Of all the bad timing in the world, Ryan chose that moment to saunter up, throw a casual arm across Jenna's shoulder and say, "Thank you, honey, for introducing me to a little piece of heaven." Before she could respond, he'd planted a kiss on her cheek, winked, and strode away, crooning, "Tonight, tonight—"

"He's crazy," Jenna said, turning back to Jake. But Jake was backing away.

"I'd better get back to work," he told her, walking away.

He'd been ready to apologize about what happened in the motel room,

Jenna thought. And naturally he hated to apologize—He's a man isn't he?—so when Ryan gave him an opening to escape, he jumped at it. Damn Ryan. And damn Jake.

Jake walked swiftly away, feeling both relief and frustration. He should have stayed and explained, but coward that he was, he ran. And the thought of her leaving tonight with that bozo—He had to walk away before he said something he'd regret. Something stupid and macho like "You can't leave with that man. You're mine!" Or something stupid and sensitive like, "I need you, Jenna. Help me through this." Or something just plain stupid like, "I'm no good right now, but as soon as I can I'm going to love you like you're a fiddle and I'm the bow and we're the winning contestants in Dueling Banjos."

Yeah, he had to walk away.

Would Nichols take her to his place or hers?

Within minutes he realized he could stand on the opposite side of the room and be miserable while he tried to catch fleeting glimpses of her, or he could walk back across the room and join her.

Jenna felt her heart start to thud when Jake once again stood by her side. She decided to keep the conversation light rather than scare him away.

"Now here's one thing I hope to place the winning bid on." She'd finally reached the cookie jar Millie had told her about. Its creamy white color glistened in the fluorescent lighting. It was shaped like a cat and resembled the fairy tale character *Puss 'n Boots*. The cat was sporting a small hat between its ears; a yellow bird perched on the rim in a taunting manner. The boots it was wearing were outlined in blue and the facial features were marked in black. The only other color came from a big red bow around the cat's neck. "It will be the perfect addition to my collection."

"You collect cookie jars?" Jake ran a finger lightly over the jar, deliberately brushing his hand against hers. Lame, he thought. Talk about a lame maneuver just to get an excuse to touch her! "It's a Shawnee, isn't it?"

"Yes." Jenna was absurdly delighted. They shared a common interest. Probably the only interest other than orchids that could get her mind off Jake and sex. "You're a collector, too?"

He laughed, his teeth white against his tanned face, his drawn features relaxing a little, his eyes sparkling with amusement, for a moment relieved of that subdued pain. A beautiful face. She wanted to reach up and stroke it, trace her finger along the scar on his lower jaw, ask how he got it, kiss it to make the memory go away.

Stay focused. She clutched the cookie jar tighter.

"My mother," he explained in a voice that implied real men don't collect cookie jars. "She loves anything Shawnee." *Not her house.* He didn't want to see Nichols driving past in the morning, his face a picture of smug conquest. "When you grow up around it, you start to recognize the style." Once again he ran his fingers over the contours of the jar. Once again his hand brushed against hers. Once again he berated himself. Lame, lame, lame.

"Yeah, I guess you would." She paused, trying to think of something else to say. "Um, I don't limit my collection to just one brand. I like to pick ones that Carlee can enjoy." Jenna said, keeping her stare glued to Puss's red bow so Jake couldn't see into her eyes and recognize how his touch unsettled her. "She'll love *Puss 'n Boots.*"

Carlee. Mention of her name reminded Jake that he was walking a tightrope, a high wire with a long fall. What was he doing? What was he thinking? He pulled his hand away and looked toward the front of the room, where a flurry of activity was drawing the crowd. "Looks like the auction is about to start. Good luck on the bidding."

Jake strode quickly off, leaving Jenna to ponder his sudden attitude change. It was when she mentioned Carlee, she realized. He really does have a thing against Carlee. That definitely puts him out of the picture. And just as well, she chided, carefully replacing the cookie jar and heading for the chair Ryan and Millie were saving for her.

Ignoring for a moment Jake's obvious flaws—his aversion to Carlee, his unpredictable mood swings—just where in her busy lifestyle did she plan to tuck a man anyway? While she was running around the state drumming up customers for her fledgling floral business? While she was gardening in the flowerbeds and greenhouses? While she was doing her bookkeeping, her ordering, her billing, her taxes? While she was searching the Internet for prospects and special plants and seeds? While she was helping Claire design brochures, newspaper ads, and now sachet tags? No and no and no and no and no. Any spare time she had was devoted to Carlee. Carlee and Claire.

So why was she continuously looking in his direction, obsessed with getting a glimpse of him?

When the *Puss 'n Boots* cookie jar went up for bids, Jenna was delighted to find herself the high bidder. Millie won the bid on a gorgeous pair of vintage earrings and a large set of china dishes. Even Ryan, who was sitting between Jenna and Millie with an arm draped across the back of each chair, alternately making wisecracks in one girl's ear, then the other, joined in the fun by bidding on an old poker set, then bidding an outrageous sum for her vase of orchids and winking at her when nobody was insane enough to top the bid. Phil Averies bought a batch of Claire's macaroons and forced the bidding up on the rest of the cookies. Jenna observed that Jake, who was sitting several rows away, bought a small, oak bookcase and a box of dog toys. As far as she could tell, he never once looked in her direction.

About 11 o'clock the evening drew to an end and it was time to head for home. Ryan offered to help Millie and Jenna load up their winnings and the three walked out together, each carrying a box. Since Millie's china made up most of the bundles, Jenna left her cookie jar on the table so she could help Millie. She'd make an extra trip back for her jar, she told Ryan and Millie, who seemed quite content with the arrangement. It was obvious to Jenna they welcomed an opportunity to say good night to each other in private.

As they pushed their way outside, a muggy gust of air whooshed in, blowing Jenna's hair into wild disarray. In the excitement of the auction and the distraction of Jake, it had been easy to ignore the approaching storm. Huge, gray-black clouds covered the moon, their edges roiling in tumultuous whirls. Thunder, much louder than when she'd arrived, cracked almost continuously.

Jenna was only too happy to seek the shelter of the hotel as she dashed back for her own things. A bright flash of lightning rent the sky, followed mere seconds later by an earth-shattering boom of thunder. Several large drops of rain splashed against her face, and Jenna shivered despite the summer heat. The thunderstorm was imminent, blowing in from the west, moving toward her house. She only had a fifteen minute drive, so if she hurried, she might be able to stay ahead of the storm. She *really* hated driving in the rain.

Jake, despite his best intentions, had watched Jenna leave with Nichols. He felt an unreasonable surge of anger. Anger at Nichols for being such an unconscionable blackguard and preying on a helpless woman. A tiny voice questioned just how helpless Jenna was, but he chose to ignore it. Anger at

Jenna for being such an innocent fool and falling for Nichols' oh-so-obvious, oh-so-lame seduction methods. The same tiny voice questioned just how innocent Jenna was, but he shoved that aside also. Anger, most of all, at himself for being such a stupid weakling that he couldn't walk away from this attraction, couldn't control his emotions, couldn't stop his thoughts, and most of all, couldn't just walk up to Jenna and say flat out, "I want you more than life itself, but I have a slight problem right now, so if you could just bear with me—"

He was still staring moodily at the door when Jenna burst back in like an avenging angel, her windblown hair a red halo about her head, her rain-specked cheeks sparkling under the lights. For a moment, all Jake could feel was awe.

She looked his way, and when their eyes locked, her brisk stride faltered. Then, brushing loose strands of hair from her eyes, she hurried over to the table. She'd come back for her cookie jar, Jake realized, while some unnamed hope that had ignited in his breast at the sight of her returning was as quickly extinguished. Leave it to Nichols to let Jenna make that dash through the storm instead of him doing the gallant thing and getting the jar for her.

Jenna set her purse on the table to dig out her keys. Then, hooking her purse over her shoulder, she carefully picked up the cookie jar. As she turned to leave, she noticed her wine glass, still nearly full, on the floor near the chair where she'd been sitting during the auction. If left sitting there, it would surely get knocked over and stain the carpet. She should return it to the bar. Sighing, she picked up the glass and, juggling cookie jar, wine, keys, and a purse that was slipping off her shoulder, she headed for the bar, maneuvering her way through a jumble of chairs that had once been arranged in nice neat rows.

She'd nearly run the course when her dangling purse got hung up on a chair back, its sudden resistance causing her to look backward just as her foot got tangled in the legs of the chair in front of her. The same diabolical fate that had been plaguing her all day had one more ace up its sleeve. She stumbled. She probably could have—would have—regained her balance given a little forward space to work with, but the forward space was blocked. Blocked by the taut-bodied, seemingly omnipresent, rapidly wearing thin presence of Jake Corbin.

He did the manly thing of course—*me Tarzan, you Jane*—grabbed her arm and steadied her. She managed to keep possession of her belongings—the precious cookie jar, her keys, her purse, the wine glass. The wine, unfortunately, eluded her and Jake's shirt suffered the same fate his shoe had suffered earlier. She'd had one sip of her wine and the glass was now half empty.

Jake held her arm in a grip that had turned to iron. Once again he studied her with that infuriating judgmental look. But Jenna had had enough. From her first brush with him at her house, he had been nothing but trouble, destroying her property, upsetting her routine, arousing unwelcome emotions, torturing her with his mood swings, walking out on her in the motel, *not liking Carlee!* Who the hell was he to be judgmental? Something snapped. "Stop sneaking up on me!" she shouted.

Jake ignored her outburst as he ignored his wine-soaked shirt. "Were you planning to drive?" His voice was icy.

"Certainly," she snapped. "Were you planning to let go of my arm?"

"In your condition?" he asked, eyeing her wineglass. She was still drinking, even with her keys in hand. His feelings were a mixture of giddy relief she wasn't leaving with Nichols and disbelief that she planned to drive while under the influence of alcohol, in a heavy storm.

Just like Barb.

"In my condition!" she sputtered. What did he think, she was pregnant or something? And what business of his would it be if she were?

"I don't think so." Jake's voice was clipped and final as he deftly snatched the keys from her hand and started to lead her from the hall.

"Are you nuts?" she said, jerking her arm free and reaching for the keys. Jake had them in his fist, which he shoved in his pocket. She stopped and looked around for a policeman—there was never one when you needed one—or something to break over Jake's head, like a bottle of wine, which would be appropriate, since his head was the only part of him she hadn't soaked. She noticed the mayor across the room, but from the wide grin on his face, she somehow doubted that he'd be any help. Men!

Phil Averies, who must have observed the whole humiliating scene, strode up and gave Jenna a cheerful grin and fatherly pat on the shoulder. "You might as well go with him, honey. He means well and you couldn't be in better hands. You don't really want to drive in this storm anyway, do you?"

"But—but—" A loud clap of thunder reverberated through the room, as though Mother Nature were adding an exclamation mark to Phil's statement. And Mother Nature, she decided, could be very persuasive. Making a noise that teetered between a sound of disgust and a groan of frustration, she let Jake lead her outside.

They were halfway to his Land Rover and she was blinking away the first drops of rain before she realized she was still carrying the glass of wine.

Although Jenna cradled the cookie jar in her left arm, held the wine glass in her right hand, and had slung her purse precariously over one shoulder, she quickly shoved her way past Jake when she realized he was circling around to the passenger side of his Land Rover. She wasn't going to give him the satisfaction of playing the gentleman. She'd open her own damned door, thank you very much.

As she moved in front of him, she swung her arm to toss the contents of her goblet into some bushes, but in an impulsive and perverse gesture, she tossed it instead straight into Jake's face. His startled exclamation and the bright anger sparking in his eyes both thrilled and chilled her.

CHAPTER SIX

Jenna drew in a sharp breath and instinctively moved away from Jake, not stopping till her back hit the side of his vehicle.

"You'll pay for that," he muttered, taking a meaningful step toward her. He spoke in a voice charged with emotion as he loomed over her, but the red liquid dripping off his nose made any intended threat seem too comical. What had begun in her throat as an instinctive screech morphed into an unexpected giggle, emerging as a strangled croak through a mouth suddenly gone dry. What had she done?

At her mixed reaction, Jake's stance changed. "You're more drunk than I thought." Reaching behind her, he grabbed the door handle and yanked the door open with a force that nearly toppled her onto the damp pavement of the parking lot. Before she could regain her balance, he'd seized her by the arm and forcefully steered her into the passenger seat.

She straightened her clothes with as much dignity as she could muster while glaring daggers at him, understanding fully for the first time the trite expression "if looks could kill." And speaking of kill, how well did she know this man anyway? A tumble in the grass with Jake and Buster, a few dances, a fizzled out trip to a motel room—that was all she had for a character reference. It didn't say much for him—or for herself, she realized, blushing. He could be a serial rapist for all she knew. And she had just meekly let him shove her into his car. Not smart.

She could jump out of the vehicle and run, she could scream for help, she could—could—smash her cookie jar against the dashboard and leave a trail of broken pieces for the police to follow when they were searching for her body. That grim but admittedly ridiculous image broke through her blanket of anger. Who was she kidding? She wasn't scared of Jake, despite his attempt to intimidate her. Besides, Phil Averies seemed to regard him as pretty okay. And Phil Averies was an excellent judge of character. He liked Claire, didn't he?

Jake intrigued her, puzzled her, sometimes he simply infuriated her. That ridiculous statement he'd just made about her being drunk. Drunk, for pete's sake. With the exception of one sip, Jake had consumed all of her drink. On his shoe, on his shirt, in his face. She stifled a giggle, picturing again the startled look on his face *every single time* she'd doused him. It was like a scene from a Three Stooges movie.

But he really thought she was drunk! It floored her that he could think that, but at the same time she, like the rest of the world, was certainly familiar with the saying, *Friends don't let friends drive drunk.* If he actually believed she was drunk, then he had done exactly the right thing. You take the keys away using whatever method works. There's no point in arguing with a drunk. If he—or she—wants to drive, he—or she—isn't going to listen to reason.

And here she was, once again, seeing the other side of an argument. First she had argued herself into believing that Buster's rampage was partly her fault. Now she was actually trying to justify Jake's heavy-handed behavior.

She would *not* let herself go there. There was no way she would take any of the blame for this fiasco!

Because she wasn't drunk. She resented the implication. And—turning to face Jake, who had by now climbed behind the wheel—she spoke between clenched teeth as she finished the thought "—and you are NOT a friend. You're a completely misguided, absolutely idiotic, totally self-absorbed, male chauvinist pig!" With Paul Newman eyes.

Jake, using the roll of paper towels he kept under his seat, was preoccupied wiping the wine from his face so responded to her with nothing more than a quizzical glance. Then, tucking the soiled paper towel into the small litterbag hanging from the glove box (he had to lean across Jenna's lap to do it), he started the Land Rover and deftly swung out of the parking lot.

A vivid flash of lightning, close enough to read a book by, was followed almost immediately by a loud clap of thunder and pelting rain. No time to count the distance between lightning and thunder, the storm had arrived. The seatbelt, thank god, prevented Jenna from curling into a fetal position. It was humiliating enough to be treated like a helpless drunk without enforcing the lie by behaving like one.

She wrapped her arms around the cookie jar lying on her lap, gingerly dangling the wine glass between stiff fingers, and willed herself to stop trembling while she watched with anxious fascination the heavy onslaught of rain slamming against the windshield and exploding across the glass.

Well, guess what, folks. She had just stolen a wine glass from a charity auction, she thought, trying to concentrate on something besides the sheets of rain beating against the windows with the vehemence of Cujo. And after that scene Jake caused, she wasn't willing to go waltzing back into the hotel tomorrow or any other day to return it. She had no desire to endure the smirks on the faces of the hotel staff.

She took several paper towels from the roll (she had to feel around behind Jake's legs to find them) and used them to pack the goblet securely inside the cookie jar.

Despite the circumstances leading up to this moment, she was glad she didn't have to drive in this storm. She cast a furtive glance at Jake to see how he was handling the near-blinding downpour. His body was tense; his knuckles as he gripped the steering wheel were a startling white against his tanned hands. Surprised at this unmistakable sign of vulnerability, Jenna glanced up at his face. His jaw was clenched and his eyes focused on the road. But as though sensing Jenna's furtive glance, he spared her a quick look, a jaunty grin, and amazingly, a wink. Then he returned his attention to the road.

Jenna wasn't deceived. That grin had been forced, his wink didn't hide the concern in his eyes, and even a total idiot would find nothing funny about this storm. It was all an act. All Powerful Male reassures Helpless Female. She leaned her head back against the seat, closed her eyes, and uttered a silent prayer. *Please just get me home safely and let me never lay eyes on Jake Corbin again.*

Jake glanced at Jenna, the frequent double and triple streaks of lightning illuminating the interior in sporadic bursts of white. Her face was white; her eyes tightly closed. She was frightened of the storm and who could blame her? But it was more than that. Her breathing was fast and furious, just like the rain outside, which was pounding on the roof and streaming in sheets down the windows. The windshield wipers, on highest speed, were little help, and the glare of bright lights from oncoming cars seemed washed out, distorted, giving a false impression of the their distance.

As he concentrated on his driving, he agonized over his actions, asking himself why he'd grabbed her keys, why he'd insisted on driving her home. Who did he think he was? What gave him the right? The questions were rhetorical, not even worthy of consideration. He did it because he had to, because he couldn't turn his back and walk away, because he never wanted to see another car wrapped around a tree. She wouldn't thank him for it, he could be sure of that, and she would probably resent it forever. But he could take her anger. What he couldn't take would be seeing an ambulance carrying her away. Or a hearse.

His glance rested for a second on the small childish drawing of a dog hanging from his rearview mirror. *This is the dog I want, daddy, with a black, shiny coat and ears that prick up when I call him, and a red tongue that sticks out like this when I give him some of my ice cream cone, and a blue collar with his name on it. I think Buster is a good name, don't you, daddy?* Familiar pain seared his heart, so sudden and intense he felt the spasm.

Lizzy, Lizzy, Lizzy. Every day. Every minute of every day he ached for her. Her shrill, childish laughter, her silly knock-knock jokes, her absorbed fascination with the animals in the zoo and the exhibits in the museum, her endless questions. Even her tears and temper tantrums. But mostly, he missed hugging her, holding her, laughing with her. The picture of the dog was the last thing Lizzy had ever drawn.

Yes, sweetheart, Buster is a perfect name.

No, he'd done the right thing, taking Jenna Kincaid's keys, even if she never agreed with him. He wanted to talk it over with her, but the roar of the storm prohibited conversation and, besides, he wanted to look at her while he talked, watch her reaction to his words. He couldn't do that and drive too. Not in this storm.

But the silence was intolerable.

Finally, raising his voice over the noise of wind and rain, he said, "I know I was presumptuous, but—"

"Presumptuous?" Jenna squawked, sitting up and glaring at him. *"Presumptuous?* Ordering a meal for me in a restaurant without consulting me—that's presumptuous. Showing up unexpectedly and inviting yourself to stay for dinner—that's presumptuous. Taking your date to the movies and buying her a hotdog without knowing whether or not she's a vegetarian—that's presumptuous."

"Are you hungry?" he interrupted with a weak attempt at humor. "You seem a little fixated on food."

Jenna was not to be distracted. "You *humiliated* me in front of my friends! You *stupidly* assumed I was drunk when I *hadn't even been drinking!* You *stole* my keys and *forced* me into your vehicle! And you call that *presumptuous?* Listen up, you pompous fool, you—you *control freak!* You went way, way, way, beyond presumptuous!"

The proper exit, Jenna thought, would be to storm out and slam the door behind her, but that not being an option, she had to settle for turning her back to him and glaring out the window. That felt unsatisfyingly anticlimactic.

The storm, however, seemed even more angry than she, whipping against the windows with a fury hell hath not. Resentful now even at the heavens, which seemed to be taunting her, she banged her head back against the seat's head rest, clenched her eyes shut, and tried to close all five senses to the outside world.

Holy jumping jackrabbits, she hated domineering men. Ned, for one. But even before that, long before that, there was her father. Dear old dad with his compulsion to rule, to be the king of his castle. Self-centered, domineering, really believing that man was the superior force and woman merely his helpmate. How had mom lived with him all those years? Before Jenna had escaped the house by marrying Ned—leaping from the frying pan into the fire—her father had all but convinced Jenna that she, a mere female, couldn't exist without the support of a man.

Apparently Jake shared that belief.

"I'm not a control freak." Jake tightened his grip on the steering wheel, his knuckles turning even whiter. "I just wanted to—stop you—prevent an accident." The words did sound dictatorial, even to himself. "Every time I looked your way, you had a drink," he argued. "I saw you stumble a couple of times, I was the victim of your staggering. Need I remind you?"

Jenna felt a stab of guilt and knew a flush had stained her cheeks, which only made her angrier. "You saw what you wanted to see. I had one drink. I carried it around with me all night. And I only took one sip of that. If you weren't always treading on my heels like the Gestapo, you wouldn't have been the *victim of my staggering.* Good grief, I can't believe you!"

"Nor I you," he said, but he was feeling the first stabs of doubt. He had to admit she wasn't acting drunk now, or even slightly under the influence. He'd lived with Barb long enough to recognize the symptoms, and Jenna just wasn't exhibiting them. Still, he wasn't ready to yield quite yet.

"You expect me to believe you took a glass of wine you had no intention of drinking and carried it around with you all night? Do you take me for a fool?"

"Certainly, but not just any old fool. More like an interfering, self-righteous, misbeguided, domineering fool!"

Jake studied her face briefly before turning back to his driving, but in that instant Jenna saw acceptance of truth glimmer in his eyes. Belief. And contriteness. The constant flashes of lightning worked better than an interior light. His embarrassment was evident—red was creeping up his neck and coloring his cheeks.

Amusement nudged her anger. She tried very hard to cling to the anger, not let it melt away as it threatened to do. She would not forgive and forget. She would not. But her lips began to twitch at the corners. She bit the insides of her cheeks to keep from betraying her amusement. When she was alone in her room tonight, she'd have to treat herself to one good long belly laugh.

"A friend handed me the drink," she explained, when she could talk without chuckling. "I didn't want to embarrass him by refusing it."

Jake didn't deserve an explanation after his highhanded behavior, but she continued anyway. "I was going to go back to the bar and get a bottle of water and drop the drink off at the same time, but I never seemed to make it in that direction." *I was too busy looking for you.* "I just never got around to it," she finished, as a clap of thunder drowned out her voice. She lapsed into silence.

Jake knew she was telling the truth. Any lingering doubts had been extinguished when he'd looked at her. Those gorgeous green eyes had been clear, not bloodshot. Her gaze was direct, not hooded or evasive. Her voice was steady, her diction precise. She wasn't drunk, not a little, not at all. He'd made a rash decision, a drastic mistake. But who could blame him? Her face had been flushed, she'd seemed unsteady on her feet, she'd kept spilling wine all over the place, or at least, all over him. And he'd jumped to conclusions.

He sighed. Barb had pulled the wool over his eyes, had lied over and over about her drinking, and he'd believed her. But he realized in retrospect that he'd believed her because he'd wanted to, wanted to give her another chance, and another and another. Wanted to shut his eyes to the numerous clues, wanted to avoid a painful confrontation. He'd let his experiences with Barb color his judgment with Jenna. And he'd served her a terrible injustice.

He owed her an apology. And fast. Her driveway was just up ahead. A flash of lightning rent the sky as he looked her way and started to speak.

"Jenna, I'm—"

"Jake! Watch out!" Jenna's warning came just in time. Through the downpour he saw a dark shape—a large dog—directly in their path.

"Buster?" Jake slammed on the brakes. The sudden action on the slippery wet pavement sent the vehicle into a sliding spin. Jake pumped the brakes delicately as he fought to get the Land Rover under control. Jenna saw the dog leap from the wheels, heard Jake's desperate "Hold on!" and felt a bone-jolting impact as the vehicle skidded front first into the foot of a tall oak tree.

They sat in stunned silence.

Finally, Jake found his voice. "Are you ok?"

"Yes." Jenna gulped. "You?"

"Yeah. You're sure you're not hurt?" He had turned to her and tentatively touched his fingers to her face, then ran his hands down her arms. "You're sure?" His face was white and Jenna realized it was fright for her that caused his deathlike complexion.

She flexed her fingers and toes, moved her arms around, twisted her head back and forth. "Everything seems to be working."

His touch on her bare arms, her face, her neck, that touch was working for sure, sending electric tingles dancing over her skin, but she'd grown a little wary of his on-again, off-again behavior. It had been an emotionally exhausting night, climaxing an emotionally exhausting week, and all she wanted to do now was get this night behind her.

She opened the door and stepped out into the pelting rain, fighting the wind as she looped her purse over her shoulder, then reached back inside for her cookie jar. That was the only bright note about this whole disastrous evening—the cookie jar. Luckily she'd instinctively clung to it when the car hit the tree, so it hadn't been damaged. Despite everything, she smiled, anticipating Carlee's delight with the new addition.

Jake climbed out and stood beside her. "Jenna, I—"

"No, Jake, no, save it," she interrupted.

The storm, in Florida fashion, had started to abate as it moved farther inland, taking the thunder and lightning with it, but leaving a steady downpour in its wake. Both Jenna and Jake were drenched in a matter of seconds. "I just want to get home. I'm wet, I'm tired, and I'm still pretty upset. Good luck with your car. I hope the damage isn't too bad."

She trudged away, leaving Jake staring after her.

Jake's first instinct was to accompany her to her door despite her objections, but decided it wasn't a good idea, under the circumstances. He owed her an apology, but it would have to wait. She'd made it pretty clear she didn't want his company or his solicitations. *Control freak, huh?* So he contented himself with standing in the pouring rain and watching until she'd reached her house and stepped onto the porch.

He shivered with a sudden chill. A hot shower would feel good right now, a fire in the fireplace, a steaming cup of coffee. *A woman beside him.* He shook the thought away, depressed at the desolate feeling of loneliness that swept over him. Resolutely he turned his attention to his Land Rover.

* * *

It didn't take long for Jenna to reach her yard. Even so, by the time she got there, she was so wet her hair was dripping water like a faucet. She climbed the single step to the front porch, then decided it might be best to go in through the kitchen. Detouring off the porch, she moved into the shadows at the side of the house. And shivered. She'd never noticed how dark this area was. She was infinitely grateful the lightning had moved off, but she could have used some light.

She stumbled over something in the dark.

"Carlee," she muttered, "why must you leave your toys scattered about?" She bent to retrieve the wayward toy, and discovered it was an empty coffee can. Carlee must have dug it out of the trash to play with in the sandbox. Tossing it aside, she once again began making her way to the back of the house. A few feet farther on she stumbled again. Frowning, she felt around in the dark and discovered a grease-covered cereal box. Yuck.

Hurrying her steps, she made it to the kitchen door, stepped inside, and turned on the yard light, certain of what she would see. She hoped she was wrong, but discovered she was right. A week's worth of trash was scattered all over the yard.

Buster had struck again.

* * *

Jake inspected the front end of his Land Rover. Fortunately, the damage seemed to be minimal, although the grillwork was messed up pretty bad. Unfortunately, parts for this particular model were hard to come by so even little things were a pain to fix.

With a sigh, Jake swiped at the water dripping into his eyes. He climbed back into the SUV, and turned the key in the ignition. After several tries, the engine finally turned over, and his relief was so great he felt like whooping.

When he turned into his driveway, his headlights swept across the yard.

"What the—Buster!" the exclamation escaped his lips even as his brain registered the trash strewn from one end of his yard to the other. Pulling to a stop mere inches from a large trashcan, now tipped and lying empty, Jake yanked his door open and yelled the dog's name.

Big mistake. Despite Jake's tone of voice, which would have cowed a Doberman, Buster gave a joyous yelp, came sailing over the fence and barreled into Jake, knocking him flat. Something soft and squishy burst under his weight. As Jake struggled to sit up, Buster leaped on his chest, flattening him to the ground and delivering his usual round of sloppy kisses. It took Jake a few breathless minutes to wrestle the very wet, muddy and stinky dog off him so he could sit up.

"I really need to teach you the proper way to greet your master," he grunted.

Somehow, despite Buster's best efforts, Jake struggled to his feet. Since he was already soaked, he took a few minutes to clean up the worst of the mess scattered about the yard. As he moved around, trying to ignore the rain assiduously drenching him, Jake's thoughts wandered back to the events of the evening. An image of Jenna Kincaid, water streaming down her face, mascara running, popped into his head. Even totally mussed she looked good. Why was he so drawn to the woman? He'd known women more beautiful. He'd certainly known women more friendly. But he'd never known a woman that had aroused such immediate and consuming excitement.

Not that it made much difference. After Tallahassee and then tonight, he'd be lucky if Jenna even drove past his house anymore. She'd probably take an alternate route, drive twenty miles out of her way, just to avoid getting that close to him.

"Yeah Buster," he said to the dog, who was thoroughly enjoying this late night romp in the rain, "I guess we both have a knack for making a mess of things."

All things considered, maybe tonight's misadventure was more good than bad, he reasoned. Put him in the same room with Jenna and every rational thought in his head evaporated like a Florida mud puddle. He knew he should stay away from her, but so far that had been impossible. Perhaps tonight fate had given him a shove in the right direction, forced him to take that first step. Now all he had to do was drag his will power out of his trousers, slap it back in his spine where it belonged, and stay the hell away from her.

"No!" he said suddenly, aloud, and then repeated it, louder. "No!"

Buster lifted his ears in a puzzled look, as though wondering what he'd done wrong.

Jake strode to the fence and gripped his fingers in the chain links, looking out at the woods. "Lizzy," he said softly, "you know I love you, princess. You know nobody can ever take your place in my heart. Never, I promise you that. Never."

He fell silent, struggling to find words, then, giving up, turned away. He took a step, then turned back to resume his post at the fence. "Lizzy, there's somebody I want you to meet. You'll like her. Her name is Jenna. She's smart, and funny, and hard working. Pretty too. And she has—she has this little girl, just about your age, Lizzy. But you'll always be number one in my heart. You'll always be my little girl, my beautiful little princess. I promise."

Buster whined as though sensing Jake's anguish. He picked up a tin can in his mouth and dropped it at Jake's feet.

Jake reached down and scratched Buster's ears, looking around at the trash but needing a shower more than a clean yard. "We'll finish this tomorrow," he said to the dog. "And you, my fine furry friend, will get some kind of restraint if I have to handcuff you to one of the hurricane anchors securing the porch."

Once inside, Jake headed for the hot shower he'd been craving. While he fumbled with the buttons of his dripping shirt, his eyes were drawn to an object on his dresser. It was a Shawnee cookie jar that he'd purchased for his mother last Christmas only to discover she already had an identical one in her collection. So his had gotten shoved to the corner of the dresser and forgotten.

Jenna would probably love it.

Her words from the auction came back to him. *I like to pick ones that Carlee can enjoy too.* He refused to be detracted by the guilt that swept over him when he let his thoughts dwell for a minute on Carlee and the delight the cookie jar would bring her.

"No one can take your place, Lizzy," he repeated, and forced his attention back to the Shawnee cookie jar. As he stared at it, the shape of the cookie jar receded into the background, superseded by an idea taking shape in his mind.

In the shower while the steaming water massaged his aching body, the idea took shape and grew. By the time he climbed between the sheets, he had a full course of action all planned out.

CHAPTER SEVEN

Jake woke at dawn, stretched, yawned, and lay in bed for a minute enjoying the luxury of a well-rested night. Before Lizzy's accident—everything, it seemed, fell into the "before the accident" period of his life or "after the accident" period—before the accident he used to enjoy storms, the rain, the lightning, the thunderclaps. While he was in the haven of his home and in a cozy bed, he found the fury outside very conducive to sleep.

Barb would always get up and pace the house, a drink in one hand, a cigarette in the other. He'd urge her to come back to bed, but she'd refuse, and he wasn't willing to abandon the comfort of his bed to keep her company in her smoky, boozy pacing. Sometimes the thunder woke Lizzy and she'd crawl into bed with Jake, snuggling her little body against the security of his broad back, and immediately fall back to sleep.

After the accident, storms always precipitated nightmares.

But last night images of Jenna had crept into his thoughts, lulling him to sleep and miraculously keeping the nightmares at bay. Jenna. He loved the way her green eyes sparked fire when she was angry, the way her lower lip trembled and aroused his urge to nibble it. He loved the way her eyes danced with merriment—so many things amused her—and her smile lit up her expressive face. He loved her wild, crazy and sexy hair, that refused to be constrained, that tumbled about her head and shoulders like a goddess of love or war. Most of all he loved those green eyes that couldn't conceal the desire she felt, that smoldered with a passion that defied reason and bound them together. Jenna. His last thoughts before dropping off to sleep had been of Jenna, and his first thoughts on waking were of Jenna.

He had really botched things last night. Now if only he could set things right. As he dressed in jeans and a T-shirt, he replayed in his mind the plan of action he had devised the night before. It might work; it *must* work, he thought as he headed for the door.

* * *

Jenna rolled out of bed at six o'clock and staggered to the kitchen, being quiet so she wouldn't wake Claire. She didn't want to face her mom's questions about last night until she'd had a pot of coffee to sustain her.

It was going to be a busy day. She had a hair appointment at Millie's Place followed by stops at several local floral shops where she planned to introduce the idea of orchid sachets. And her van, thanks to Jake's high-handed attitude, was still parked at the hotel. She'd have to get Claire to drive her, which would give her mother plenty of time to ply her with questions. She didn't look forward to it.

But first there was trash in the yard to clean up—Thank you very much, Buster—and then an hour or so with her orchids, so she quickly donned her favorite denim cutoffs and a flowered halter top. When she was through outside, she'd shower and dress in something more appropriate for a trip into town.

While she pulled on her clothes, she mulled over her sleepless night. She hated driving in storms and was terrified of lightning when she perceived it as a threat, but once inside her house, the security of four sturdy walls wrapped around her like a cocoon and her fears subsided. Then an onslaught of rain beating helplessly against her windows enhanced her feeling of security in the haven of her house, and especially when that cocoon of safety was reinforced by soft, enveloping blankets as she nestled in bed. Normally, storms lulled her to sleep like Claire's bedtime stories had when she was a child.

Last night, relaxing after a hot shower and slipping between fresh sheets, she couldn't sleep. Last night, images of Jake Corbin kept stealing into her thoughts. Every time she started to doze off, he'd intrude. And Buster the vampire slayer was never far behind. Within moments, she'd see Buster tearing through her yard, knocking over trashcans, digging up plants, and destroying all her orchids. Mr. Sandman had hastily retreated before the boisterous image.

When she'd finally managed to put those disturbing memories at bay, others had intruded and she found herself agonizing over memories of Jake's kisses, his touch, his hard body.

Then, reminding herself of Jake's erratic behavior, his desertion in Tallahassee, his reaction to Carlee, his high-handed behavior after the auction, she'd end up pounding her pillow instead of sawing logs. To add insult to injury, last night when she'd taken a moment to examine her cookie jar, she'd discovered it also was a casualty of that evening's fiasco. The cat was now missing the tip of one ear. Jake Corbin had a lot to answer for.

Jake. She loved his hard body. She'd explored quite a bit of it during those passionate kisses in Tallahassee. She loved his brilliant blue eyes, the unexpected flashes of mirth that cancelled the fleeting glimmers of pain he strove to keep buried in his macho way. She loved, most of all, the smoldering passion that drew her inexorably to him. She sighed. For better or worse, Jake Corbin had gotten under her skin. More than that, he was in her blood. It was a stupid thought, impossible to believe, yet she knew it was true.

There's good news and bad news, she thought. The good news: Jake Corbin was in her blood. The bad news: Jake Corbin was in her blood.

The good news was Jake had shaken her from her sexual torpor, had reminded her that she was a woman, still young, still healthy. He had awakened responses in her she'd not dreamed possible. Not reawakened, she realized, but newly awakened. Ned had never elicited such deep, compelling, overpowering responses. Not just sex, but her essence, her being, had responded to Jake. If they had made love in Tallahassee, she knew that every cell in her body that made her a woman would have rushed joyously to welcome the lover. And, in a primitive sense, the woman fulfilled would have belonged to its creator—Jake Corbin.

When he'd walked out, she'd felt more bereft than she'd ever felt in her life, because for the first time she'd had a glimpse of love's potential. Is that what made women have affair after affair, she wondered. Is that what made nymphomaniacs? Had they become aware of love's potential and were embarked on a relentless pursuit to realize the potential?

Jenna knew she would never travel that path, would never journey from bed to bed seeking fulfillment. Her quest had begun and ended with Jake Corbin.

This desire Jake aroused in her was so novel, so exciting, so shattering, that she couldn't ignore it or even scarcely describe it. Urges born in a more primitive age and carried forward from woman to woman through thousands of generations had surfaced. She wanted Jake not just for a one-night stand, but for a mate. And instead of being terrified of the craving, as a more civilized, educated woman should be, she exulted in it. Like a Neanderthal stalking a mammoth, her instinct was to stalk Jake Corbin, sling him over her shoulder, and carry him to her cave. And, oh, how she loved that feeling!

The bad news was Jake came with a backpack of problems too big to fit in her cave, Carlee being the biggest, insurmountable problem. If Jenna had to choose between her own happiness or Carlee's, it was no contest.

So while it didn't seem possible to banish Jake from her thoughts or her hormones, she was just going to have to live with them and without him. In the meantime, she had orchids to tend and trash to clean up. Again.

When Jenna stepped outside a few minutes later, she was temporarily blinded by the bright morning sunshine. It was just starting to creep over the tree line, bathing her yard in brilliant hues, millions of diamonds sparkling on the wet grass. That was why she didn't see Buster until he'd launched himself at her, nearly bowling her over. He was attached with a chain to a tree, but it had enough lead to allow him to reach her as she stepped through the sunroom door into her back yard. Doggie kisses that smelled like rotten eggs and yesterday's gravy slurped over her face. What had she ever done to the canine world to deserve this dog's attentions?

"Get down!" she commanded, her voice ringing with irritation, while her racing pulse reminded her that Buster's master was undoubtedly somewhere about. Buster, obviously not attuned to nuances of voice, yelped playfully and laid his head on her shoulder, looking at her with beseeching brown eyes.

"Buster, sit!" Jake's command, issued in a strong voice, startled Jenna, though it had no effect on the blissful dog wagging his tail.

She couldn't take her eyes off Jake as he strode over and grabbed Buster's collar with one hand and wrestled him to the ground.

"What are you doing here at—" she managed to tear her eyes away from Jake to glance at her watch "—six fifteen in the morning?"

"I'm sorry," he said as he pulled Buster away from her.

"That dog's got the manners of the proverbial bull in a china shop," Jenna said, determined to keep her hormones subdued under a barrage of righteous indignation. "He needs obedience training."

"You're right," Jake said in an abstract way. He couldn't take his eyes off Jenna. Those cutoffs and halter-top should be outlawed. Her tanned legs looked incredible, and that halter concealed what it should, but left enough bare skin to make his fingers twitch.

"Preferably some obedience school far away, in a foreign country," Jenna added, suddenly terribly conscious of her scanty outfit. "And you didn't answer my question. What are you doing here? And why is Buster tied up in *my* yard?"

"Well…" Jake spread his hands wide and Jenna realized he was holding a handful of wet, soggy trash. "I came to apologize."

"And the break of dawn struck you as a good time to do that?"

"I wasn't exactly thinking about the time." Jake grinned sheepishly. "Anyway," he continued, "when I got here, I realized that Buster must have made this awful mess, so I figured it would help my position considerably if I cleaned it up before knocking on your door."

"Your position?" Jenna spoke tartly, deriving wicked pleasure in his discomfort. It was payback time. "You have no position here." As she spoke she stepped off the patio and began gathering trash. She wasn't an adept liar and knew if she looked at Jake, if she met his gaze, he would see the truth. He did have a position there. He'd slipped smoothly—sometimes not so smoothly—past all her defenses and was firmly *positioned* in her thoughts, her fantasies, her desires. *Not my heart though!* She forced that thought to the fore, then sighed in resignation. She was not an adept liar. Not even to herself.

"I meant," Jake said, joining her in the cleanup operation, "you might be more willing to listen to my apology." He spoke without looking her way, and as he finished what he was saying he suddenly became absorbed in an empty soup can he'd picked up. Jenna found his awkward discomfort very appealing.

He isn't used to making apologies. The thought came unbidden. A man like Jake doesn't have a lot to apologize for, she guessed. This should prove interesting. *Payback time.*

"You want to apologize," she said, more a statement than a question. A simple "I'm sorry" wasn't going to cut it. He had too much to apologize for. Last night. Buster. Tallahassee. Carlee. No, a simple "I'm sorry" was way too easy. If it were painful, difficult, if he couldn't get the words out, that might be a point in his favor. If he choked over the words, that would help. If the words stuck in his throat like a Brazil nut, if she had to perform the Heimlich maneuver to save him, that would help. Would she save him? Or would she just turn her back to him and walk away, keeping her chin up where it belonged and her shoulders squared against his appeal?

"You want to apologize," she repeated in an effort to still her thoughts before they reached their inevitable conclusion. Of course she'd wrap her arms around that chest she was itching to stroke right now and save the wretched man's life. It took tremendous willpower to keep her voice level while her Stone Age instincts still commanded that she throw all six feet of him over her slender shoulder and cart him to her cave.

He didn't answer until they'd carried the last of the trash over to the trashcan and dumped it inside. In fact, she'd decided he was studiously ignoring her when he finally spoke.

"If it's any consolation, he pulled the same stunt in my yard last night."

He looked so genuinely contrite that Jenna felt the smile twitching again. She forced it away.

"And you were right about Buster," he said, following Jenna to the tree where Buster was watching them with reproachful looks. "About his jumping the fence. When I got home last night, he came sailing right over it to greet me." He grinned ruefully. "Caught me by surprise, knocked me for a loop. Then jumped on me and knocked me the rest of the way down. A rotten banana broke my fall—slammed my elbow into a melon rind—my head landed in some coffee grounds—my…"

Her smile twitched again. "Stop. I'm getting this urge to spray you with Lysol."

For a second, their eyes made contact, silent laughter uniting them. She turned quickly away, noticing for the first time an object sitting on her picnic table. It looked like a cookie jar.

She walked slowly over and picked it up. It *was* a cookie jar. She looked at Jake.

"It's a gift," he said simply, shrugging his shoulder as if it were no big deal.

She examined it. It was shaped like a dog that looked remarkably like Buster. The dog was sitting on his haunches with his paws raised, his big droopy brown eyes begging for something. A note was taped to one of the paws. Jenna read the note:

I'm begging forgiveness.
I know I was wrong.
Jake

There was a muddy paw print below the writing that obviously belonged to Buster. Jenna glanced at Jake. He was standing there with his hands up at his chest, in a stance similar to the cookie jar dog, a pleading look on his face that implied he *was* begging forgiveness. And beside him sat Buster. Somehow, in the few seconds it had taken her to inspect the cookie jar, Jake had positioned Buster on his haunches with his paws at his chest. The two looked totally comical together. She burst into laughter, and Jake dropped his hands and joined her.

"Does that mean I'm forgiven?" His voice was casual and he shoved his hands in his pockets and looked around while he spoke, but Jenna had seen the intent gleam in his eyes and realized her answer was important to him.

She sighed. "How can I stay mad at a man who can make me laugh before my first cup of coffee?"

"About last night," he said, speaking quickly, his nervousness showing. "I know I was way off base. You weren't drunk and I was the biggest fool this side of Pluto. I was just going to tell you what a dammed fool I was when Buster showed up and we had that close encounter with the tree."

"Well, the cookie jar fits the occasion perfectly. Where on earth did you find it, and on such short notice?"

A sneaking suspicion crept over Jenna, causing a frown to wrinkle her brow. She carefully removed the lid from the jar, then flipped the base over, exposing the bottom. In raised letters were the words 'Shawnee USA.' She lifted accusing eyes to Jake.

"You bought this for your mother, didn't you? You told me last night that she collected Shawnee stuff."

Jake had the good graces to look embarrassed. "Originally, yes. But…"

"I can't accept it." Jenna tried handing the jar to Jake.

"No, no. You have to keep it."

"But you bought it for your mother."

"And after I bought it, I found out she already has one in her collection. It's been sitting around my house collecting dust for months. Waiting for you, I guess."

Jenna wavered. It was such an adorable jar. Carlee would love it.

"Your little girl will love it."

Could he read minds? Her startled green eyes met his enigmatic blue ones. "Okay." She grinned, giving in gracefully. "Carlee *will* love it. Thanks." She gently set the cookie jar on the picnic table.

"I also brought your van back," he said, handing her the keys. "It's in the drive."

Jenna glanced toward her driveway. "How on earth did you manage that?" Even Jake couldn't drive two vehicles at once.

"A friend drove me."

"I hope you didn't wake him up at dawn just to drive you to town."

"Well, actually, yes I did."

"And he's still a friend?"

"He owed me a favor. Besides, it was the least I could do, after last night."

"Well, thank you. I appreciate it." She stuffed the keys into her pocket. She hesitated, avoiding any devastating eye contact. "Umm, I'd better get busy. My orchids…" She waved a hand toward the two greenhouses. "I like to get all the plants taken care of before Carlee wakes up."

She headed across the yard and Jake followed, leaving Buster tied to the tree.

"Is there anything I can do to help?"

"No, thanks. I'll just move some of them into the sun and see how my show entries are shaping up."

"You actually use those greenhouses?" Before Jenna could respond, he continued. "I'm impressed. I know Charlie Schwartz ran a nursery out here for years before he retired, but he let the greenhouses fall into disrepair toward the end. Then they stood empty for over a year before you bought the place. I'm surprised they're still useable."

"They weren't." Jenna grimaced, remembering the broken windows, rusted pipes, cracks in the floors, leaks in the roofs. Her mom had bought this property and financed the repairs. She owed her mom a lot.

"It took over a month to fix this one up," Jenna said, unlatching the door to the smaller of the two buildings.

"Whew," he said with a low whistle, clearly impressed as they stepped inside. "You've done wonders." He ran a hand over the windows. "You've replaced all the glass. What is this stuff? Some kind of plastic?"

"Corrugated plastic. It's better than regular glass panels. It diffuses the sun's light, distributes it evenly."

"You really know your stuff, huh?"

"Yeah, I love it." Jenna slowly made her way down rows of hanging orchids, carefully inspecting each one for early signs of disease or other problems.

"Is it hard to raise orchids?" Jake asked.

"Not really hard, but time consuming. Basically, they just need four things—sunlight, consistent temperature, food and water. And it's important when growing non-native orchids to match their habitat here to their native habitat."

"Are these all orchids, then?" Jake asked, glancing around. There were large plants, some six feet in length, and small plants that fit in four-inch pots. They were all shapes and sizes, some standing tall, others twisting in fascinating shapes, and many had no blossoms at all. He wondered how anyone could tell they were orchids. The blossoms he did see ranged from the large familiar big-lipped plant he associated with orchids to tiny button-sized blossoms. Very small plants were in pots, not planted in dirt, he observed, noticing their roots tangling around a clump of straw or something, he couldn't tell what. The larger plants were hanging in pots that allowed their roots to move freely in the air. "I never knew orchids grew like this, their roots so exposed," he said.

He stopped before an orchid whose stem was loaded with buds. Three years ago, when Charlie Schwarz ran the nursery, he remembered, he'd brought Lizzy here to pick out a plant for Barb for Mother's Day. There'd been a table of pansies here then, their velvety petals a profusion of deep, rich colors. *This one, daddy. Mommy will love this one. Purple's her favorite color you know. But I just love this pink and white one. Oh, I guess— I guess we should get the purple one. Do you think the purple plant will be lonely all by itself, daddy? Do you think we should get two?*

Jake clung to the memory, seeing again the anxiety in Lizzy's soft features, her troubled blue eyes, as she tried to choose between the one she thought her mother would like and the one she, herself, wanted. *Yes, sweetheart, let's get both of them. What a good idea. What a smart little girl you are.*

Jenna's voice pulled him back to the present. "Yes, I remember how surprised I was, too, when I first got into orchids. You can't plant them in the earth. It would smother them. They grow quite comfortably on trees, getting their food from the droppings of birds and dead leaves, washed down by the rain. And there are so many different species, 25,000 around the world. They're on every continent, you know, except Antarctica. There are 168 species in Florida alone. But every orchid in Florida is on the endangered species list."

She stopped abruptly, realizing her enthusiasm for the subject was rarely shared by others, whose eyes quickly glazed over.

"I'm sorry. I get carried away." A quick glance at him surprised her. He actually looked interested.

She touched the orchid hanging near his head. "Hello, beautiful," she purred to the plant. "How are we today?" She glanced with some embarrassment at Jake, who was watching her with amused interest. "You probably think I'm silly, but I always talk to my orchids. I tell them how beautiful they are, and then they give me more beautiful blossoms."

"Not silly at all," Jake assured her, though his eyes still glimmered with amusement. "Studies have proven plants thrive better exposed to soothing sounds than plants exposed to raucous noises. Same way with cows, the milk's better."

"This one's going to the show," she said of the orchid. "Aren't you, beautiful? And you're going to bring home an FCC."

"An FCC?" Jake asked.

"First Class Certificate," she said. "It's the highest rating an orchid can get."

Jake looked dubiously at the orchid. The buds seemed to be dragging the stem down. That didn't seem like a good sign.

Jenna laughed, reading his doubts. "This many buds on one spike is quite amazing. That alone might win it an award. And if we're lucky," she added, turning to speak directly to her plant, "your blossoms will be so big and beautiful, your parents will be extremely proud of you, and the judges will all be amazed."

She turned back to Jake, ignoring the heightened amusement showing in his face. "One of the things that judges base their decision on is how the orchid compares to its parents. Bigger and brighter is better."

"Its parents?" Jake asked, trying to control a telltale twitch of the lips.

"You're laughing at me," she accused.

"I'm sorry," he said, unable to deny it. "But I hasten to add, my admiration is greater than my amusement. You're lucky, to be able to make your living doing what you love—and to be good at it." His thoughts went fleetingly to the untouched manuscript in his office. Would he ever feel that joy again?

Jenna felt her cheeks redden with embarrassment. She wasn't comfortable with compliments. "I—I guess you're one of the lucky ones too. I mean, being a writer and all."

"Yeah, I guess I am," he agreed in a noncommittal tone, but she saw that pain flick through his eyes, there and as quickly gone. "And," he said, reaching around her to touch a small pot and turn it slightly as he inspected the plant, "I can see why a dog like Buster is an anathema to you."

"Oh, Buster's not so bad," she said faintly, and then frowned, not believing she'd heard herself correctly. Jake's nearness was having its usual effect on her, enhanced by his fresh outdoorsy scent. Her father had used a musk cologne, one she'd always associate with him, to the detriment of any man wearing it. Ned had preferred a sharp cinnamon aroma, another unpleasant reminder of the past. Jake's scent was his own, and she found it nearly irresistible.

Jake enjoyed listening to Jenna's voice, soft yet passionate, as she talked about her orchids. He wanted to keep her talking. He wanted to keep her close. He wanted to touch her.

"How many kinds of orchids do you have?" he asked. He waved his hand to take in the entire greenhouse, his arm brushing against hers in the process. Lame, lame, lame.

Heat coursed through Jenna's skin at the light touch, radiating out from the point of contact. To steady herself and put some inches between her and Jake, she leaned back against a small wooden table on wheels, careful not to send it rolling. "I've got about seventy varieties—well, maybe closer to fifty right now," she said, remembering Buster's rampage. "Those are just babies," she added, pointing to another table.

This time it was her arm that brushed his, and again she felt her skin tingle, pores waking up with a whoop and a holler, ready to party. He must have felt it too. He turned his face to hers, his eyes raked over her and fastened on her lips. Her stomach did a flip-flop.

"I keep them on these tables so I can wheel them outside every day for sun and air," she said, her voice barely above a whisper. "They need direct sunlight every day, but not when the sun's overhead, so I bring them in and out." She straightened from the table and started to roll it toward the door.

"I've heard of taking a dog for a walk, but never taking your flowers for a walk," Jake joked. He leaned beside her, gripping the table and helping her control its path. Bent over as they both were, he could see the cleavage her halter-top revealed. He forced himself not to stare, but averting his gaze did not erase the image and did not stop the electric contact as thigh brushed thigh, shoulder touched shoulder.

Despite their mutual attraction and distraction, they somehow managed to maneuver the table outside with only one or two minor bumps along the way.

Once outside, Jenna straightened up quickly and stepped away from Jake, determined to marshal her emotions, which threatened to spin out of control. "One down, three to go," she said, backing toward the greenhouse. "You don't have to help. I'm sure you have more important things to do and I can manage by myself."

"Not on your life," he said, following her back into the greenhouse.

Oh damn. Was she destined to yet again make a fool of herself, falling all over Jake Corbin? Absolutely not, she vowed. Probably, she admitted.

"This is one of the more fascinating varieties," she said, pointing to another hanging orchid. "It's not native to Tampa, so I hope it survives." She had decided to use Jake's interest in orchids to keep things on an impersonal level.

"Oh? What makes it fascinating?" he asked.

"Well," she said, "this is the male blossom." She pointed to a large blossom. "And this—" she pointed higher up the spike, "is the female. You want to know how they pollinate?"

Jake nodded, looking intrigued, she noted with gratification.

"The male attracts the pollinator, in this case a particular bee, which lights on the landing pad." She indicated the orchid's lip. "Then the sneaky orchid lambastes it with a blast of pollen that knocks the silly bee clear off the lip. The bee gets madder than a hornet, and flies straight up, as bees tend to do when they get mad."

"Sort of flying off the handle," Jake suggested.

Jenna laughed appreciatively. "Yes, straight up and lands on the female blossom, carrying all that pollen with it. That's how the female gets pollinated."

"So," Jake said, thinking about it, "you loose some poor unsuspecting bee in here to be taken advantage of by the horny male?"

Jenna wasn't sure she liked the way the conversation was going. "Er, no. If I did that, the bee would fly willy-nilly from plant to plant, and I'd never know who the parents of the offspring were, would I?"

"Ah, I see. So, you play the role of pollinator. Sort of like the orchid's pimp, wouldn't you say?"

Jenna knew he was teasing her, but any kind of sexual conversation with this man was suggestive and dangerous.

"Well, um, next table." She quickly walked to another table and started to push it. Jake joined her, a little too eagerly, she thought. She suspected his interest in orchids wasn't what accounted for that familiar gleam in his eye as he bent beside her and placed his hands next to hers.

So once again they were joined at the shoulder, joined at the hip, each pretending not to notice while each knew they both did notice. They had only pushed the table a few feet when the path was blocked by some low-hanging pots. They stopped and looked at each other.

That's when it happened. Up to that point Jenna had carefully avoided making eye contact with Jake. She'd glanced at him, she'd slid her gaze over him, she'd looked at him and looked quickly away. But she hadn't looked him directly in the eye. This time she was caught off guard, looking up at him automatically to see which way they should turn the table. Their eyes met. Their gazes locked. Desire leaped between them. With mutual accord, they turned to face each other.

"Jenna," Jake said softly, placing his hands on her upper shoulders. Jenna stepped into his embrace as though it were the most natural thing in the world. His arms tightened around her as she wrapped her arms around him, laying her head against his chest. She could feel the beat of his heart, thump, thump, thump. It was a comforting sound, a very sensual sound, and it felt wonderful to be in his arms.

He stroked her hair, then laid his cheek against it. His fingers trailed a path from the nape of her neck around to her face. He cupped her chin and lifted it, looking into her eyes for any sign of resistance. Her lids were heavy, her eyes smoldering.

"Jenna," he said, his voice husky, lowering his lips toward hers.

"Mommy! Mommy!" Carlee's frightened scream tore through the air. Jenna and Jake jerked apart and ran for the door. The scream had come from the direction of the patio, and it had been filled with terror.

CHAPTER EIGHT

Carlee's scream echoed in Jenna's ears as she and Jake rushed toward the sound. The sudden quiet following the scream was as terrifying as the scream itself had been. What had happened? Was she hurt? Did she fall out of a tree, crack her head?

As they rounded the house, Jenna's heart leaped to her throat. Carlee *was* lying under a tree, silent and still, her frail little body nearly obscured by the hulk of the dog standing over her, its mouth close to her face. Before Jenna could scream, could leap on the dog and tear him away, she heard Carlee's girlish laughter. She and Jake reached Carlee at the same time. Buster was straddling Carlee, one huge paw resting lightly on her chest while he smothered her with wet kisses. And Carlee was absolutely ecstatic.

Jake grabbed Buster's collar and hauled the dog away from Carlee, but not before Jenna made an amazing discovery. That monster dog, that delighted in bowling over Jake and Jenna, seemed to sense Carlee's helplessness. He was treating her more gently than lotion-laced tissue.

Jenna gave Jake an incredulous look and he seemed as surprised as she. Relief was written all over him, but his face was still white and his eyes still retained a hard, ready-to-do-battle glint.

"I just felt in my gut it had something to do with Buster," he said in a hoarse whisper. "I thought he'd attacked her." He gave Buster's collar a sharp shake. "Don't ever scare me like that again."

Jenna lowered a hand to Carlee and helped her stand. "I heard you scream, munchkin."

"I didn't see him. He scared me. But he's a nice dog, mommy. He doesn't bite."

Carlee pulled loose from Jenna's grip and ran to Buster, throwing her arms around his neck. "See, mommy, he doesn't bite. He just kisses," Carlee said laughing as Buster slurped her cheek.

Jenna looked, but what she saw was Carlee in close proximity to Jake, who still held Buster's collar, and not showing one sign of fear. Carlee was so enthralled with Buster she forgot to be afraid of the dog's owner.

Well, Jenna thought, giving Buster a grateful look for the first time since they'd crossed paths, that certainly proves the old adage "It's an ill wind that blows no good."

Carlee turned pleading eyes up to Jake. "Can I play with your dog?"

Jenna glanced at Jake. Would that ill wind called Buster blow a little good Jake's way too? Would Carlee's delight in the dog, and Buster's obvious delight in Carlee, soften Jake's aversion to Carlee? But he was gazing with unseeing eyes at some memory in his head. Like the night at the auction, she thought.

"Daddy, can I have a dog? Suzie's dog had puppies and she said I could have one. Can I, daddy"?

Lizzy's eyes were enormous, hopeful, pleading. "Can I, daddy? I'll take care of it. I won't let it chew on your shoes, or go to the bathroom in the house. I promise."

Barb's harsh voice cut into the child's pleas. "There'll be no dirty, flea-bitten dog in this house, Lizzy. How many times do I have to tell you? No dog!"

Lizzy's blue eyes filled with tears, but she wiped them away soundlessly. Barb got mad at her when she cried, and Jake didn't know how to bridge the gap between mother and daughter. Damn Barb, anyway. She wouldn't let Lizzy be a child.

"Jake?"

Jenna's voice drew Jake back to the present. She was staring at him, and so was Carlee. Carlee with her little girl eyes, enormous, hopeful, pleading. Jake successfully fought down an impulse to turn and flee from those eyes.

Carlee repeated, "Can I play with your dog?"

This was tough. This was so damn tough. He felt brittle, like one small tap would shatter him to pieces.

He swallowed with difficulty and composed himself before answering in a teasing voice, "Well, if you promise not to hurt him."

Carlee's sharp little mind recognized the humor and she giggled. "I promise."

The byplay between man and child brought a lump to Jenna's throat and she had to turn away to hide the tears that suddenly flooded her eyes.

When she had composed herself, she turned back to Carlee. Her petite little girl had reached up to grasp Buster's collar and was walking the monster dog around the tree while Jake watched attentively, ready to spring to the rescue if necessary. Buster followed Carlee's lead as demurely as a Victorian maiden, taking only an occasional liberty with his slurpy kisses.

"This is the best dog in the whole world, mommy," Carlee said, noticing Jenna watching her. "He didn't mean to get in the trash all those times. He just wanted to play and he didn't have anybody to play with. But now he's got me, so he won't be bad again. Will you, boy?"

"His name is Buster," Jake said in a voice that sounded strained.

Buster, whose head was about level with Carlee's, slurped her on the ear.

Carlee squealed and hugged Buster. "I love you, Buster, I love you," she said, before continuing to walk him around the tree.

Only a four-year-old could fall in love with a dog that fast, Jenna mused. Then, remembering her willing surrender to Jake's attraction, she felt like a hypocrite belittling Carlee's quick capitulation.

"Thanks, Jake," Jenna said, turning to him.

Jake's face was white, his expression strained, his eyes haunted. He waved away Jenna's thanks, then said in a tight voice, "I'll be going now. If you have any problems with Buster, give me a call. I'm in the phonebook. Oh, and don't worry about bringing him back. I'll wait a couple hours, then come and get him." He turned to Carlee. "Keep Buster on the chain, okay?"

Seeing her nod, he left quickly before he fell apart before their eyes. He'd just made a major step. He knew it. He also knew it had hurt like hell. In fact, it was tearing him apart.

As he tried to walk off his pain, he suddenly realized that in the tortured shock of dealing with Carlee, he had completely forgotten about the near kiss in the greenhouse. And he'd walked away without giving any indication to Jenna that it had meant anything to him. Okay, he thought, I'll have to make it up to her. The thought intrigued him.

During the rest of the walk home, his thoughts continued to dwell on Jenna. She was an amazing woman, strong, self-possessed. And funny! Maybe he liked that about her more than anything else. It felt so good to laugh again, to tease and joke and trade friendly insults. Even their arguing contained an element of humor. He could not imagine her ever being a clinging vine, demanding a man's total attention and adoration. He suspected such a role would bore her to tears. She was too busy with life to begrudge anyone else his share of it.

Jake savored the memory of those moments in the greenhouse. He had been hesitant about kissing her, afraid she would reject him after his boorish behavior in Tallahassee. He wouldn't have blamed her. But she hadn't rejected him. She'd been ready to meet him halfway, and after Tallahassee he knew how good halfway was. Yes, he promised himself, walking with an unaccustomed spring to his step, he would make it up to her. Anticipation quickened his pulse and soothed his hurting heart.

Jenna watched Jake until he was out of sight. Then she turned back to Carlee. "Why don't you come inside, get dressed and eat some breakfast before you play with Buster?"

"Can't I eat out here? Buster might get lonely if I stay inside too long."

Jenna smiled. "Ok, but not till after you're dressed. You can't run around in your jammies all day."

Carlee giggled and took Jenna's outstretched hand. They were almost to the house when Carlee remembered why she'd been looking for Jenna.

"Wait! I left my new book by the tree."

She ran back and got the book and rejoined Jenna at the door.

"Will you read it to me, mommy? Gramma read it to me last night while you were at the auction, but I want to hear it again. I like Wendy. She's a wood nymph you know. And the Butterfly Queen is so pretty. You should see her wings! They're pink and purple and silvery!" Carlee flipped open the book and held it up for Jenna's inspection. "See? And Wendy's tree is cool too. I wish we had a tree like that in our yard." Carlee pointed to another part of the page, where an intricately drawn tree dominated the background. "It has special branches where all Wendy's visitors can sit while they visit her. Do you think we can get a tree like that, mommy?"

* * *

The acrid smell of perming chemicals assaulted Jenna as she stepped into Millie's Place a few minutes before eight. Millie already had one customer, early as it was. Jenna caught Millie's eye and waved, then took a seat on one of the three cushioned chairs in the waiting area. Picking up a magazine, she idly flipped through the glossy pages. Finding an article on gardening that drew her attention, she attempted to read, but her interest in the topic couldn't stop her thoughts from wandering back to Jake. Despite her best intentions, ten minutes in his company had reduced her backbone to wet noodle consistency. I'm hopeless, she thought, shaking her head.

It's not my fault, she argued, sounding in her mind like a 10-year-old trying to squirm out of a misadventure. It's science, biology, physics, whatever it is that makes the love hormones zone in on each other. Pheromones, isn't that what they're called? A gene we're born with or something like that, she vaguely recalled from an article she'd read about a year ago. Something to do with smell, as she remembered it. They seek out similar genes and when they find what they're looking for, whamo, more powerful than Cupid's arrow. It's all chemistry. The sexual pull between Jake and her was preordained the moment they were conceived in their mothers' wombs. *Not my fault, can't be helped.* Breathing a sigh of relief, she absolved herself of all blame. And, by extension, admitted that future attraction was inevitable. *Can't fight it. What will be will be.*

Having logically and scientifically reasoned away any question of misbehavior, she felt free to relive those moments in the greenhouse. Jake had very artfully reduced her to putty in his hands. If Carlee hadn't screamed, would they have picked up where they left off in Tallahassee? The reaction in her body just thinking about the possibility made her aware of how fervently she wanted that to happen.

But she couldn't ignore the fact that Jake had some sort of issue with Carlee. This morning was the first time he had actually interacted with Carlee, and the strain it put him under would have been obvious to anyone with eyes.

Which brought her full circle to her original resolve. Pheromones or not, science or not, Cupid or not, she would not allow a relationship to develop that would place Carlee in a situation with a man who couldn't abide her. She'd move to Timbuktu if that's what it took to outrun their sex-maniac hormones.

Thinking of sex-maniac hormones brought her thoughts back to those few minutes in the greenhouse when Jake had almost kissed her. She knew what his kisses could do to her. She *loved* what his kisses could do to her. *Not my fault.*

She sighed. Would her mom be terribly upset when Jenna broke the news to her that they would be moving to Timbuktu? She sighed again.

"Jenna?" A gentle tap on Jenna's shoulder accompanied Millie's enquiry. "That's the third time I've called your name. I bet you were thinking about a certain dark-haired writer." Millie grinned and winked. "How'd it go last night? Did the handsome brute take you straight home and walk you to your door like a perfect gentleman? Or did you run out of gas on the way?"

Jenna felt her face grow warm at Millie's words. "How'd you find out about that? You left before we did."

Millie laughed. "I'm a beautician, aren't I? And you know how women love to talk."

"You were talking about me?" Jenna squirmed uncomfortably.

"Nope. You know me better than that! Just listening to them. Something about taking your car keys?" She quirked an eyebrow. Jenna frowned. Could everybody on the whole darned planet except for her quirk an eyebrow?

"Besides," Millie continued, "I knew you had an appointment this morning, and I'd get the scoop firsthand. So, come on, out with it. What happened?"

"Well, he might have done the perfect gentleman thing if a tree hadn't got in the way." She sat in the chair Millie indicated.

"What do you mean? Were you in an accident?" Since Jenna was obviously all right, the question wasn't spoken with much alarm.

While Jenna submitted to Millie's expertise, she related the events of the night before. In retrospect, the whole situation had been kind of funny, and

Millie was laughing so hard by the time Jenna finished that tears threatened to spill onto Jenna's freshly shampooed hair.

"But I still think it was damned presumptuous of him to take my keys," Jenna said, shaking her head.

Millie laid a hand on her head. "Hold still, hon. I've got two blades of steel in my hand that will clip your ear off as quick as you can say snip."

Properly chastised, Jenna did her best not to move again. "He's a strange man," she said reflectively. "Kind of weird, actually."

"Mmmm," Millie murmured noncommittally. "Not so weird, really, all things considered."

Jenna's ears perked up, though not enough, she hoped, to get snipped. "What's that supposed to mean?"

"The accident, you know, that killed Barb and little Lizzy."

"Accident," Jenna exclaimed, shocked. "I had no idea. What happened?"

"It was an automobile accident, and so unnecessary. It happened a couple of years ago. Barb was taking Lizzy to the doctor, so the paper said. There was a storm, much like the one we had last night, and Barb was drunk, which was her usual state. Well, same old story—drunk driver, slippery roads, driving too fast—"

"That's terrible. Barb was his wife?"

"Yeah. Jake hasn't gotten over it—keeps blaming himself. He never talks about it, but he's carrying a heap of guilt around, weighing him down like a lead harness."

"But it wasn't his fault—was it?"

"Course not. But you know how people are. If only I had stayed home, if only I had taken Lizzy to the doctor, if only this, if only that. The night it happened he was at the library, doing some research for one of his kid's books. Wanted to finish it in time for Lizzy's birthday. She was going to be four in two days. I saw him when I went to check out a book, said hi to him, we chatted for a few minutes. Everything was fine, normal, except Jake was a little anxious about finishing the book in time for Lizzy's birthday. Then, two hours later, it was a moot point, and his life was down the toilet."

"It would be so horrible to lose your child." Jenna didn't know what she would do if anything happened to Carlee. Jenna had divorced Ned, torn apart their family, alienated herself from Ned's world, mainly so Carlee could have a fair chance at enjoying life. And she would do much more than that, fight lions if she had to, to protect Carlee. She would rather die than have Carlee hurt.

She shook her head. "I still don't see how Jake could blame himself for what happened."

"Oh, hon, you don't know how your mind can be your worst enemy. Now Jake and I, we go back a ways. We went to school together and we've remained friends. Nothing romantic, you know, the chemistry's not there. Just buddies. We'd have lunch once in a while when he was in town doing research or whatever. Sometimes he'd talk about his family. He had debated divorcing Barb because he couldn't handle her drinking, said she was a lousy mother to little Lizzy, drunk all the time and talking mean. But then he got her to join AA and he thought that was a positive sign. He wanted things to work out, you see. He really wanted to keep his family together. But I guess Barb kept a bottle hidden in the house somewhere. Then the accident—"

"That's why he says it's his fault?"

"Oh, he doesn't *say* it. I just know him so well, I know what's going on in his head. He should have divorced her, he should have stayed home that night, that kind of thing. But goodness no, he never talks about it. Not to me. Not to his mother. Not to anyone. Just keeps it all bottled up inside."

Millie was silent for a few minutes while she concentrated on Jenna's hair.

"Lizzy was just four years old?" Jenna asked. "Carlee's birthday is next week. She'll be four too."

"Yeah, two days shy of her fourth birthday, and such a sweet little tyke." Millie's voice softened as she reminisced. "Jake doted on her. They were always off on adventures. Girl stuff, like hunting butterflies and picking wildflowers, but not just girl stuff. He was teaching her how to bat a ball, how to swim, even the proper way to run. They were a familiar father/daughter team in local charity races. And she would come strutting in here with her dad, proud as a Siamese cat, to get her hair trimmed. She was precious."

"I guess that explains why he overreacted when he thought I'd been drinking last night."

"Yeah," Millie agreed. "The darned fool meant well."

She finished trimming Jenna's hair, and swirled the chair around so that

Jenna could check the results in the mirror. "All done."

Jenna nodded absently, smiled and paid Millie automatically; scarcely aware of what she was doing. Her mind was absorbed with the story Millie had told her. Now she understood those fleeting glimpses of pain she'd seen in Jake's eyes. It was there, it was real, and it mirrored a pain so intense she couldn't even begin to imagine it. And, she realized, it also explained his aversion to Carlee. Carlee would be a constant painful reminder of his loss. Which was one more reason to keep Jake out of her life. It was hard enough to fight live competition. It was impossible to fight a ghost.

* * *

When Jake came to pick up Buster, Claire told him Carlee and the dog were in the butterfly garden. He strolled slowly in that direction, anticipating the pain awaiting him but determined to see it through. He paused when he heard Carlee's childish voice talking earnestly to Buster. He peered over a bush.

Carlee was crouching beside Buster, explaining the intricacies of her butterfly garden to the contented dog, who was lying at her feet.

"Now this one's a milkweed plant, Buster," Carlee was saying in the schoolteacher tone she adopted when explaining the garden to those she thought less knowledgeable. "It's poison, so don't ever eat it."

Buster emitted a noisy sigh and thumped his tail.

"And this," Carlee continued with the pride of a mom showing off her new baby, "is Willy. 'Cept you can't see him cuz he's inside his cryslis. When he comes out, he's going to be a beautiful monarch, probly the most beautiful in the world I think."

This grandiose pronouncement seemed to ignite Buster's interest enough to prompt him to touch a nose delicately to the vulnerable chrysalis. Carlee tugged on Buster's collar and the dog obediently lowered his head. Jake was astonished that Buster obeyed the child so well. He knew it was because the dog instinctively recognized a helpless child and behaved accordingly, but it still amazed him to see Buster so docile.

Jake watched silently, buoying up his resolve to approach Carlee. Her childish voice evoked a rush of memories, but he refused to let them master

118

him. One more step, he reminded himself. One more step toward healing.

It hurt. It hurt like hell, the pain slicing through his heart. *My salvation or my destruction.* At that moment, he didn't feel remotely close to salvation.

"Oh, look." Carlee's voice dropped to an excited whisper. "Another caterpillar. This one's smaller than Willy, but isn't he pretty? No, Buster," she added sternly, placing a small hand over the dog's big snout, "you can't kiss it. Caterpillars don't like dog kisses. See those?" she asked, pointing to small holes lining the sides of the caterpillar. "That's where the caterpillar breathes. If you kiss it, your doggy slobber will get in the speercals and it can't breathe."

Spiracles, Jake thought, remembering the word from a story he'd written about a master gardener the summer before.

Buster had his ears pricked forward, exhibiting polite interest in the lecture, and laid his head back on his paws when Carlee paused for breath.

Jake took the opportunity to approach, forcing each step in front of the other. When Carlee saw Jake appear suddenly from around the bush, she scrambled quickly to her feet and moved behind Buster, putting the dog between them. Jake stopped, surprised. There was no mistaking the little girl's body language. She was afraid of him. Well, that put them on equal footing, he thought wryly, since he was afraid of her.

Buster raised his head and thumped his tail at Jake's approach, but kept his position in front of Carlee.

CHAPTER NINE

Jake and Carlee stared at each other for a moment. Jake didn't miss Carlee's frantic glance toward the house, obviously debating escape, but she'd have to pass Jake to get there.

"Hello, Carlee," he said, keeping his voice as calm as possible.

"H-hi," she answered, her little hand opening and closing convulsively on the dog's collar.

Jake squatted, putting himself at eye level with the little girl. "I'm sorry if I startled you. I just came to get Buster."

"Oh," she said, inching around the dog to keep space between them.

"I see you took him off the chain," he said, frowning.

Carlee's eyes filled with tears and she started to tremble. "I—I just wanted to show him my butterfly g-garden," she sobbed. "I was going to tie him b-back up."

"Well," he said gruffly, her tears unnerving him, "it's okay this time, I guess. I just didn't want you to get hurt, and Buster's kind of unpredictable."

Carlee looked at Jake, brushing at her tears with the backs of her fists. Her eyes were still filled with fright, but there was uncertainty now also.

What did she think I was going to do, Jake wondered. Scold her? Beat her? Lock her in a closet? Her look reminded him of Lizzy. Everything since the first day he'd set eyes on Carlee reminded him of Lizzy. Lizzy had never looked at Jake that way, but he had seen that look on her face whenever Barb was angry with her, yelling at her. For the first time, Jake wondered what Carlee's father was like. He knew from what he had observed that Jenna would never be the cause of Carlee's fear, so it stood to reason it was the father. He felt anger stir inside him, helpless frustration, but for once it wasn't a reaction to his loss. It was a reaction to the realization that some man had so misused this beautiful, intelligent little girl that she cringed at the least sign of disapproval from a man.

Still squatting, he reached for Buster's collar. Carlee actually flinched when his hand came her way. Jake's body tightened, his protective instincts aroused. He'd like to throttle the person responsible for causing Carlee's fear.

"I'm going to take Buster home now," he told her, striving to keep his voice normal. The look on her face—fear, disappointment—was wrenching. A four-year-old shouldn't have to fear any man. He recalled the first day he had seen Carlee, how she had clung tightly to Jenna's hand while hiding behind her legs. She'd been afraid of him then, he realized now, but he'd been too wrapped up in his own shock to notice. Earlier today she hadn't seemed afraid, and he gave that credit to Buster, who was enough of a novelty and distraction to make Carlee forget her fear. But apparently the novelty had worn off, allowing her fear to resurface.

"Would you like to play with Buster again tomorrow?" he asked gently.

Carlee wiped the last of the tears from her eyes and nodded.

"Good," Jake said. "Buster will like that. I'll bring him over after lunch." With that promise, he turned and hurried away, unable to look a minute longer at the small, tear-streaked face.

* * *

Jake hammered another nail into the wooden receptacle he was building around his trashcan. He was no carpenter, but to paraphrase an old axiom, necessity was the mother of prevention. He had to figure out some way to thwart Buster's foraging in the trash, and enclosing the trashcans made the most sense to him. He'd made a trip to the local hardware store and came home with his SUV loaded to the max with tools, boards, hinges, and a how-to book.

He found the manual labor a pleasant change from writing. He had the immediate gratification of watching the structure take shape, and while he worked he could let his mind dwell on other matters, something impossible to do when writing.

He'd been sawing and hammering away for the past two hours and the 'other matters' occupying his thoughts were Jenna and Carlee.

He knew he was making progress with Jenna, knew the attraction between them was mutual, knew it was inevitable that they wind up in bed together. And he knew he wanted more than a brief fling.

Which brought his thoughts to Carlee. One plus one equaled three, and adding Carlee to the equation was every bit as tough, as torturous, as he'd expected it to be. But the alternative—a life without Jenna—was not acceptable. He'd already made that decision and the challenge of Carlee wasn't going to scare him off. He was confident that given time and circumstance, he could win Carlee over, erase her fears, convince her to accept him. It was himself he was worried about. Could he accept Carlee? He *wanted* to, but want could be an exercise in frustration with no resolution.

A small voice inside him suggested that maybe, possibly, the woman at the funeral had been right. Maybe time did heal all wounds. He would never stop loving Lizzy, he would never stop missing her. He would carry that scar till the day he died. But maybe that's all it would be—a scar. Maybe the wound would heal, leaving only a scar. There would be days when the scar would itch and ache, but the wound would be healed. Was Jenna the balm that would stop the festering, heal the wound? In his heart, he knew she was. And Carlee was the rub that would cause the scar to itch and ache.

He picked up another nail and hammered into the wood. Carlee was the toughest mountain he'd have to climb, he knew that. She reminded him so much of Lizzy, and every reminder hurt. He thought of Carlee laying her tiny hand over Buster's huge mouth and in her funny little schoolteacher voice ordering him not to kiss the caterpillar.

Lizzy had wanted a dog so badly. He despised himself now for not getting her one, Barb be damned. But he hadn't known, couldn't know, what a short time she had.

He wouldn't dwell on morbid thoughts. He closed his eyes and pictured his little Lizzy with Buster, leading the furry hulk around by the nose, imperiously issuing orders Buster meekly obeyed. The image made him chuckle. And he realized with a wonder that brought tears pricking his eyes that this was the first time since Lizzy had died that he'd been able to think of her and laugh.

Eventually, after many bent nails and a sore thumb, Jake hammered the final nail into the receptacle. He stepped back to admire his handiwork, inordinately pleased with his attempt at carpentry. The front opened for trashcan removal on trash pick-up days, and the top lifted for easy access when throwing things away. It might not earn an A in woodshop, but it darn sure would stymie Buster. Buster, and the raccoons and coyotes too, all of which were adept at getting in the garbage.

He looked around the yard. The next task would be installing cyclone fencing, but that would have to wait until his order came in, about 10 days from now, according to the salesman. In the meantime, he had a fifteen-foot length of sturdy chain and a monster metal tie-down used to anchor mobile homes in the event of a hurricane. He'd dig a deep hole, encase the tie-down in cement, hook the chain to it, and Buster's roaming days would come to a screeching halt.

He tucked his garbage cans into the new receptacle, pausing more than once in the process to admire the effect. "Not bad," he said several times. "Not bad at all." He was inordinately pleased with his carpentry. And having practiced on his own trash container, he was ready to build one for Jenna. She could use one even after Buster was effectively fenced in, he reasoned. If raccoons and coyotes hadn't paid her a visit yet, they would sooner or later. They were ingenious in their efforts to ferret out man-made trash. It was even possible that Buster really wasn't guilty of all those crimes he was accused of.

Yes, tomorrow when he took Buster over for Carlee to play with, he'd take along his tools and enough lumber to build a trash bin for Jenna.

* * *

Jenna placed the last of the groceries into her van with a sigh. It had been a long morning and she was glad to be heading home. The usual heavy weekend traffic on U.S. 19 impeded her progress, but once off the freeway Jenna was able to let her thoughts wander over the day's events.

Between now and the time she'd left Millie's yesterday she had called on a dozen prospective buyers, visiting floral shops, funeral homes, lawyer's offices, and hotels. Through perseverance and determination, she'd signed on two clients yesterday and three more today. Not a bad percentage. In fact, she considered it pretty darn good.

Tonight, there'd be a celebration! She'd bought everyone's favorite foods, and she would dig out her grandmother's china to dine on. Carlee would love that, she thought. And so would she and her mom. They'd even have candles. So what if China and candles weren't the normal setting for pizza (Carlee's favorite), Chinese (Claire's favorite), spaghetti (Jenna's favorite), and chocolate cream pie (everyone's favorite)? She'd wrapped up her business meetings early in order to do the necessary shopping and was looking forward to an enjoyable celebration.

So much for your predictions, Ned. The taunting words rang through her thoughts. A song bounced in her heart. *You said I'd come crawling back. Well, ha-ha and ha!*

She thought back to the day she'd signed the divorce papers. "You can't make it on your own, Jenna," Ned had told her, trying to sound concerned, but obviously relishing the certainty of her failure. "You need me. When you wake up and admit that, you'll come crawling back." He was trying to undermine her confidence, as he had for the five years they'd been married, and had pretty much succeeded, but that final jab had not had the desired effect. Instead of panicking her, it had made her more determined to succeed than anything else he could have said.

Even had she believed him, and in her heart maybe she had believed him, she had known that leaving Ned was the best thing for Carlee. His critical behavior had often reduced Jenna to tears, but it had not sent her flying to the nearest divorce lawyer. She had married him for better or worse, after all. He had been totally domineering, making every major and minor decision about the house, their friends, their activities, everything, treating her like his possession, not his partner. That had eventually pitched her to the brink of depression, but still she hadn't sought a divorce lawyer.

He found subtle, psychological ways to punish her when she'd displeased him. He would embarrass her by canceling plans and explaining the broken commitment in ways that made Jenna seem disorganized or "under the weather," which everyone knew meant drunk as a skunk, even though Jenna didn't drink. He'd come home for dinner so late the food would be ruined, especially, it seemed, when she'd spent hours preparing something special. Once, on the very night of a dinner party, he had taken a pair of scissors to a new dress she'd bought for the occasion, leaving her no choice but to wear an older style that made her look gawky next to the other chic women. That's when she began to be afraid of him. She'd seen the excited glitter in his eyes as he'd cut the dress to shreds. He wouldn't actually hurt her, she had thought. He wouldn't use the scissors on her. But she couldn't reason away the stab of fear. Even that, even that, had not pushed her to seek a divorce.

But when he had started exhibiting the same behavior to Carlee, the criticism, the total domination, the psychological cruelty, Jenna knew she had to take her child and escape. His outbursts of anger had been coming more frequently and with greater intensity. Carlee, having more acute instincts than Jenna, it seemed, had feared Ned almost as soon as she was able to recognize him as an individual. The child's fear both enraged and excited Ned. He would deliberately goad her into behavior that warranted punishment. And that was the most frightening thing of all.

That's when Jenna found a lawyer. Carlee was almost three, withdrawn, on the verge of stuttering, afraid of her shadow, terrified of Ned. At first Ned was going to fight for custody of Carlee, more as a magnet to assure Jenna's return, she suspected, but Jenna had negotiated, agreeing to forego child support if Ned gave up visitation rights. In the end, he'd agreed. What had Carlee been to him after all, he'd said caustically, but a sniveling disruption of his daily routine. When the divorce papers were finally signed, Jenna only hoped for Carlee's sake that she hadn't waited too long.

That memory made her think of Jake. Millie had said Jake was debating getting a divorce, but had waited and now had to live with the self-imposed guilt of his failure to act. Jenna wondered what she would have done if she had waited too long and something terrible had happened to Carlee. She would feel exactly as Jake felt. Guilty, racked with pain, and sunk in deep despair. How could he ever come to terms with that, she wondered.

As she turned a corner onto the road home, she shuddered for what seemed like the thousandth time at the huge ugly sculpture that passed as art in front of the strip mall. It must have cost thousands of dollars, and was so— so—*ugly!*

It always reminded her of Ned. Not Ned the husband, but Ned the sculpture, for that was the name she'd given a hideous "work of art" Ned had installed in their front yard. Without consulting her first, of course. It was too big for the yard, tremendously ugly with its gargoyle features, and made of some kind of rough metal that gave it a scaly look. It was ugly, ugly, ugly. Ned had bought it shortly after their marriage, and every time she drove into her drive, for five long years, she had to see that pop-eyed monster. As her marriage to Ned quickly manifested itself as a master-slave relationship, she came to associate the statue with Ned's personality. It epitomized their marriage. Big, ugly, scary, domineering. She named the statue Ned. She reached a point in their marriage where she hated going home, home to that ugly statue, home to her ugly marriage.

And now, here in Florida and a long way from Ohio, every time she exited the freeway and saw the sculpture rising in front of the shopping center, she was reminded of Ned and that ugly statue that epitomized their marriage.

How different things were now, she mused. She loved her yard with its native plants, its trees, her orchids. She loved going home to Carlee and her mom. Oftentimes on this last stretch toward home she caught herself speeding, and sometimes couldn't force herself to let up on the gas. She was speeding now, she realized, and dropped down to an acceptable—in her opinion—ten miles over the limit.

She'd wasted several years trying to please Ned, but she'd never really tried to analyze him. He was who he was. She knew from conversations with other women she'd met in club meetings, while shopping, even in church, that Ned was not unique. A lot of men believed their wives were their possessions, subject to their desires, their will, their whims. Men like that did not appreciate a woman who was self-assured, capable of independent thought, or pursuing personal interests. Women were killed every day by men who resented the fact that "*my* woman" had stepped outside her male-dominated role.

Jenna realized she was working herself into a rage against domineering men. She took a deep breath and tried to shake off the feeling. Ned was history. The gargoyle was history. And that horrible sculpture in front of the strip mall was just that—a sculpture. Somebody must have liked it very much or it wouldn't be standing there. Some man, undoubtedly.

She still couldn't understand people like Ned. Marriage was a partnership, teamwork, two people respecting each other's opinions and wishes. Where did people like Ned come from? And God help anybody married to one.

As Jenna turned into her driveway and exited the car, she heard hammering coming from the rear of her house. Curiously, she headed in that direction, but paused when she spotted Jake's Land Rover. What was Jake doing here? She continued around the corner and discovered Jake hammering a nail into a wooden structure. What was he building—and in *her* yard?

Thoughts of domineering men were still foremost in her mind. Thoughts of ugly sculptures brought up a close second. And here was a man taking it upon himself, without the courtesy of consulting her, building a—she wasn't sure what—in her yard. It wasn't a gargoyle, but it wasn't Michelangelo's David either.

She hurried over to him, saw the sweat soaking the handkerchief tied around his forehead, saw the shapeless structure looming up, saw the look of pure male self-satisfaction he wore as he pounded contentedly away without so much as a glance in her direction.

It was the look of male self-satisfaction that drove her over the edge.

"What do you think you're doing?" she challenged, anger and disbelief throbbing through her.

Startled, Jake missed the nail and hit his thumb.

"Damn!" he said, none too mildly, causing Jenna to wince at his tone. He inspected his thumb then shook his hand to help relieve the pain. "Don't ever sneak up on a man with a hammer in his hand!"

The tone was half joking, but Jenna focused only on the implied criticism, and the scene was all too familiar. Ned yelling at her, telling her what to do and what not to do. Ned making plans without consulting her, Ned installing that damnable, god awful, bug-ugly gargoyle statue.

She narrowed her eyes at Jake in a look so piercing, so indignant, so full of malice that Jake halted with the hammer mid-swing.

"Who the hell do you think you are, building that—that—" she waved her hand, "whatever it is—in *my* yard?"

Jake was surprised at her vehemence and the accusation burning in her eyes, but before he could respond, Buster came bounding around the corner of the house, a laughing Carlee riding on his back.

"Look, mommy," she shouted. "I can ride him like a horsey!"

"Carlee, get off him, now!" Jenna admonished.

"But, mommy," Carlee turned toward Jenna to protest, and lost her precarious hold on Buster's collar. With a startled "Oh!" Carlee slid off Buster's back and fell the short distance to the ground. Still laughing, she scrambled to her feet and ran after Buster, whose happy yelps mingled with her excited shrieks.

"It's okay, mommy. Jake said I could play with him." Her voice trailed off as she rounded the corner.

Jake said she could play with him? Fuming, Jenna stalked up to Jake and poked a finger in his chest. She narrowed her eyes and spat out the words. "What gave *you* the right to tell *my* daughter what she can and cannot do?"

"Well," Jake began, before Jenna interrupted him.

"What gave you the right to build this gargoyle in my yard?"

Gargoyle? Jake gave the receptacle a brief, critical look. It was a masterpiece, a work of art. He didn't know how to respond to Jenna's anger. And why *was* she so mad, anyway? He'd expected her to be pleased. He'd *anticipated* her pleasure. "Well," he began, scratching his head.

"And what gives you the right to criticize how I approach people in my own yard? I did not sneak. But if I wanted to sneak, I would damn well sneak." She poked his chest to emphasize each word.

That was too much. Jake took Jenna by the shoulders, holding her firmly. "What's wrong with you?" he asked.

"What's wrong with me? What's wrong with *me?*"

Jake placed a finger over Jenna's lips to silence her angry sputters. "Shhh," he said softly. Something had worked her into a royal snit, and if he could get her to calm down, maybe he could get to the bottom of it.

Jenna was not about to "shh." She shoved his hand away. "Are you telling me I can't speak in my own yard?"

His sigh was long-suffering, like the time Buster had chewed up his fine leather belt. His finger pressed against her lips again, exerting a little more persistent pressure than the first time, bringing with it a faint taste of sweat and sawdust. The reminder of things macho ignited her anger to a higher pitch, and she started to shove his hand away again. He caught her wrist in a steel grip, and spoke softly. "Sweetheart, stop yelling in my face or I'll be compelled to either turn you over my knee or kiss you quiet."

The gleam darkening his eyes, the determined grip on her wrist, the way his look traveled to her lips and stayed there penetrated Jenna's fury. He would do it. She pressed her lips together.

"Okay," Jake said, feeling a stab of disappointment. He would have enjoyed kissing the pout off her lips. "I didn't ask your permission to let Carlee play with Buster because you weren't here. But you seemed okay with it yesterday, and nothing bad happened then, so I assumed it would be okay today."

Carlee and Buster came barreling back around the house just then, shrieking and yelping.

Jake watched Jenna as her look followed girl and dog, saw the smile curving her Kiss Me Quick lips until the noisy duo had disappeared around the corner.

Then she turned back to him and her smile evaporated. "What is this— thing?" she asked in a controlled voice.

Still holding her wrist, he dragged her to the receptacle. "This *thing* is a trash bin. I'm sorry you think it looks like a gargoyle. Actually..." he paused, contemplated the possibilities, then dismissed them with a shake of the head, "...I wouldn't know how to make a gargoyle," he said, disappointment evident. "But this *thing* will keep Buster out of your trash. As well as any wild animals that might choose Chez Kincaid for their dining pleasure."

Oh. "You could have asked—" Jake's finger pressed against her lips.

"And as far as your sneaking up on me, well, honey, you can sneak up on me any time of day—or night."

Jenna avoided looking at the eyes that were doing a good job of penetrating her anger and arousing her ardor. "You could have asked about the—the—bin," she repeated stubbornly.

"I would have asked you, but you weren't here." He held up a finger to still her argument. "So I asked Claire. *Claire*, I might add, thought it was a great idea."

Silently Jenna pulled away from Jake. Her anger had dissipated, leaving her feeling foolish at her shrewish outburst. She turned away, unwilling to face him.

"I'm sorry, Jake," she said. "You didn't deserve any of that. I guess I just had about five years' worth of rage built up inside me, looking for an excuse to erupt. You caught the brunt of it, I'm afraid."

He stepped up behind her and placed his hands on her shoulders. He'd already formed his own opinion of her ex-husband and thought he understood her anger. "Feel better?" he asked, his mouth close to her ear, her flowery fragrance an aphrodisiac. So good, so good.

She turned to face him and a slow grin spread across her face. "Yes," she answered. "Surprisingly, I do."

"Well," he said, "I guess we're even now. I assumed you were wrong when you accused Buster of trashing your yard all those times, and now you assumed I was presumptuous, or overbearing, or whatever it was you read into my act of carpentry. Truce?"

"Truce," she agreed, holding out her hand.

He looked at the hand, laughed, and kissed her soundly.

CHAPTER TEN

"I think," said Claire, with a faint hint of disapproval in her voice, "that with company coming for dinner, the menu should be just a little bit more sophisticated than pizza, spaghetti, Chinese, and chocolate pie."

Jenna laughed softly. "You're the reason we're having company tonight. You're the one who invited Jake. Besides, it's a fun menu." She opened a pack of cheese and started grating it into a bowl.

"I know, I know, but then you went and invited Phil Averies."

"Serves you right. You played Cupid first. Turnabout's fair play. And Phil was delighted to be asked. He told me anything we cook is his absolute favorite food."

"Of course he said that. What man is going to turn down a home-cooked meal? But do you really think he's expecting this strange conglomeration?"

"I think it was something other than a home-cooked meal that tempted him," Jenna said, giving her mother a sideways glance.

Her mom, to Jenna's amusement, had changed into a flattering pants suit that emphasized the green in her eyes, which gleamed brilliantly with suppressed excitement. Her brushed and sprayed hair sparkled with silver glitters, and her carefully applied makeup was perfection itself. Bold, colorful, but perfection.

Jenna found her excitement contagious. When her mother had learned of Jenna's plans for a celebration, she'd run outside and invited Jake, who was finishing up the trash bin, to join them. After some persuasion he'd accepted and gone home to shower.

The end result left the two women feeling like they were double dating. The whole thing was ridiculous, Jenna thought as she sprinkled cheese on the pizza.

"Both Jake and Phil know the menu," Jenna said. "They're not expecting a five course dinner with flambé and roses."

She glanced around the kitchen; the variety of savory smells assailing her senses. Had they forgotten anything? The chocolate pie was chilling in the fridge. A big pot of water for the noodles was just coming to a boil and the spaghetti sauce was simmering on the stove. Carlee's pizza, topped with homemade sauce, thin slices of ham and tons of cheese, just the way Carlee loved it, was sitting on the counter ready to be popped into the oven. Cubed chicken and a tempting variety of vegetables were ready to go into the wok.

Had they forgotten anything? Their guests would be here in less than thirty minutes and she still had to dress.

"Go," said Claire as though reading her thoughts. "I'll finish up here."

Jenna gave a last glance around, then started toward the door.

"The garlic bread," she said, turning.

"I'll take care of it," Claire answered. "Now go. Make yourself look desirable."

"I'm not going to make myself desirable," Jenna argued. "Presentable is good enough."

"Well, at least scrub the sauce off your cheek," Claire suggested humorously. "It will hardly pass for rouge."

Jenna, conscious of the time and her need to shower, turned to leave.

"Should we have a salad?" she asked, turning back.

Without answering, Claire marched to her side and shoved her through the doorway.

"Wash behind your ears," she joked as Jenna obediently started toward the stairs. It was a refrain Jenna had heard often as a child when she was going through her soap-shy sevens. Although more appropriately directed at Carlee these days, it still tumbled in Jenna's direction when her mom was in a playful mood.

And her mom was certainly in a playful mood tonight, Jenna thought, wondering if it was because Phil was coming or because she thought one of her matchmaking schemes might finally bear fruit.

As she passed the dining room, she saw Carlee carefully placing a large vase of flowers on the table. Her little arms and hands wobbled as she hoisted the vase, balanced it on the table's edge, scrambled into a chair, then slowly shoved it toward the center.

"Don't look. It's a surprise," Carlee cried, catching sight of Jenna in the doorway.

"I won't look, munchkin," Jenna said, turning hurriedly away.

Jenna recognized the flowers as ones that grew in the flowerbox along the side of the house. Carlee loved the long-stemmed glads and her desire to grace the table with a gladiola centerpiece indicated just how importantly she viewed the occasion.

Jenna smiled, thinking not only how the glads added color to the table, but how Carlee herself had blossomed since they'd escaped Ned's domination.

"Mommy," Carlee said, running up behind her as Jenna started up the stairs, "can I wear my special dress tonight? The one daddy bought me?"

Jenna knew which dress Carlee referred to. The floor length, frilly pink and purple dress had been a favorite of hers for several weeks after Ned bought it. But every time Carlee had worn the dress, Ned had criticized her for running in it and had demanded she sit like a lady. He had brought her to tears with angry shouts when she'd splashed water on it by accident and had even yelled at her once for not holding the skirt high enough to keep the hem from dragging the floor.

Carlee had quickly lost all joy in wearing it. Until now. It was a big step and Jenna was delighted that Carlee felt confident enough in herself to take the risk. Of course, the dress would probably only hang to just below Carlee's knees, and despite the fact that the top had been pretty loose a year ago, it would most likely be a snug fit now. Still, if that's what Carlee wanted, Jenna definitely wouldn't argue.

She was glad now she hadn't left the dress behind with a lot of other bad memories.

"Of course you can wear it, munchkin. Bring it in to my room after I shower and we'll get dressed together."

It was a fast shower, and because of the late hour, Jenna wore a shower cap to keep her hair dry. Back in her bedroom, pulling on her pantyhose, she eyed the silky white blouse she'd laid out earlier. It had a cool, soft look, yet it clung in the right places. There was only one four-letter word for it, and it wasn't 'cute.' The blouse was sexy.

Tonight sexy was exactly the way she wanted to look, partly because she wanted to eradicate that shrewish image she'd portrayed earlier, and partly because she felt sexy. Yes, she felt sexy, and alive, and impatient to see Jake, to see his eyes gleam when he saw her in this sexy, sexy blouse. She held it against her and laughed.

"Why are you laughing?" Carlee came in carrying her dress, the pink and purple rayon material folded neatly over her arm.

"Oh, I'm just happy, darling," Jenna said, turning to Carlee. "I love parties, don't you?"

Carlee nodded eagerly, but as she stepped toward Jenna, the slippery dress slid from her arm onto the floor.

Her eyes widened in horror as she stared apprehensively at Jenna, then quickly scooped up the dress.

Jenna felt tears smart the backs of her eyes. Carlee still had a long way to go. She plucked her white blouse from the bed and let it fall to the floor.

"Goodness, look at us. What a couple of fumble fingers we are."

She laughed as she grabbed up the blouse, held it to her body, and did a couple of spins, causing the bottom of the blouse to swirl out around her.

"Bet I can spin my blouse faster than you can spin your dress," she said.

Carlee squealed with delight as she snatched her dress to her body and spun clumsily around. Then she collapsed in Jenna's arms.

"I'm dizzy!" she giggled.

"Okay, little dizzy dean, let's get dressed before our company comes and eats up all our favorite foods. You help me zip my skirt and I'll help you with your dress."

"Hurry up you two slowpokes!" Claire's clear voice reached them from the stairs. "Jake's already here and Phil will be arriving shortly."

A few minutes later, Jenna descended the stairs behind Carlee, feeling supercharged in her sexy white blouse topping a flower print cotton skirt that hugged her hips and flared gently where the hem touched just above the knees. Carlee was snuggly zipped into a now mid-length dress, her curly red hair crowned with Jenna's pearl choker.

Claire was looking up at them with undisguised love shining in her eyes.

"I'm a princess!" Carlee declared, reaching up to pat her pearl crown.

"You most certainly are!" Claire said, stooping and hugging her as the child reached the bottom step.

A smiling Jenna was right behind Carlee and spotted Jake at about the same time Carlee did. He was standing a few feet behind Claire, watching Jenna's descent with eyes that darkened with desire. Jenna swallowed, wondering if wearing the blouse was such a good idea after all. It would be hard for her mother or Phil to mistake that predatory gleam if it persisted through an evening meal.

She nearly stumbled over Carlee as the little girl faltered, her hand reaching back to cling to Jenna's. The dress had probably awakened a lot of bad memories in Carlee too, Jenna thought.

Jake saw the apprehension on Carlee's face. He took a step toward her and dropped to one knee, like a subject paying homage. Before Carlee realized what was happening, Jake had lifted her small hand to his lips and kissed it. "Your humble servant at your command, your princessness."

To Jenna's relief, Carlee giggled, and loosened her grip.

Jake's eyes traveled over Carlee's head to rest on Jenna, who had paused at the foot of the stairs.

The way his eyes darkened when he looked at the soft, clinging blouse, his reluctance to lift his eyes from her breasts, left her short of breath and big on doubts about her choice of wardrobe.

Jake pulled his gaze upward to Jenna's face and his heart leaped at the dazzling smile she gave him. He stood and brought his hand from behind his back, holding a bouquet of flowers.

Carlee clapped her hands with glee.

"They're pretty. They're so pretty."

She eagerly reached for them, face glowing. "Thank you, Jake," she said in her childish voice.

Jake quickly filled the awkward silence with a laugh as he, Claire and Jenna exchanged glances.

"Nothing's too good for a princess," he said, handing the bouquet to her.

Carlee took them and buried her pert little nose in the blossoms.

"Mmmm," she said. "These smell like mommy."

"Almost as good as mommy," Jake said, making Claire laugh and Jenna blush.

"What does the card say?" Carlee asked, handing it to Jenna.

Jenna took the card. The brief message, written in neat, bold script, was, *"Congratulations! It won't be long till you have as many clients as the petals on these flowers.—Jake"* Carlee could make out several simple words in children's picture books, but luckily she couldn't read cursive writing.

"Um. 'Congratulations. Tonight you get to party with the grownups. Have fun.' Well, I think that's a very nice message." She looked at Jake and smiled and her voice was softer than she'd intended as she added, "A very nice message indeed. Thank you."

She turned to Carlee. "There's an empty vase in the pantry. Why don't you run get it for the flowers."

Carlee scurried off.

"I also brought this." Jake stepped to the hall table and picked up a tall bag with a bottle inside.

She gave him a curious look. Could it be champagne? According to Millie, Jake hadn't taken a single sip of alcohol since the night his daughter died. She took the bag from him and peered inside. It certainly looked like champagne. She pulled the bottle out and looked at the label.

"Sparkling Grape Juice," she read aloud.

"It's surprisingly good. A nice substitute for champagne, and one that allows everyone—" he nodded toward Carlee who was returning with the vase "—to join in when toasting your success."

"Carlee—and me," Jenna said. "I'm pretty much a teetotaler myself. Thank you. It's perfect for tonight."

She was reminded of the hotel wine glass she had walked off with the night of the auction. It had survived the car accident intact, cushioned as it was inside the cookie jar, and was sitting on her dresser. Why she'd set the souvenir of disaster on her dresser she couldn't answer, not even to herself. But there it sat, practically the last thing she saw at night before turning out the lights, glistening in the lamplight, reflected in the dresser mirror. And there it sat, practically the first thing she saw in the morning after opening her eyes. But when she looked at it, she didn't think of the disastrous auction night at all. She thought of Tallahassee and how her body had responded to Jake's touch.

Claire took the bottle from Jenna and walked off with Carlee to find a perfect spot for the flower arrangement. Jenna was very much aware that she and Jake were alone at the foot of the stairs, standing close together, and he was watching her with that hooded look that sent prickles of anticipation racing through her veins.

He reached out and touched her hair, then let the strands run through his fingers as he lowered his hand to her throat and caressed it with his thumb. At his touch, the prickles of anticipation flamed into waves of desire. His gaze had dropped to her breasts and was riveted to the sight. She knew her breasts had peaked like the two-inch meringue on the chocolate pie sitting in the refrigerator.

He seemed incapable of speech as he raised his eyes to look at her. And lowered his lips to taste her.

The chime of the doorbell announced Phil's arrival. Jake's lips lightly brushed hers as he pulled away, his softly muttered oath an indication that he was as reluctant as she to settle for that brief contact.

"Later," he promised in a low growl, and released her so she could answer the door.

With Phil's arrival, the gang trooped into the dining room, and everyone raved over the home-cooked goodies as they sampled all the entrées. Jenna was glad she'd made plenty of each dish.

Phil's light banter and Claire's sparkling repartee kept them laughing, while Carlee basked in the adult celebration. Jenna and Jake talked about literature and plants. Jake was gratified to discover that Jenna seemed to enjoy reading as much as he did, and Jenna appreciated Jake's keen interest as she talked about all the things she wanted to accomplish with her fledgling business.

He seemed especially interested when she mentioned the upcoming orchid show.

"How many orchids do you plan to enter?"

"Well, for sure that hanging one I showed you the other day. Then there are a couple of others I have high hopes for. I'm waiting for them to bloom before I definitely decide. And of course, I'll use many, many more to accent my displays, as backdrop and to create a theme or mood."

"And if one of Mommy's orchids wins," Carlee piped up, "I get to name it! She promised me."

"Name it?" Jake looked questioningly at Jenna.

"Winning orchids are given a personal name and registered."

"Cool." Jake turned to Carlee. "So what name have you picked out?"

Jake's direct look and direct question made Carlee nervous. She hesitated before responding, as though afraid to give the wrong answer. When Jake waited patiently, she finally ducked her head and whispered, "Carlee's Beauty."

Jake chuckled. "Hmm, now I wonder where on earth you got that name?"

"A lot of the winning orchids are named after people, especially wives and daughters," Jenna explained.

Phil proposed a toast to Jenna's success, and glasses were quickly filled with grape juice. Carlee, thrilled to be included in the toasting, dribbled some of the red liquid on her dress while trying to handle the unfamiliar stemware. A look of horror came over her face and she started to tremble.

"I'm s-s-sorry," she sobbed. "It just s-s-spilled." She was looking at Jake, not Jenna as she spoke.

"Well, your highness," Jake said, "it's my understanding that when a member of royalty as high up as a princess starts a new style, everybody follows suit." With that, he dipped his finger in his glass and flicked a few drops of juice on his shirt.

"Yes, I believe you're right, sir," Phil said, flicking a few drops on his starched shirt.

This sort of play was right up Claire's alley. "I follow the princess's lead," she said, flicking drops on her front.

Carlee watched the byplay, her tears forgotten. "You guys are silly," she said with a giggle.

Heads turned to Jenna and she willed herself to smile and dip a finger in her glass. What was grape juice going to do to her sexy, sexy, white blouse?

"Carlee, munchkin," Claire said before Jenna could do the juicy deed, "this is a perfect time to pass out your invitations."

Everyone looked expectantly at Carlee. Flushed with the importance of the moment, she rose excitedly. "I'll be right back," she said.

Jenna sent Claire a grateful look, which Claire acknowledged with a wink. Her mom was the best.

Jenna spoke softly to Jake. "You've been wonderful with Carlee tonight, defusing situations. Thanks."

Jake shrugged without speaking.

This evening must be torture for him, she thought. Absolute torture. Despite the considerate and imaginative way he'd handled Carlee, she'd sensed his restraint. His manner was relaxed, his words light, but the pain was still there, reflected in his eyes in those fleeting moments when his grief overrode his self-control.

Carlee returned with a handful of invitations and importantly passed them around. When Jenna got hers, she read it with surprise. She had expected it to be an invitation to a party celebrating Carlee's fourth birthday, which was in a few days. Instead, it was an invitation to Willy's coming out party, when the caterpillar would emerge as a butterfly. Jenna felt a twinge of guilt. She'd forgotten all about it.

The little folded invitation, obviously computer generated, had a small monarch butterfly fluttering away from its opened chrysalis. Inside it read, "Please join Willy and me on the day he begins his butterfly adventure. We'll gather at the picnic table for Kool-Aid and cookies and a ringside seat on Thursday, Friday, or Saturday at a time to be determined depending on Willy's schedule."

"Gramma helped me make them," Carlee confessed. "But I picked out the pictures." She handed Jake a second invitation. "That's for Buster," she said.

After the meal was over Claire and Phil insisted on kitchen duty. Jenna objected, but was shooed from the room. As she followed Jake and Carlee out to the sunroom, she noticed a satisfied smile on Phil's face. Why, the old coot was enjoying playing the domestic with Claire! And judging by Claire's look, she didn't mind one bit either.

When they reached the sunroom, Jenna started opening windows, to let the night breeze in through the screens.

"Let's catch lightning bugs," Carlee said, picking up a jar near the outer door and heading out into the yard.

Jenna saw Jake blanch at Carlee's request. It seemed, from Jake's reaction, that Carlee had pushed one button too many. She remembered Millie saying Jake had chased lightning bugs with Lizzy. Maybe she could make this easier on him, let him know it was okay to leave if he wanted to.

She sat down beside Jake as he lowered himself onto the wicker loveseat. "Jake, you're welcome to stay as long as you want, but don't feel obligated to hang around. Nobody's going to think you're unsociable if you decide to skip this kid stuff and leave."

He looked at her and she could tell he was considering the option. Then his eyes seemed to harden with determination and his jaw clenched.

Jake had thought about leaving several times during the evening, but he was determined to stick it out as long as he could. He figured the more exposure he had to Carlee, the easier it would get. He definitely did not want to leave Jenna, and after the camaraderie tonight, the thought of going home to an empty house was depressing.

"I'll hang here for awhile," he said. He managed a crooked grin. "I'm still looking forward to that *later* I promised myself before dinner."

"Oooh, yeah," she agreed, remembering the unsatisfyingly brief kiss. That *later* appealed to her too. But she continued to watch him, thinking about the little girl he had loved and lost, feeling his pain.

"I know about Lizzy and Barb," she said softly, hoping he wouldn't resent her for bringing up the subject. "Millie told me. I'm so sorry."

He looked away from her and she felt him emotionally drawing away. She swallowed. "That's why I said if you want to leave, it's okay. I'd understand."

He drew a deep shuddering breath and leaned back, resting his head against the seat and looking up at the stars. Sensing he was going to speak, she waited without moving. When he did speak, it wasn't the words she had expected to hear.

"Barb and I were—well we weren't married in the true sense of the word, that last year before the accident. Any feelings—any *good* feelings between us had died. Slowly, painfully, completely, long before the accident." His voice sounded strained and hollow. Jenna just looked at him, not quite knowing how to respond.

"I just wanted you to know," he said heavily. "I didn't want you to think I was some cold bastard who forgot all about his dead wife while I was, was…" His voice trailed off. Then he turned to her, took her hands in his and said in a low, husky voice, "While I was doing my damnedest to get you in bed."

Jenna's insides leaped. He could seduce her with a look, a word, a touch. He was seducing her now, though she suspected he wasn't even aware of it.

"I'll hang loose for a while longer if it's okay," he repeated.

"Come on, you guys!" Carlee yelled. She was waiting in the yard, darting back and forth as the lightning bugs flitted past her.

Jake looked quickly away from the little girl. "You go ahead," he told Jenna. "I'd rather watch."

She nodded and stood up. She walked to the sunroom door, then glanced back at him.

"Later," she said softly. She gave Jake an encouraging smile and joined Carlee in the yard.

"Bet I catch more than you," Carlee said, laughing. Her voice floated back to Jake in the still night air.

He watched with unseeing eyes, his thoughts straying to an uncannily similar scene.

"Daddy, daddy, look! I caught two at once. Look!"

The blond hair swirled in the breeze, the bright moonlight turning it a pale gold. The blue eyes reflected the moonlight and shone with an inner excitement. "That makes me the champion, doesn't it, daddy? I caught twelve lightning bugs and you only caught five!"

"I guess that means you get to carry the lantern," he said with a laugh, helping her add the two bugs to the collection in the jar. "Lead on, oh little lamplighter. Your mighty lamp can light your way to bed."

"But I don't have to go to bed now, do I, daddy? I want to catch more lightning bugs."

"Not tonight, Lizzy. It's getting late."

Her face drooped with disappointment. "Can we catch lightning bugs tomorrow?"

"Yes, my eager little hunter. Tomorrow and tomorrow and a thousand tomorrows."

Jake wrenched his thoughts from the past, his heart slamming with pain. After that night, Lizzy hadn't had a thousand tomorrows. She'd had exactly six.

Dimly, he was aware of Carlee's excited cries and Jenna's laughter buzzing in the distance like an unreal scene from another world. He was removed from it and felt alien, an intruder, with no place in this laughing, active family. Leave! his instincts shouted.

The impulse was so strong he actually stood, but just then Jenna looked his way. Even in the darkness, he saw her eyes, luminous in the moonlight, gaze inquiringly at him. She looked almost ethereal standing there, the breeze playing with her moonstruck hair, the shadows flitting around her. Then a stronger breeze pinned her blouse against her, outlining the gentle curves of her breasts, the shape of her thighs, and nothing about her was ethereal. She was real, and alive, and so damnably beautiful, and he felt a surge of desire so powerful he groaned.

As though responding to a summons, Jenna took a few tentative steps toward him.

"What is it, Jake?" she asked in a whisper as she neared him.

He looked at her, knowing desire must be naked on his face. He didn't answer her question. There was no need. Once again, their thoughts were in total sync. Jenna stepped into the sunroom and Jake took a step toward her, their minds already melded, their bodies closing the distance.

"We've brought lemonade!" Claire's upraised voice coming from behind Jake jerked him from the hypnotic trance, and he turned as though awakening from a dream.

Claire carried a tray with glasses and Phil followed with a large pitcher of lemonade.

As they all gathered in the sunroom, finding comfortable positions with their cold, sweet drinks, Jenna mulled over the last few minutes. What had happened? She had often read in novels about a sudden emotional moment so intense that 'time stood still,' but although she'd always been willing to suspend belief for the sake of the story, she'd never taken it seriously.

Now she knew it was no trite phrase, but a real phenomenon. A few minutes ago she had stood in the yard looking at Jake and the world beyond the two of them had ceased to exist. Sight, sound, smell—nothing existed but Jake standing before her and their slow steady steps toward each other. If Claire's sudden appearance had not broken the spell, she would have continued straight into Jake's arms, right there in front of God and everybody. And only God knows what would have happened then.

She stole a glance at Jake, who sat a few feet away. He looked as confused as she felt.

"Just the thing to cool one off after a long lightning bug hunt," Claire said. "Right Carlee?"

"Mmhmm." Carlee nodded her head, then walked shyly to Jake. When she was in arm's length she held the twinkling jar out to him. As he took it, she said, "You can take them home. We'll catch more."

Jake made a strangled sound in his throat, stood up, and started to walk rapidly away.

Carlee's eyes filled with tears. "Is he mad at me?"

"No darling, of course not," Jenna said. She turned to look helplessly at Claire, then at Jake's retreating figure. She couldn't let him walk off like that, alone, full of pain and suffering. "I'm going after him," she said. She'd confided earlier to Claire about Barb and Lizzy, so she knew Claire had a pretty good idea what was tormenting Jake.

"Yes, go after him," Claire said, and for once it wasn't matchmaking fervor that glistened in her eyes. It was moisture.

By the time Jenna caught up to Jake he was about halfway home. She walked silently beside him catching her breath. He accepted her company without comment, and she couldn't be sure if he resented or welcomed it.

As they neared his house, he suddenly stopped by a path leading into the woods. "I—I have to do something," he said. "Will you walk with me?"

Jenna stared dubiously into the dark woods, but she nodded.

The path was narrow and she had to follow behind him. The woods closed in around them. Somewhere in the distance a coyote howled. She inched closer to him, practically treading on his heels. Where were they going? "Lucky you've got that lightning bug lamp," she said, talking to keep a creepy feeling at bay.

Jake made a low, indescribable sound.

The path wound around, sometimes turning back on itself, sometimes twisting between trees. Jake seemed very familiar with the route. He must have traveled it many times. After what seemed like miles, though Jenna knew that was impossible, Jake stopped. Jenna, caught off guard, smacked into him.

The path had widened to a small clearing and Jenna moved to stand beside Jake. She was trembling, both with cold and nervousness. Jake took her hand, but his attention was focused on the giant live oak tree that dominated the clearing. Its moss-covered branches reached skyward, and horizontally in several directions, weaving wood paths between the trees. It must have been hundreds of years old. It was beautiful, awesome, mystical. Jenna felt very insignificant in front of such majesty, and totally entranced.

"This is Wendy's tree," Jake said, his voice charged with emotion. "I stumbled across it shortly after Lizzy was born. It was the inspiration for the Wendy books I write. Wendy the wood nymph," he added by way of explanation.

Jenna nodded, recognizing the tree now from pictures in Carlee's Wendy book.

"I used to bring Lizzy here a lot. She liked to sit in that perch right there," he said, pointing to a flat spot where a branch met the trunk. "Then I'd read to her and she would pretend she was Wendy. It was—just a game we played," he added, glancing quickly at Jenna to see if she thought he was nuts.

Jenna squeezed his hand. "It's a beautiful spot," she said.

He took the jar of lightning bugs and placed them on the branch where Lizzy used to sit. "Lizzy loved to make lightning bug lamps. Then, we'd come here and sit and talk. We'd talk about things Lizzy had done during the day and anything else that came to mind, while the bugs twinkled in the jar. When we were ready to go home, we'd let the bugs go." Jake reached up and opened the lightning bug jar. Slowly, the lightning bugs flew into the air, one by one, their lights tiny beacons as they made their way into the surrounding woods. Jake and Jenna stood in companionable silence and watched till the last bug had made its escape.

When they were all gone, Jake placed both hands on the tree and rested his forehead against the knobby trunk. He stayed in that position while he spoke. "Her grave is in a cemetery in town. But she's not there, in that little broken body. She's here. Her spirit is here."

He turned to face Jenna, his back against the tree. "Do you think I'm crazy?"

Jenna walked over to him and wrapped her arms around his waist.

"No, I don't think you're crazy. If you feel Lizzy's spirit here, then this is where her spirit is."

Jake put his arms around Jenna then and held her like he'd never let her go. "Will you go home with me, Jenna?" he asked softly.

Jenna leaned back and looked up at his face. In the moonlight filtering through the leaves of the tree, flicking shadows across his face, Jake looked like a mythical creature that belonged there, in that place, bound to that tree. Then as he moved his face closer to hers and the moonlight struck it more fully, he didn't look supernatural at all. He looked like a man. A man in a great deal of pain.

"Yes," she said.

He raised a hand and gently stroked her face. "I don't want to make love to you. Not tonight. I just want to hold you. And—and—I want you to hold me."

When they reached Jake's house, he ignored Buster's exuberant greeting and led Jenna into the bedroom. Moonlight streaming through the window bathed their bodies in dancing shadows. In silent agreement they undressed and slipped between the sheets of his double bed. Jake pulled her into his arms with a strangled moan that seemed to come from the depths of his soul. He shook with spasmodic tremors. She put her arms around him, pulled his head onto her shoulder, and held him tightly, gently stroking his back with her fingers.

She didn't know how long they lay like that. Her arm went numb where his weight pressed against it. Her stomach grumbled once. She felt herself getting sleepy. But she lay there and held Jake tightly, protectively, in her arms, held him until the tremors became less and less frequent and finally stopped, until his breathing was the deep even sound of a person in peaceful sleep, until his arms around her relaxed their hold. Then she slipped carefully out of bed, kissed him tenderly on the lips, pulled on her clothes and walked home.

CHAPTER ELEVEN

As the sun's rays stretched over the tops of the trees in a blaze of color, Jenna was reminded of the aptness of Homer's frequent references to "Dawn with her rose-red fingers." If this morning's sunrise, visible and beautiful through the greenhouse's open door, was any indication, it promised to be a beautiful day.

Jenna had been working with her orchids for a quarter of an hour, anticipating another couple of hours of uninterrupted work before Claire and Carlee awoke, so she was surprised to suddenly see her mother approaching in short summer pajamas with her hair tousled.

"What's wrong? Is Carlee all right?" Jenna asked, her heart starting to thump. What else would bring her mother out in her pajamas and no makeup? She dropped the hose and took a few steps forward, meeting Claire in the middle of the greenhouse. Only then did she notice the cordless phone in Claire's hand.

"Mr. Right is on the phone," Claire said, arching a brow. Can't you two cool it at least until a decent hour of the morning, her teasing look seemed to be saying.

"Oh Claire, I'm sorry the phone woke you up," Jenna said.

"Jake has already apologized and I've already forgiven him," Claire turned to a nearby orchid and sniffed its fragrance. "Yum. I like this one." She sniffed the one beside it, then started moving systematically around the table, testing each blossom's fragrance.

Jenna rolled her eyes at her mother and silently shooed her away.

Claire assumed an exaggerated air of injured innocence, but she obediently left.

"Hello," Jenna said softly into the phone.

"Hi." Jake's voice held a note in it Jenna hadn't heard before. Incredibly sexy, as always, but now more intimate. "I wouldn't have called at this ungodly hour, but I know what an early bird you are."

"Yeah, it's okay. Are *you* okay?"

"Yeah, I'm okay. Last night you were—I was just—nobody's ever—"

"You're welcome," she said.

Jake laughed. "I guess I sound like a babbling fool. And I'm supposed to be a writer. Jenna, do you have any idea what a good person you are?"

"Oh gorsh," she said in an effort to downplay the compliment.

"I mean it. I told you what I needed and you gave it to me. No more, no less, no questions asked, no suggestions offered, no judgments made. Do you know anybody else who would have done that?"

"Jake," she said, embarrassed. "It's okay. Someday I'll need a hug too. Maybe you'll be there for me."

"That's a favor I'd love to return." He spoke lightly, then asked hopefully, "Do you think you'll need a hug soon?"

She laughed. "You rake."

When he spoke again, his voice was serious. "I'm going to be busy for the next few days. I have several newspaper assignments I'm committed to, and then I've got a personal project to finish up. It's something I started quite a while ago. I guess it's time I stopped procrastinating."

"Isn't procrastination the middle name of every writer?" she said, ribbing him. Why was he telling her all this? He seemed to be leading up to something.

"The reason I'm telling you all this," he said with uncanny timing that made Jenna grin, "is because if I make myself pretty scarce for a few days, I don't want you to think I'm avoiding you or that I consider you a one-night hug."

"Oh," she said weakly. She was remembering that hug. In fact, she had never stopped remembering it. In the cold light of dawn, the events of last night seemed unreal, dreamlike. From the first time their bodies had made contact during the tumble in the back yard, the sexual attraction between them had been immediate, powerful, and all consuming. Yet last night, in his bed, in each other's arms, the only emotion she was aware of was her compulsion to soothe his wounded spirit. Sex had not even occurred to her, incredible as that seemed now. In a sense, she had been like Buster, she thought. Buster was a wild dog with her and Jake, but in Carlee's tiny hands he turned gentle and docile. Some instinct in Buster recognized Carlee's helplessness and responded to it, overriding the dog's normal instinct to pounce and play. Last night some instinct in Jenna, probably born with the dawn of woman, some instinct to nurture, to heal, had recognized Jake's state of shock and responded, overriding the sexual mania that had been dominating their relationship.

Jake's words broke through her thoughts.

"Whenever I think of you, which seems to be most of my waking hours, I definitely do not think of you as a one-night anything," he said.

She realized as his words washed over her, bathing her in electric desire, that her nurturing instinct had gone back to sleep and sexual mania was back with a vengeance. She wanted to say something bright and witty, but her little gray cells seemed to have dried up like her mouth. She took a hasty swallow from the water bottle she always kept close at hand while working in the greenhouse.

"You're awfully quiet," he said. "I hope I didn't say something offensive."

"No. No, not at all. I—um—" Her voice trailed off. She was afraid if she talked too much her voice would betray the shaky state of her feelings. She wasn't sure of them herself, only aware of a sudden clarity that seemed to have been absent last night. In his bed she had been immersed in his pain, conscious of his tremors and labored breathing, his devastating grief. Although they were lying body-to-body, sexual desire had not been present. Now, with their bodies physically separated by a quarter of a mile, just the sound of Jake's voice aroused her as though it were his hands caressing her skin, and she was remembering those hours with a different and brilliant clarity. His tumbled hair and thick lashes, his male scent, so arousing, his chest with its soft curling hair rising and falling with a rhythm that now sent her pulse pounding, his flat stomach, his lean, strong limbs, his hard, hard body.

Last night she had been aware only of a man in deep distress, in need of succoring. This morning she could only remember the man himself. How could she have lain next to him last night and never thought of sex, when now she had to sink weakly onto a stool and lace her feet around the rungs to keep from running out the greenhouse door, along the path, and into his arms?

After a moment, Jake continued, "There is one other thing. Would it be okay with you if I drop Buster off to play with Carlee for a couple hours every afternoon? They really enjoy each other's company, and Buster seems to behave a lot better after a workout with Carlee. I guess he wasn't getting enough exercise before."

Jenna swallowed and forced herself back to mundane circumstances. "Yes, that's fine. Carlee would like that."

"I'll bring him over after lunch," Jake said.

With that promise they said their good-byes and Jenna returned to her orchids, replaying the conversation over and over in her mind. Although nothing had been spelled out, it seemed to her Jake had certainly implied he wanted a long-term relationship with her. Would she dare to encourage that idea? If she were the only one involved, the answer would be yes, yes, yes. But she wasn't the only one involved. Carlee was very much involved in any long-term relationship, and it wouldn't be fair to the child.

Long before last night she had known Jake's interaction with Carlee was strained, forced. Last night as she had watched them together, she had seen not only a lessening of Jake's reserve, but also a lessening of Carlee's fear. But just when she'd started to believe—to hope—that her doubts were exaggerated, one simple little thing like the lightning bug jar had knocked away all Jake's defenses. Carlee ended up in tears, Jake ended up with the shakes, and Jenna ended up with doubts that had ballooned bigger than ever. How many times would scenes like that be repeated? How many times would Carlee be hurt?

No, in all fairness to Carlee, Jenna could not encourage a committed relationship with Jake. In fact, she should discourage it before it went any further. When Jake brought Buster over in the afternoons, she decided, she'd be busy somewhere else.

After breakfast Claire and Carlee sat at Claire's computer creating Carlee's birthday party invitations. Jenna sat at her computer in the same room updating records to reflect the sales she had made during the week and the pod seeds she wanted to buy to replenish and expand her inventory. She was too engrossed in worksheets to be aware of the two women in her life until Carlee's voice, close to sobs, suddenly demanded, "Why can't I invite Buster?"

Jenna glanced up to see Carlee's eyes filled with tears. "He's my friend. My bestest friend in the whole world!"

"My best friend," Jenna corrected automatically. She had never talked baby talk to Carlee and was quite proud of her child's command of grammar. She never ceased to be alarmed at the poor grammar she heard coming out of the mouths of high school students, and she never ceased to be amazed when she heard a preschooler use good grammar. She much preferred amazement to alarm.

"My best friend," Carlee mumbled. She sniffed as a giant tear escaped her eye. It rolled down her cheek, still chubby with baby fat, and landed with a plop on the tip of Claire's purple shoe.

Claire glanced helplessly at Jenna. If Jenna was a pushover when Carlee was happy and laughing, Claire was an even bigger pushover when Carlee cried.

"Momma?" Carlee turned hopefully to Jenna. "Can Buster come to my party?"

Jenna sighed. "Carlee, you know if your grandmother tells you no, you're not to come to me and try to get me to say yes. That's very disrespectful to your grandmother."

Carlee's lower lip quivered.

"I think you should apologize to her."

"I'm sorry, gramma," Carlee said in a tiny voice. Her lip quivered harder and tears slid silently down her cheeks.

Jenna tried reasoning. "Buster can't play games like 'Pin the Tail on the Donkey' or 'Duck, Duck Goose'. And he can't sing happy birthday or..."

"He can too sing. He was singing yesterday, wasn't he gramma?"

Claire nodded, shrugging at Jenna's skeptical look. "While you were shopping and Jake was building Gargoyle." Claire had jokingly dubbed the new trash bin with that name after hearing about Jenna's tirade. "Buster's howl accompanied Celine Dion when I had my player out on the patio. You know that duet she sings with Luciano Pavarotti, that one line "Then I love you more" where he holds the notes so long you could bake a cake before he draws a breath? Well, Buster was right there with Pavarotti, note for note." Claire smiled, remembering, and said with a little awe in her voice, "It was really quite tuneful. The dog's got talent."

"It was funny," Carlee said, forgetting tears, "We laughed so hard. Even Jake was laughing." Then, remembering her mission, she pleaded, "Please let Buster come, gramma."

Carlee turned beseeching eyes from Claire to Jenna. Claire, giving in to Carlee's tears, but wanting Jenna's blessing, turned beseeching eyes to Jenna.

Oh damn, Jenna thought. I'm being beseeched. She tried to strengthen her backbone by envisioning all the havoc Buster could wreak. He could put the cake in flight with a swish of his tail, send kids somersaulting across the yard, swallow large pieces of Carlee's presents.

The eyes won. "Well," she said in a very stern voice so they wouldn't think she was a wimp, "if you promise me Buster will sing Happy Birthday."

"Yippie!" Carlee shouted.

"Wimp," Claire mouthed silently, laughing at Jenna.

Behind Carlee's back, Jenna stuck her tongue out at her mother.

Claire and Carlee turned back to their invitations, and Jenna resumed her work. But she couldn't concentrate. Claire's mention of the love song "I Hate You Then I Love You," which as far as Jenna was concerned was one of the greatest love songs ever written, especially when sung by Celine Dion and Pavarotti, kept intruding. Jake had been there working on the trash bin and must have heard it. Did he think of her when Pavarotti sang, "I never, never, never want to be in love with anyone but you," she wondered. The line kept playing through her head, haunting her, blinding her to the sterile numbers scrolling across her monitor. Finally, she gave up.

"I guess I'm done here," she said, shutting down her computer. She stretched, rolling her shoulders and neck. "Whew, after two hours bending over orchids and another hour at the computer, I'm stiff. I think I'll take a jog in the woods. Then I'm going to treat myself to a slice of that homemade bread I smell."

"It should be ready to come out of the oven," Claire said, glancing at her watch.

Jenna turned to Carlee. "Want to come? Get the old blood pumping?"

"I've got to help gramma with the invitations," Carlee said, quite proud of her role in the process.

"Well, we're almost done," Claire said, pushing the print key. "The first one's printing as we speak."

"I'll give that one to Buster," Carlee decided, watching with avid interest as the colorful sheet inched into view. "Can we jog over to Buster's, momma?"

"No," Jenna said, too quickly. She inwardly groaned at Claire's penetrating look. "Err—Jake is pretty busy. I don't think he would want to be disturbed."

Carlee's little brain worked fiercely, then she smiled. "He probly won't get mad if we invite him too."

"Not bad," Claire said. She pointed to Jenna. "Your turn."

"You can invite Buster—"

"And Jake," Claire interrupted.

"And Jake," Jenna said, scowling at Claire, "when they come over here this afternoon."

"But that's a long time," Carlee protested. "Can't we go now?"

"Well, you'd certainly be doing me a favor," Claire said.

"How so?" Jenna looked suspiciously at Claire, wondering what she was up to now.

"When Jake called this morning and I forgave him for waking me, I also promised him a loaf of homemade bread."

"Our bread? You promised him our homemade bread?"

"Don't get your tail in a spin. I made two loaves. So if you could just drop one off for Jake, he can enjoy it while it's still warm."

"And we can give him Buster's invitation," Carlee said happily.

"God save me from the machinations of old ladies and little brats," Jenna muttered to herself, heading upstairs to change into jogging shoes.

* * *

Jake sat at his desk, trying to concentrate on the article he was writing. He couldn't. Statistics about West Nile Virus were losing out to thoughts of

Jenna. Last night he'd had her in his arms, in his bed, out of her clothes. At first he hadn't even thought about sex. He was still shaking his head in bewilderment over that. Thinking back on it, he realized he must have been suffering from a mild case of shock.

She had pulled him into her arms, holding him safe in her warmth, keeping all the demons at bay. Her comfort, her strength, had seeped into his body until the horrors that had possessed him were gone and he was himself again. And he was a man again, excruciatingly aware of Jenna's soft body, her intoxicating fragrance, her gentle touch. As the demons faded, his desire for Jenna had surfaced, clamoring to be sated. New tremors had shaken his body, less painful but far more insistent. He had been lying half on his back, his thigh pressed against her body, and it had taken an iron will to stop himself from turning to her, stroking that beautiful body into a state of frenzy, and taking her with the exultant release his body craved with manic insistence.

The song he'd heard Pavarotti singing that afternoon had taunted him as he lay beside Jenna. "I never, never, never want to be in love with anyone but you." Turn to her, his body urged. Take her, love her, it urged, an insistent whisper boiling his blood. Love her.

He hadn't given in to the urge. It would have been an enormous and unforgivable betrayal of Jenna's trust. She had entered his bed, trustingly placed herself in that vulnerable position, because she had recognized his pain and wanted to soothe it away. He had asked her to hold him, had needed her to hold him, and she had answered that need. She had come to him like an angel and, like an angel, she had brought him peace. Their bodies had merged, not sexually, but spiritually, and the bond that merging created was so powerful, so soul-shaking, that he knew he'd been given a rare gift few men would ever experience, a glimpse of what complete understanding could exist between a man and a woman, an understanding on a higher plane than intellect, an understanding of spirits, of souls. He had somehow summoned enough control not to defile that gift by turning it into a sexual orgy.

He had no doubt in his mind that when he and Jenna did consummate their desire it would be a sexual orgy. A wild celebration of sex, with steamy kisses, electrified foreplay, frantic couplings, and when their appetites were sated enough to allow it, slow, exploratory, sensual lovemaking far, far into the night.

So he had lain beside her, burning with desire, aware of every move she made, her soft breath against his neck, her whispered sighs. He didn't turn toward her, not even an inch, for fear it would destroy his self-control, and eventually he had relaxed in the circle of her arms, relaxed and drifted into sleep.

Jake sat in front of his laptop and relived that beautiful, torturous night. It had been heaven. It had been hell. He uttered a low sound of frustration. Buster, in his habitual place on the rag rug, pricked his ears and echoed Jake's groan with a soft sound of his own.

Jake hit the save button on his computer and stood up. He needed to do something physical. A good, hard jog would help clear his mind. He doubted that he could run Jenna out of his system, but he might be able to tire out his hormones and enjoy a little peace.

Jenna had sounded a little strange on the phone earlier, he thought as he went to the back door for his jogging shoes, and that fact reinforced his opinion that he'd done the right thing by not initiating anything sexual the night before. If she regretted crawling into his bed last night when the encounter had been so innocent, how much greater would be her regrets if they'd had sex? If she didn't want their relationship to go any further, and that was sort of the impression he'd got from the phone conversation, then she would really have resented him for taking advantage of her compassion, using it to satisfy his own desires and push their relationship to a level she didn't want.

He sank into the chair in his office to change his shoes. He was confused, and he admitted it. He knew the sexual attraction between them was mutual, mutually irresistible, yet he sensed a reserve in her, a holding back, that indicated she didn't welcome what was happening.

Buster, seeing the running shoes, scrambled to his feet, his tail wagging. "That's right, big boy, we're going for a run," Jake said. Buster's joyful bark was interrupted by the phone ringing. Jake answered it and was surprised to hear Claire's voice.

"I've just baked some bread," Claire said. "I wondered if you would like a loaf. It's still warm."

Homemade bread. "Claire, you said the magic word. Did a duck just drop down from the ceiling and give you a hundred dollars?"

Claire laughed. "Either you're about 30 years older than you look, Jake,

155

or you have a weakness for Groucho Marx quiz shows."

"You bet your life," he quipped back. "Every Halloween when I was a kid I dragged out my Groucho Marx glasses and moustache."

"Be still my heart. A young person who has an appreciation for the finer things past. Well, that certainly justifies the little—er—loaf of bread I baked for you. Jenna and Carlee will bring it over."

Jake thanked her and hung up, grinning at Buster's eager expression. He couldn't stop grinning. Homemade bread *and* Jenna! He glanced at his watch. "We've probably got ten or fifteen minutes before they get here, fella, so we can't go far. C'mon."

Outside Jake was amused at Buster's aversion to the new hurricane anchor cemented into the back yard with the 15-foot chain attached to it. He put Buster on the chain whenever he had to leave the dog home alone, knowing Buster would leap the fence in a heartbeat now that he'd discovered a soul mate in Carlee.

They had advanced only a few feet into the edge of the woods when they spotted an armadillo rooting in the ground for insects. Jake slipped his hand under Buster's collar in case the dog mistook the little critter for a doggie treat.

"Sort of missed your curfew, didn't you, soldier?" Jake said to the armadillo. "What are you doing poking around in the daylight?" Buster strained against Jake's grip, wanting a nose to nose with the creature, and Jake slid his hand further under the collar for a better grip.

Suddenly Buster did an unexpected about face, slamming into Jake's legs and knocking him off balance. Then Buster leaped forward like the first horse out of the gate at the Kentucky Derby, with Jake stumbling along beside him, uselessly yelling, "Whoa! Heel! Sit! Stop! Halt! Damn you!" Jake's watch band had caught in Buster's collar, and he galloped along beside the dog trying to free it without breaking it. It took him several seconds to work the watch free, and when he'd finally accomplished it, Buster forged ahead while Jake's forward momentum landed him face down in the dirt.

Jake raised himself to hands and knees, wincing as a scraped knee protested the pressure. Two running shoes stepped into his point of view, topped by two beautiful tanned legs he'd come to know intimately on more than one occasion.

CHAPTER TWELVE

Jake looked up with a rueful grin. Beyond Jenna he saw Buster sitting docilely at Carlee's feet, slurping her face with kisses.

Jenna patted Jake's head, scratched behind one ear. "Nice doggy."

He scowled into emerald eyes sparkling with laughter. "I'll show you nice doggy," he growled, lunging forward and tackling her around the knees, rolling so she landed on top of him. She came down amid shrieks of laughter, and immediately tried to roll away from him, but Jake wrapped his arms around her and they rolled together, picking up leaves and twigs along the way. When they stopped, Jake was on top. He rested his elbows on either side of her, supporting his weight and effectively preventing her escape.

He watched her face, exalting at the transformation she couldn't control. Her laughter died, replaced by awakening desire, manifested in her flushed face, her smoldering eyes, her trembling lips, the whispered sigh. She was so damnably desirable, such a turn-on, and the biggest ego trip he'd ever experienced.

He lowered his lips to her left ear. "Woof, woof," he murmured.

"You big dope," she said with a shaky laugh, but the words ended with a gasp as Jake's tongue traced the contours of her ear, then plunged into its depths. "Woof," he murmured, dragging his lips across her face and kissing the corners of her mouth with his tongue. He traced his tongue across her upper lip, then her lower lip, savoring the taste, this delicious appetizer that gave so much and promised so much more.

Her arms reached for him, encircled his neck, and he lost himself in the power of their kiss. Without ending the kiss, he rolled onto his back, pulling

Jenna on top of him, and let his hands rove the gentle curves of her body. She felt so good. He curved his hands around her hips and pressed her closer against his body, aroused by her response, urgent with his need, and feeling in every pore of his body the perfect rightness of it.

Jenna's senses were swirling under the onslaught of Jake's hungry kisses, her body frantic to press closer to his, breast to breast, stomach to stomach, pelvis to pelvis, thigh to thigh. The fingers of her right hand splayed through his hair, claiming that territory as hers, while her left hand pushed impatiently under his shirt to stroke his body. His male hardness, pushing between her legs against the constraint of clothes, stimulated and tantalized her beyond reason.

"Yes," she sighed. "Oh, Jake, yes."

She felt a tremor travel through his body, felt an answering tremor in her own, as he reached down to caress her and unzip his pants.

"Momma?" The voice, at first sounding far away, on a distant planet, but suddenly in their faces, jerked the two adults back to Florida. They stared at each other for a minute, their feelings mirrored in each other's face. Passion, not yet ready to yield to the demands of a child. Surprise that they had been so lost in each other, so oblivious to their surroundings. Regret, promise.

Jenna dragged her gaze to Carlee and pushed herself to a sitting position atop Jake, excrutiatingly aware of his hardness beneath her.

"What, Punkin?"

Carlee's worried look traveled back and forth between Jake and Jenna. One little hand rested on Buster, who was now favoring Jake with slurpy kisses. The other little hand reached for Jenna.

"I thought you were fighting," she said in a small voice. "But I guess you were just kissing."

Just kissing. Jenna croaked out a laugh. "Yes, we were just kissing," she said, while forcing herself to sit still and ignore the heat radiating between herself and Jake. A quick glance at Jake's strained face showed his feelings were on a par with her own.

Carlee offered two envelopes to Jake. They were a little damp and wrinkled, apparent victims of Buster's exuberance. "Here," she said. "These are for you and Buster."

"You already gave me invitations to your caterpillar's party," Jake said.

"Oh, these are for my birthday party," Carlee said. "I'll be four. That's old enough to go to preschool."

Jake felt like he'd been hit with a sledgehammer. He sat up, keeping Jenna on his lap. "Four," he said, struggling for a normal tone. "That's a—a wonderful age, Carlee."

"Can Buster come to my party? And you."

Jake recognized the "and you" for what it was. An afterthought. A bribe. That was okay. He didn't want an invitation. "I'll be pretty busy," he began.

Seeing Carlee's mouth droop, he finished rapidly, "But Buster can come, if you're sure it's okay with your mom."

He glanced at Jenna. She was watching him with an analytical expression. *Does she wonder if I'll bolt and run like I did last night over the lightning bugs?* For some reason, the thought angered him. He'd carried his grief like an albatross for too long, he needed to reassert his manhood, stand on his own two feet (although at the moment it didn't seem prudent to do so).

"Are you sure you want Buster at Carlee's birthday party?" he asked her, reaching over to pluck a twig from her hair.

"Well," Jenna said, "Carlee assures me Buster can help sing Happy Birthday." The remark reminded her of Pavarotti. "I'll never, never, never want to be in love with anyone but you."

"Buster can do that," Jake agreed. He remembered Buster singing with Pavarotti. "I'll never, never, never want to be in love with anyone but you."

They looked at each other. There was no way each could know what the other was thinking, but there was no mistaking the look in their eyes.

* * *

Jenna sat on the edge of Carlee's bed, *Wendy and the Butterfly Queen* open on her lap. Carlee was tucked under the covers, her head on the pillow, her eyes wide with excitement.

"I don't think this is such a good bedtime story," Jenna teased. "I'm through page six and you're more wide awake now than when I started reading to you."

Carlee sighed happily. "I love Wendy, she's so brave. And the butterfly queen is so beautiful. Don't stop. This is the good part."

"You say that about all the parts," Jenna said with a laugh. She and Claire must have read the book to Carlee at least twenty times since Jenna had given it to her. The child could quote whole passages by heart. When Jake brought Buster over to play with Carlee, the child would sit on the patio beside the attentive dog and "read" the pictures to him. Jenna turned back to the story and resumed reading aloud.

In the early dawn Rebecca Blazing Star opened her soft purple-pink petals to the sun and looked around. All her sister blossoms on their tall, thin stems were starting to wake, the woodsy air perfumed with the sweet scent of their stirring.

The butterflies had not come.

Wendy must have failed, Rebecca realized. Our species will die. Soon Rebecca and all her sisters would grow old and die, dropping from their tired stems to the ground, where they would mingle with the earth, giving it life as the earth had given them life. That was the natural order of things, Mother Nature's great plan, and they were proud to be a part of it.

After they were gone, new blossoms, young, fresh and beautiful, would take their places. Tiny new buds, born of their flesh, born when their pollen was carried from blossom to blossom, would bring new healthy life to the blazing star plant and life would go on and on. That was also part of Mother Nature's plan, the great cycle of life.

But without the butterflies to pollinate the blossoms, there would be no new buds in the spring.

Jenna liked the way Jake wrote. He used simple concepts, easily grasped by young children, but he didn't talk down to them. He didn't hesitate to throw in an occasional adult word or phrase when it expressed his thoughts concisely and its meaning could be understood. The stories, besides being gripping little dramas, were educational vocabulary builders. No wonder parents and teachers, as well as children, loved them.

But thoughts of Jake reminded her all too vividly of their insanity that morning. With Carlee not twenty feet away, they had practically—

She felt a red flush heat her face. And why should their near copulation surprise her? Isn't that the way it had been since their first meeting? On the grass, at the motel, during the auction, in the greenhouse, and now that little episode outside Jake's house.

She would have to be an idiot not to realize she and Jake were speeding recklessly down a one-way street. They kept hitting stop signs, but the stops only momentarily interrupted their journey. It was only a matter of time before their pell-mell flight crossed a point of no return, before they arrived at the inevitable conclusion of that headlong race.

The thought of that inevitable conclusion filled her with a sudden anticipation so intense her body tingled from head to foot. The primitive longing to mate raced through her body, from her head, from her heart and even from her extremities, to settle with hot urgency between her legs.

"But the butterflies had not come," Carlee prompted.

Jenna drew a shuddering breath and continued reading.

```
    But the butterflies had not come. The cycle
of  life  would  stop  with  Rebecca  and  her
dwindling family. Eventually, even the shrub
itself, without happy baby buds tugging on
its wise old limbs, would lose all joy and
wither away.
```

"And 'Becca's tiny blazing star heart lost all hope and was filled with dread," Carlee quoted.

"With great dread," Jenna agreed. "And now, my funny little peanut, it's time for you to go to sleep."

"Just read a little more," Carlee begged. "I 'specially like the part where Wendy's tree wakes her up. I wish I could sleep in a tree."

"If you slept in the crook of a tree, you'd be sure to wake with a crook in your neck," Jenna said. "But I'll tell you what. I'll read a couple more pages and you can shut your eyes and pretend you're sleeping in a tree."

"In Wendy's tree," Carlee amended, closing her eyes. Jenna smiled at the little face so precious to her, its soft features framed by tangled wisps of red hair, thick lashes fluttering as Carlee strove to keep her eyes shut. Jenna read.

> Far away from the blazing star blossoms, on the other side of the great woods, Wendy was curled in a tight ball. She was sound asleep in her favorite spot, the thick flat branch growing out of the trunk of her massive live oak tree.

Lizzy's tree, Jenna always thought when she came to that sentence.

> In her sleep she felt soft leaves caress her cheek. In her delicate pearly white ear she heard a murmured whisper. A breeze rustling through the branches of the ancient oak whispered the tree's urgent message. "Wake up. Wake up. Wake up."
>
> Wendy stirred and brushed her ivory ear, trying to make the whispers stop. She was dreaming of rainbows and bluebirds and didn't want to wake up. Suddenly the branch she was sleeping on began to shake, bouncing Wendy awake. "Okay, okay," she grumbled, sitting up and rubbing the sleep from her eyes.
>
> "Blazing star, blazing star," the oak whispered through the rustle of its leaves.
>
> Wendy jumped up, all three feet of her wide awake. Rebecca! The blazing stars! She had to save the beautiful shrub from extinction. She

had to lead the butterflies to the hidden grove. Otherwise the very last shrub of blazing stars in the great woods would die, its lavender beauty and sweet fragrance gone forever. She had to save the blazing stars, for their sake, for the butterflies' sake, for the great woods' sake—and for her own sake. For Wendy loved nature's beauty above all things.

The butterfly queen would help her. The butterfly queen would summon all the butterflies to the big circle in the woods and explain the problem to them. She would order pollinators to follow Wendy to the forgotten grove where they would carry the life-renewing pollen from blossom to blossom.

Except the butterfly queen was missing, and nobody knew what had happened to her. There were terrified whispers of a monstrous lizard, green and quick and clever, that the beetles had seen darting among the branches of the red maple trees. There were exaggerated rumors of a hawk-like bird that was terrorizing the queen's butterfly bush.

Had the butterfly queen lost her way in the forest, was she lying trapped, her wing caught under a fallen rock, had she been eaten, was she dead? The butterfly kingdom was in a state of turmoil, and had refused to help Wendy until they found their queen.

Wendy had to find the queen before it was too late, before something dreadful happened to her. If it wasn't already too late.

Jenna stopped reading, gently stroked the cheek of her sleeping child, and silently left the room.

* * *

Jake jogged along the path to Jenna's house, the noon sun hot on his back. Buster loped beside him, occasionally stopping to snuff at a new scent or explore a sound, then galloping to catch up. Buster could have climbed a tree and Jake wouldn't have noticed. His thoughts were consumed with Jenna. He hadn't seen her or talked with her for three days. Not since she'd brought the homemade bread over Monday morning. Today was Thursday and every day when he'd brought Buster to play with Carlee, Jenna had been gone.

She was avoiding him, that much was obvious. He could hardly blame her after the bizarre exhibition they'd put on in front of Carlee. He'd picked up the phone at least a dozen times to call her, but each time had backed down. She wouldn't appreciate his hounding her when she was trying to cool their relationship. It would only make things worse if he made a nuisance of himself. So he'd struggled to keep Jenna pushed to the back of his thoughts while he concentrated on finishing up his stories for the paper. He'd e-mailed the last one to the editor this morning, along with a note saying he wouldn't be available for assignments for a while.

During the three days he had been writing stories for the paper, Jake had debated the wisdom of refusing more assignments. But now that he'd made the decision to finish his Wendy book, he knew the newspaper stories would not only be a time-consuming distraction, but they'd also be a crutch. Completing his Wendy book would be a giant milestone in his struggle to conquer his grief, and he needed to get rid of his crutch if he wanted to reach that milestone.

The lightning bug jar had nearly been his undoing. And his reaction when Carlee had handed it to him certainly seemed to put a big dent in his relationship with Jenna. But the whole incident had made him more determined than ever to become the master of his destiny, rather than the victim. And achieving that mastery meant, in part, finishing his Wendy book.

When he and Buster arrived at Jenna's house, he was not surprised to see her van gone, but he was disappointed. He missed seeing her mischievous smile, hearing her wisecracks, seeing the desire smolder in her eyes. Buster took off with a bound toward the butterfly garden and Jake followed, confident the dog would lead him straight to Carlee.

He heard the heart-rending sobs at about the same time he spotted Carlee. She was sitting on the ground by the milkweed plants, crying as though her little heart would break. Jake froze, the poignant scene immobilizing him, then steeled himself to approach her.

He crouched down beside her. "What's wrong, Carlee?" he asked softly.

Carlee looked up at him, her little face ravaged with grief, huge tears spilling over her eyes and raining down her face.

"W-Willy's dead," she sobbed. "He's killed."

Jake looked quickly at the plant holding the chrysalis, afraid at first that Buster might have done something. But a closer inspection made it obvious what had happened. A wasp had taken advantage of the soft vulnerable chrysalis to lay its eggs inside, and the wasp larvae had killed the caterpillar. Jake had heard about things like that happening. Last year when he'd interviewed a master gardener, she had mentioned it. He'd forgotten about it until now.

"How come that had to happen?" Carlee said between loud jerky sobs. "I hate that wasp, I hate it!"

Jake felt Carlee's pain tear at his heart. "Come here, sweetheart," he said, opening his arms to her. She flung herself against him. Her short, chubby arms wrapped around his neck in a tight grasp. Her tear-streaked face burrowed into his shoulder just above his heart, and the little body shook with hard, racking sobs.

Buster paced around them, whining his distress.

Jake held Carlee, stroking her hair, gently massaging her back, murmuring soft sounds into her ear. He wasn't going to belittle her loss with meaningless platitudes like "It'll be okay," or equally meaningless suggestions like "Don't cry." He understood about grief.

He held her, oblivious to anything but the child in his arms and her pain. Then, slowly, he became aware of another feeling—a tenderness curling around his heart, a warm compassion that had somehow seeped in and around his grief to find an empty spot in his heart and fill it.

His eyes fell on a book lying open on the ground. It was *Wendy and the*

Butterfly Queen, and it was open to a picture of Wendy's tree. It gave him an idea.

"You know what I think?" he said to the sobbing child, turning her so she was sitting on his lap and he could see her face. "I think," he said, pulling his T-shirt off and using it to mop up her face, "that a caterpillar as fine as Willy deserves a very special funeral."

Carlee stopped crying and looked at him, sniffing back sobs.

"I know a very special place," he said, continuing his mop-up operation.

"Wh-ere?" Carlee asked, a hiccup turning the word into two syllables.

"I'll show you," he said.

A few minutes later, after explaining the situation to Claire, Jake and Carlee headed into the woods. Jake carried Carlee piggyback and Carlee carried what was left of Willy wrapped in a white tissue, covered with flower petals, and lying in a pretty plastic container supplied by Claire. One of Jenna's garden trowels poked from the back of Jake's jeans.

It took about fifteen minutes to reach the tree, and Carlee's youthful enthusiasm for the adventure had already started to heal the pain by the time the clearing came into view. Carlee gasped when Jake slid her off his shoulders and stood her before the tree.

"It's Wendy's tree," she squealed, staring for a moment in awestruck silence. Then she ran to it and threw her arms around it. Her small limbs stretched around only a fraction of the tree's fat trunk, but Carlee didn't notice. She laid her face against the tree and quoted two lines from the Wendy book, the lines Wendy said at the end of each story. "You are my tree and I am your wood nymph. Our spirits are one forever and ever."

Jake felt tears spring to his eyes. *You are my Lizzy and I am your blood. Our spirits are one forever and ever.*

Jake used the trowel to dig a small grave beneath the tree, and Carlee reverently placed the plastic coffin in the hole. Jake told Carlee that as Willy's closest friend she must throw in the first shovel-full of dirt. She swallowed back a sob as she tipped the trowel over the hole and let the dirt scatter over the container. After he'd finished burying the caterpillar, they searched around until they found a pretty rock and placed it on top of the small mound of dirt. The activity reminded Carlee of her loss, but it also helped her say good-bye. They stood beside the grave for a moment, Carlee's small hand clutched in Jake's. "Good-bye, brave Willy," Jake said. "Sleep with angels."

"Good-bye, brave Willy," Carlee said in the same solemn tone Jake had used. "Sleep with angels."

Jake stared up into the tree. "Good night, sweet princess. And flights of angels sing thee to thy rest."

Carlee tugging on his hand brought his attention back to her. She was looking at Jake with a puzzled expression.

"Is Wendy a sweet princess?" she asked, trying to wriggle her fingers.

"Hmmm?" Jake realized he was clutching her hand too tightly and loosened his grip. Such a little hand. So familiar. "Wendy? No," he said, scooping Carlee up in his arms and settling her on the flat branch of the tree. "No, Wendy is a wood nymph. Lizzy is—was—my sweet princess."

"Who's Lizzy?" Carlee squirmed around until she was comfortable.

"Lizzy was my little girl. She died. When she was your age." For some reason, Jake found it comfortable to talk to Carlee about Lizzy. She didn't show pity or horror or any kind of judgmental looks, just frank curiosity.

Carlee digested that. "I wish she didn't die. She could have been my friend. It would be fun to have someone to play with. Do you miss her?"

Jake blinked back tears. "Yes," he said gruffly. "But I feel closer to her when I'm here. Sometimes I feel her spirit here and I think maybe she can hear me when I talk to her." Becoming aware of Carlee's wide, solemn eyes, he changed the subject. "She loved this tree. We used to come here a lot. She liked to sit right where you are sitting and eat her lunch. She'd pretend she was eating with Wendy." He stopped talking and walked a few steps away, memories piercing him.

"Do you feel her spirit now?" Carlee asked curiously.

"Yes," Jake said. He rested his hand on the trunk of the tree and looked up through the leaves.

Carlee placed her hand on the trunk and looked up also, searching through the shimmering leaves, sprawling limbs and hanging moss. "I feel Lizzy's spirit too," she said.

Despite the turmoil in his chest, Jake had to smile at Carlee's imagination. "It's time to head back," he said, whistling for Buster, who had pranced off into the woods.

"Can we come back tomorrow and eat our lunch here?" Carlee asked.

Jake thought about the task he had set himself to finish the Wendy book, but decided a short afternoon break might be very welcome.

"Aha. So you want to pretend you are dining with Wendy the wood nymph too," he said, lifting her by the armpits to stand her on the branch, then holding out his arms for her to jump into them.

"No," she said, answering his question. "I want to pretend I'm having lunch with Lizzy." With a happy shriek, she leaped into Jake's arms.

CHAPTER THIRTEEN

"On vacation!" Jenna squawked into the phone. "Well you surely have more than one person who can repair my fans. This is an emergency. The temperature in the greenhouse is already rising and it's not even nine o'clock. I need somebody out here now." Jenna heard the panic in her voice and took a deep, calming breath.

"I'm desperate," she said in a gentler voice, trying to sound like a helpless female. She had discovered that here in Florida, southern chivalry was alive and well and she could catch more flies with honey than with a fly swatter.

She'd risen with the sun that morning as usual, planning to put in a couple of hours with the orchids before starting preparations for Carlee's birthday party. Since her little guests wouldn't be arriving until noon, she knew she had plenty of time. But the minute she'd walked into the greenhouse and felt the hot, stifling air, she'd had a sinking premonition that it was not going to be a good day. A quick investigation disclosed that the air circulation and cooling unit she'd had installed was not working properly. The blades in the fan were barely spinning, and every once in a while they stopped altogether. It would happen on a day the weatherman had forecast record-breaking heat, she thought.

Orchids fared best when outside during the morning hours. However, they couldn't stay in the midday heat. Even the air in the greenhouse had to be stabilized before eleven or it would be too hot inside, and she hadn't been able to reach a repairman before ten minutes to nine. It's no wonder she was panicking. The man on the other end of the line seemed to have only one sentence in his vocabulary, which he repeated with a patient, slow drawl: "I'm sorry, ma'am, but our repairman is on vacation and won't be back until a week from Monday."

After some pleading, wheedling, and near sobbing, Jenna finally solicited his promise that he would call around to the self-employed electricians he knew until he found one and "send him right over, ma'am. Now don't you fret your head over it. I'll see that he gets there right quick."

Jenna had rolled her orchids outside earlier while trying to rouse a repairman. Now, making a mental note that they would all have to be rolled back in again, she turned her attention to the next task. Carlee's cake. There was another minute of near panic when she opened the refrigerator and realized the egg tray in the door was empty, but a frantic search uncovered a dozen eggs on the bottom shelf shoved to the back. It took only a few minutes to beat the cake mix, pour it into two round pans, and shove them in the oven. Soon the stomach-growling aroma of baking chocolate wafted through the kitchen.

Claire had whisked Carlee out of the house earlier, promising her breakfast at McDonald's and a trip to the library. They wanted her cake to be a surprise.

Jenna went to the pantry and carefully removed a baking sheet from an upper shelf. Yep, the cake topping was finished, and it was beautiful. Claire had pushed her artistic talents to new heights. She had made a replica of Wendy's tree for Jenna to stand in the center of the cake. It hadn't been easy, but following the illustration in Carlee's book and cutting the shape from stiff cookie dough, Claire had managed to create a very good likeness. She'd baked two mirror images and glued them together with frosting, creating a thick tree that would stand upright. Then she'd swirled chocolate frosting over it, creating dark and light shades. She'd fashioned leaves from flaked coconut colored green and the hanging moss from shredded coconut. She'd spent hours on it, and it was a masterpiece. She'd even made a little cookie figure to represent Wendy, brightly sparkling with colored frosting and sprinkles.

"Tough act to follow," Jenna muttered, hoping her cake didn't do anything unsociable like fall in the center.

While the cake was baking she started hanging crepe paper and other party decorations in the sunroom, very glad that she could close the windows and crank up the air to keep the room cool. She kept looking at her watch, every ten minutes having another nervous spasm because the electrician hadn't shown up. If he didn't show up soon, she'd have to start carrying orchids into the house, although where she'd put them with a party in the making, she had no idea.

She was hanging a six-foot birthday banner along one wall when the electrician's truck finally rolled up the drive. Thank you, God. She hurried to meet him and walked with him to the greenhouse, explaining the problem on the way. He looked about seventeen, although she knew he had to be older than that. She'd reached an age, pushing thirty, when everybody looked about seventeen—doctors, teachers, corporate executives, and, of course the dot.com folks, who probably *were* only seventeen.

She showed him the air circulation and cooling unit, which by now had started making an awful screeching sound. He walked around it a couple of times, scrutinizing it, nodded as though he understood the problem, and winked at her with the air of an expert who has everything under control. He rattled off several sentences describing the problem and solution in techno-babble that drove home the point that she was a mere orchid grower, not a nuclear scientist.

"Make it so," she said, refraining from adding "Number One," and walked with captain-like dignity back to the house.

As she approached the kitchen, she broke into a run. The heavenly scent of baking chocolate had changed to the horrifying smell of burned cake. "Please, please, please don't be ruined," she prayed to the big Doughboy in the sky as she grabbed a mitt and opened the oven door. Smoke pouring out and stinging her eyes told her how insignificant was her standing with Doughboy.

Claire and Carlee, returning minutes later, found her slumped in a kitchen chair staring dejectedly at the cake.

"I don't like that smell," Carlee said, pinching her nose.

Claire walked over to the counter and gave the cake an appraising look. "Not one of your better efforts," she said sympathetically. "I saw the electrician's truck parked in the driveway. I guess that means the cooling unit's not working yet."

171

They both glanced at the clock. It was 10:30.

Jenna felt an ulcer mushrooming in her stomach. It would take at least 45 minutes to wheel all the orchids back into the greenhouse. Plus, she still had to hang crepe paper, blow up a few dozen balloons, bag the party favors, make Kool-Aid, put the paper tablecloth on the picnic table, lay out the plates and tableware, napkins, cups…at least the pizza was being delivered.

She sighed and pushed herself out of the chair. "I think I can cut away the edges," she said, indicating the cake. "Maybe the middle will be okay."

It was one of the few times in her life when Claire looked totally scandalized. "I think," she said with asperity, "that you can go back to the sunroom and finish the decorations while I take care of the cake." She was reaching in the cupboard for another cake mix as she spoke.

Jenna gave her a grateful smile.

Claire silently mouthed a question. "The tree?"

Jenna glanced at Carlee, who was still pinching her nose and studying the burned cake with revulsion. Jenna motioned with her eyes in the direction of the panty. "Beautiful," she breathed, giving Claire a thumbs up sign.

Claire beamed. "Carlee can help you," she said. "I know you have enough to keep you busy *out of the kitchen* while I finish up in here."

Jenna nodded guiltily. She was supposed to have had the cake finished and hidden before Claire and Carlee got home, but the best laid plans of mice and mothers…

At 10:45 Jenna began pushing the orchids back into the greenhouse. The cooling unit was humming reassuringly, the electrician was paid and gone, and the orchids looked none the worse for wear. Carlee was busy in the sunroom, setting the picnic table and filling the bags with party favors.

At 11:30 Jenna was through with the orchids and back in the house, hot, sweaty and tired. If none of her guests arrived early—fat chance—she had thirty minutes to shower, make herself presentable, blow up 24 balloons, and wrap presents. She ran upstairs to wrap presents, kicking herself for not taking care of that last night. In ten minutes she was back in the sunroom putting the presents on the card table set up for that purpose. Carlee was upstairs changing into her party clothes.

It was decision time. Should she shower first, then blow up balloons? Or vice versa? If she went for the balloons, she'd be sure to be in the shower when the guests started arriving. That wouldn't do. But if she did the shower first, she'd be sure to be blowing up balloons when the party started. That wouldn't do either.

The doorbell rang. "What now?" she muttered, heading for the front door. Surely they weren't delivering the pizzas yet. She had impressed upon them the importance of delivering them between 12 and 12:15. She jerked the door open, brushing stringy locks off her sweaty face, ready to release some tension by yelling at a hapless delivery boy.

Jake stood at the door, holding Buster on a short leash.

"Er—I'm sorry I'm early," he said, looking her up and down. He hadn't seen her for almost a week, since the infamous Monday morning madness. She looked disheveled, distraught, and delicious.

"Early? You're just in time." Jenna grabbed him by the front of the shirt and jerked him into the living room. Buster, with unerring instinct, headed upstairs to Carlee.

"I was just going to drop Buster off and leave," Jake said, a little startled.

"Over my dead body." She shoved him onto the sofa and handed him a bag of balloons. "Nobody's ever accused me of looking a gift angel of mercy in the mouth." She paused for breath. "Jake, I'm in a dreadful time bind. Would you mind blowing up these balloons while I grab a shower?"

This wasn't the way he'd planned it. His plan had been to drop Buster off early and disappear before the kids started arriving. Should he try to explain it to Jenna? Lizzy was two days shy of her fourth birthday when she was killed. They'd planned a party for her too. Even Barb had shown some enthusiasm for the event, buying invitations and mailing them out, ordering a specially decorated cake from the bakery, hiring a clown. For a week Lizzy had been dancing around in a state of fevered excitement while Jake kept the bike he'd bought for her hidden in the garage. They had the funeral the day after her birthday. He would never be able to separate the two events.

Things were happening too fast. He and Carlee had forged a bond. He had returned to his Wendy book, was almost finished writing it. A few more paragraphs and he'd be typing that closing signature line: "You are my tree and I am your wood nymph. Our spirits are one, forever and ever." He had come that far in his journey toward healing. But this, this fourth birthday party, to shove it in his face—it was asking too much.

"Jenna," he said in a choked whisper, keeping his face averted, "I—"

"Oh, Jake," Jenna whispered, stricken. How could she have been such a blundering fool? One look at his face, so white and drawn, his eyes haunted, and she should have realized. Even without those signs she should have realized. Lizzy had died just before her fourth birthday. How could she expect him to participate in Carlee's celebration?

She laid a hand softly against his cheek. "I'm so sorry," she said, shaking her head. "I wasn't thinking, fool that I am. Can you ever forgive me?"

He laid his hand over hers, pressing it more firmly against his face. He closed his eyes briefly, savoring her touch. Then he looked at her and smiled, a crooked lift to one side of his mouth. He wouldn't let his ghosts spoil this day. When he spoke, his voice cracked only a little. "There's nothing to forgive. Of course I'll blow up the balloons for you."

"Are you sure?" She leaned closer, searching his eyes.

He was still holding his hand over hers. He moved it across his lips and nibbled gently on her fingers. "I've missed you, Jenna."

"I've been—busy," she faltered. How could I have deliberately avoided him for even one day, let alone five days, she wondered? Five days, and—she glanced at her watch—two hours, thirty-three minutes, but who's counting? She stepped closer and with her free hand brushed the stray lock of hair from his forehead. He captured that hand too, and brought them both behind her back as he circled her waist and pulled her to him.

"Are you crazy," she gasped as she was pulled off balance, toppling against him. Her momentum carried them both backward, into a sprawled position on the sofa, and brought laughter to their lips.

"No sex," she ordered, panting, struggling to sit up.

Jake sat up with her, his arms encircling her waist. "The farthest thing from my mind," he said, giving her a wide-eyed innocent look.

"And if I believe that, you've got a bridge you'll sell me, right?" It felt good to be back in his arms. It felt really, really good.

He stroked his hands up her back, buried his fingers in her hair, and pulled her face to his. The kiss was not quick and perfunctory or slow and sensual. It was more like a branding iron, immediate and searing. The week's separation had kindled their appetites, their previous encounters had fueled their expectations, and the touch of lips was like a spark on dry tinder. Desire flared into conflagration.

Jenna could not stop the small sounds of pleasure that escaped her as Jake's mouth teased and his hands caressed. She wasn't even aware she made them.

And they drove Jake crazy with desire.

"Ahem. And I repeat, ahem ahem."

Jenna and Jake pulled themselves from the depths of delirium to see Claire standing over them.

"I of all people am not unhappy to catch you two *in flagrante delicto,*" Claire said, her tone reproving but her eyes laughing. "But do the words 'birthday party' ring any bells?" She tapped her watch.

Jenna gasped, jumped up, and dashed for the stairs, her face crimson.

"I, um, guess I'm going to blow up balloons," Jake said, red creeping up his neck.

The balloons went pretty fast, he discovered as he tied off the third one. He could blow one up in three or four good puffs. There were only twenty-four in the bag, according to the label. Apparently they were for a game, because folded sheets of paper had been inserted into some of them. He took another, puffed into it three times and tied it off.

At this rate, he would be done in a few minutes, done and gone before the party started. If he hurried, he could even be gone before Jenna came down, turned her eyes on him, and persuaded him to stay. He grabbed another balloon and puffed furiously into it.

Since Jake was able to do two things at the same time, puff and think, he thought of Jenna while he blew up balloons. Specifically he thought of the explosive kiss they had just shared. He thought of the way her lips tasted, the way their breaths mingled, her velvety tongue, those exciting little noises she made. His thoughts raced, fast and furious, as fast and furious as the puffs he blew into the balloons.

The next time I have her in my arms, I'm carrying her off to some remote location where there are no kids, no mothers, no stopping The next time puff puff *I have her* puff puff *in my arms* puff puff *I'm carrying her* puff puff *to some remote* puff puff—he was getting light-headed just thinking about it.

By the time he was down to a half dozen balloons, his thoughts had drifted from Jenna's face to her body. His cheeks ached, but his puffing was as fast and furious as ever. He was definitely feeling lightheaded by the time he grabbed the last balloon, blew it up and tied it. Just in time, he thought as he heard voices at the front of the house. The kids were arriving.

He stood quickly, intending to make his escape out the sunroom door and through the backyard. Before he could take a single step, the room began whirling around him.

"Whew," he said, collapsing back on the sofa. From what seemed like a long distance, he heard Claire shout. And then everything went black.

"Come on daddy, catch the grasshopper!"

Lizzy raced across the yard, the overgrown grass nipping at her knees, her excited shrieks trailing after her. She reached the fence and ran alongside it.

"There's one, daddy. Catch it, quick, before he hops away!" Jake was there beside her, lunging for the insect, but it was too fast for him, hopping this way and that, always just out of reach.

Lizzy's laughter followed the progress. "Watch me!" She chased a grasshopper, stooping every few seconds to reach and grab.

"I caught him! I caught him!" Lizzy ran to Jake, her small hand scrunched into a fist. Cautiously she opened her hand to show her prize. The grasshopper lay still, its body crushed. Lizzy began to cry.

Is he dead, daddy?" she sobbed. "Is he d-dead?"

"Is he dead?" The voice wasn't Lizzy's. It was a child's voice, a boy's voice.

"He looks dead," another voice said, another boy.

Jake could hear the voices, knew they were in the same room, understood what they were saying, but he was in a dreamlike state, like the caterpillar in its cocoon, unable to respond.

"He's not dead. Gramma says he fainted from blowing the balloons up too fast." Carlee's voice.

Real men don't faint, Jake said, but he knew he wasn't really saying the words aloud, just hearing them in his head, their echoes bouncing off the walls, then fading. In his dreamlike haze the words seemed hilariously funny, like the punch line to a joke he'd heard a long time ago and couldn't remember.

"Are you sure he's not dead? He's not moving."

"Poke him and see if he moves."

"Yeah, poke him."

"I'm not gonna poke him. You poke him."

"It was your idea."

The buzz of voices grew louder, more distinct. Jake opened his eyes and saw a small boy reaching toward him with a finger extended. Immediately behind him another boy watched avidly.

"Boo," Jake said.

The boys screamed and scrambled for the door, falling over each other in their haste.

Carlee was standing by Jake's head. She laid a hand on his forehead in a humorously professional manner. "Don't mind them, boys are so stupid," Carlee said. "Are you okay? Momma told me to take care of you until she gets back."

"Yeah, I'm okay. Where is your mom?"

"She's out in the sunroom. The pizza man came and she has to pay him." Carlee picked up Jake's arm and pressed her thumb on his wrist.

"What are you doing?" he asked.

"Checking your pulse," she said with childish authority.

"Really. What are you checking for?"

"Well," Carlee said, puzzling it over for a minute. "I think if I don't feel a pulse, that's really, really bad."

"Ah. And do you feel anything?"

"Nope," she said with a worried frown.

Jake laughed and took her hand, showing her where to press her fingers. "Do you feel the blood pumping?"

Carlee's eyes got round. "Yes," she breathed.

"Good. Then you can tell your mother that nobody is going to die on her sofa today. And maybe you should go join the party. You don't want to miss out on the pizza, do you? Those boys are liable to pig it down before you get a bite. You know how boys are."

Carlee dropped his hand and ran toward the sunroom.

Jake rose cautiously to his feet, still feeling a little woozy. And feeling a lot foolish. *I fainted?* The realization was quite a blow to his ego. *I fainted over some balloons?* Boy, that would go over big in the locker room. Luckily he didn't belong to any club that used a locker room. Okay, John Wayne, let's see if you can make your escape without bringing down any more embarrassment on your head. He weaved his way to the front door.

He had his hand on the doorknob when he felt a tap on his shoulder.

"Where do you think you're going?"

It was Claire. He half turned to her, keeping his hand on the door.

"Oh, you know, parties aren't really my thing." He waved a hand toward the sunroom, where sporadic shouts and laughter erupted. "I was hoping to slip out unnoticed." No point in lying to Claire. She wouldn't believe him if he tried.

"Jenna sent me to check on you," Claire said, stepping in front of him and leaning her back against the door. "She's swamped with half a dozen kids clamoring for food." She studied him with a keen look Sherlock Holmes would have envied. "I never thanked you properly for being so kind to Carlee when her caterpillar died."

Jake shrugged dismissively. "She's a great kid."

"Yes, she is," Claire agreed absently, as though her thoughts were elsewhere. "I wish you wouldn't leave so soon, Jake. It's boiling hot out there, you've got quite a hike to get home, and you just fainted. You're liable to faint again if you walk home in this heat." She grinned mischievously.

Jenna's grin, he thought.

"Hang around. Maybe Jenna will walk you home after the party. Just to make sure you don't faint on the way."

Hmmm. Tempting. More peals of laughter erupted from the sunroom.

"N-no, I'd better go."

She laid a hand on his arm. "Jenna won't understand if you leave without saying good-bye, without giving her a chance to thank you for helping."

Jake laughed, a short humorless sound. "Helping? I don't think keeling over in your living room could be called helping."

"Blowing up a bag of balloons was a big help. And although you didn't realize it, your "keeling over" kept all the kids entertained until the pizza man came." Her mischievous grin again. "After that, of course, you lost out to pizza."

"Maybe I will just go say good-bye to Jenna." He didn't want to go another week without seeing her. It might even be a good idea to hang around until she'd agreed to a lunch date or something. Besides, he *was* still feeling a bit light-headed.

He stepped into the sunroom and found himself amidst chaos. Six excited kids were all talking at once, raising their voices to be heard over the rising din, while Buster added his resonant barks to the clamor. He edged along one wall and stopped in a corner, next to a box containing some craft supplies and party games.

Jenna was standing at the head of the table, looking slightly overwhelmed. She was trying vainly to get the kids' attention, but they were having too much fun shouting jokes and insults at each other, swapping pieces of pizza, teasing Carlee because it was her birthday, and in general behaving like normal, noisy, rambunctious four-year-olds. One of the boys rolled his paper plate into a horn and began tooting loudly. In a moment, six horns were tooting, their racket almost equaling Buster's accompanying howls.

Jenna spotted Jake and her eyes lit up. "Are you okay?" she asked. He couldn't hear the words, but knew what she'd said. He nodded. She spread her hands to encompass the kids and shrugged helplessly.

Jake pulled several sheets of paper from the box at his feet and walked up to stand beside Jenna. He laid the papers on the table and selected the top one. With a few deft strokes he transformed it into a swan. Two girls sitting at the end of the table nearest him watched, transfixed. He handed the swan to one of them. "I want one, I want one," the other girl demanded. Jake put his fingers to his lips. She grew silent as he took another sheet and fashioned her a dog. By now the other kids saw what was happening and started begging for a figure. Each time they asked, Jake put his fingers to his lips, hushing them, and when he finished a figure, he gave it to one of the children sitting quietly.

It didn't take the kids long to catch on. Soon the table was so quiet you could have heard the paper drop, had Jake's deft fingers been that clumsy.

Jenna watched in amazement. She had always had a healthy respect for those fingers, but this was really something. "Where'd you learn to do that?" she asked.

"In the navy," he said. "The cook could make anything from a ship to a helicopter. He gave me a few pointers."

Quite a few, Jenna thought, fascinated with his fingers.

After Jake had restored order, it was easy for Jenna to get the games started.

As she explained the first one to the kids, Jake carried a folding chair to a corner out of the way, straddled the seat backwards and rested his arms on the back. He'd just hang around long enough to talk to Jenna, then slip away, he thought.

It was tough to watch the laughing kids and not think of Lizzy, although not as tough as he'd thought it would be. He found that if he kept focused on Jenna, it was easier to keep Lizzy and his grief submerged, while the kids' laughter receded to background noise.

He watched her and let his thoughts recapture that explosive kiss. Yes, he thought, reiterating his vow, the next time I have her in my arms, I'm going to tote her off to some remote location where there are no kids, no mothers, no stopping. He let his imagination play out the scene that would follow the no stopping moment.

Jenna faltered in her explanations on how to play Pop-a-Prize when she saw the gleam in Jake's eyes. She recognized that gleam, and felt her body snap to attention.

Hope that springs eternal whispered to her heart. Maybe there *was* a future for her and Jake. Claire had told her how Jake had comforted Carlee when the caterpillar had died. And tonight, when Jenna had asked Carlee to stay with Jake until he came around, she hadn't blinked an eye. Maybe, she thought hopefully. Maybe.

"Can we start?" Carlee asked impatiently.

"Uh—yes!" Jenna said, forcing her thoughts back to the party. "Okay, everybody, remember. If you pop a balloon with a number inside, you win a prize."

A chorus of okays assured Jenna that she'd done enough explaining.

"All rightee then, on the count of three, everyone start popping!"

"Wait!" Carlee ran over to Jake. "Come on, you gotta play too." She tugged on his arm. "You have to help Buster."

Jake looked at Buster, who was prancing around a little too boisterously, eager to join in the fun. It might be a good idea if he kept close to the dog and made sure he didn't get too rough during all the excitement.

Jake let Carlee tug him to stand by Buster, and took the balloon she pushed into his hand.

"Okay, mommy, we're ready now."

Jenna called out, "One…two…three! Start popping!"

For several minutes chaos reigned. Six kids were tearing from spot to spot, shouting at the top of their lungs. Twelve hands were grabbing balloons, and twelve feet were stomping and popping them. Buster barked happily and chased the balloons around the room.

Jake watched Buster, wanting to be any place but there. After a few minutes, Carlee ran up to him and grabbed his hand.

"Come on, Jake, pop the balloon!" she demanded. When he just looked at her, she snatched it from his hand and dropped it on the floor. "Pop it, pop it," she shouted, jumping up and down. Obligingly, he stomped on it. A small piece of folded paper flew onto the floor. Carlee whooped. "A prize! You won a prize for Buster!" Her gleeful excitement was contagious, and he laughed as she grabbed his arm and pulled him toward the prize table. Kids were dashing every which way, bumping into them, threatening to stomp on any foot that got in the way. Jake scooped Carlee up and carried her across the room. Her arms circled his neck as though they belonged there.

After they had retrieved Buster's prize, Carlee brought Jake another balloon. With an expectant grin, she laid it at his feet. Looking at the happy, upturned face, he was reminded of his first glimpse of her, when she'd shrunk from him in fear. As he'd come to know her better, he'd discovered, first subconsciously and now on a conscious level, how much he enjoyed making her laugh, seeing those too-somber brown eyes light up with merriment. So he placed his hands on his hips, made a comical face, and did a heel-kicking Scottish jig around the balloon before leaping in the air and coming down on it with both feet.

Carlee whooped with delight and the other kids gathered round. Another balloon was dropped at his feet. "Do the dance again," the kids urged. Jake obliged to their delight, but when a third balloon landed at his feet, he placed Carlee's hands on her hips and showed her how to do the jig. The other kids didn't need any coaxing to join Jake and Carlee. Their stumbling, out-of-step efforts to dance the jig were so comical, as they jounced and bounced and bumped into each other, and Jake laughed so hard, he had to wipe tears from his eyes. When another balloon was dropped at his feet, he held up his hands in surrender and backed away, leaving them to their fun while he watched from the sidelines.

Jenna came to stand beside Jake. She wanted to tell him she had never seen Carlee so happy, but she was afraid that would be a painful reminder of Lizzy. Instead, she said, "So, I saw you stomping those balloons like a madman bent on revenge. Was that your way of getting back at them for causing you to faint?"

He gave her a long, measuring look. "I intend to get back at *you* for that," he said, his eyes gleaming.

"Moi?" she asked with feigned astonishment.

"Oui, cherie," he said, reaching for her.

She sidestepped his grasp, though her pulse was beating a rhythm the Indians would have swapped their eagle feathers to learn. "Pizza," she gasped. "Claire saved you some pizza in the kitchen, if you'd like to take a break from this madhouse."

Not giving him a chance to answer, or advance further, she turned to the room and clapped sharply to draw the kids' attention. "Next game, kids," she said. "Line up right here."

Jake retreated to the kitchen and pizza. Balloon popping worked up a man's appetite.

He hung around for the remainder of the party, waiting for a chance to talk to Jenna. He watched the kids play their games, laughed at their antics, and realized he was having a good time.

"Love is a mysterious circle."

Jake turned to see Claire standing beside him.

"The more people you love, the more your love grows to include them," Claire said. "Did you ever notice that?"

Jake shook his head, not sure what she was getting at.

"Hypothetical situation," Claire said. "Suppose love could be measured, like water, for example. Now suppose some woman's total love in her heart measured one gallon. Do you follow me?"

Jake nodded.

"Now suppose this woman had a child and she poured that whole gallon of love onto her child."

Claire paused and Jake nodded warily.

"Okay. Now she has a second child. And she loves her second child. Where did that love come from? Did she take it from her first child? Does each child get only half a gallon of love? Or does she still love the first child a whole gallon AND love her second child equally?"

Claire watched Jake like a robin watching a worm. Jake squirmed. "I suppose," he said haltingly, "she loves each child equally, but does not love the first child less."

"Which means the woman's love has grown to encompass both children. It would now measure two gallons. But the mystery is, she will love her first child with all her heart, and she will love her second child with all her heart. So how much love is in her heart now? Two gallons? Four gallons? And if she has more kids, four, six, a dozen?"

Jake was baffled. He shrugged.

"Exactly. It's a great mystery. The more she loves, the more her love grows. And the more her love grows, the more she loves. A never-ending circle."

She smiled at Jake. "Well, time for the cake. Don't go away." She headed for the kitchen.

Jake understood what she was getting at, and it even made some kind of sense. When he was at Wendy's tree with Carlee and Carlee had said she'd eat lunch with Lizzy, he'd felt a jolt of love flow through him. Love for Carlee for including Lizzy in her thoughts. And that "gallon" of love he'd felt for Carlee had not made him love Lizzy less. If anything, it had made him love Lizzy more.

Claire came out carrying a large layer cake, its four candles flickering. Jenna had supervised the seating of the children, and they waited in eager anticipation as Claire placed the cake in the middle of the table. Carlee squealed with delight when she saw the cake and the kids oohed and aahed.

Jake hung back, his gaze fixed out the window, still mulling over Claire's words. He heard the kids and adults sang Happy Birthday, with Buster accompanying the song, and turned to watch Carlee make a wish and blow out the candles. Then Jenna began to cut the cake.

He turned and started to walk in that direction. Carlee's excited, piping command to her mother came to him over the chatter of the children.

"Be careful, Mommy. Don't break the tree."

Jake froze, suddenly knowing what he would see. He was about a yard from the table and had to stretch his neck only a little over the kids' bobbing heads to get a good view of the cake. His stomach starting to churn while his head began a fierce pounding that threatened to knock him out. Wendy's tree. Four candles and Wendy's tree.

"God help me," he groaned.

It was Lizzy's birthday, but Lizzy was dead. Tomorrow they were putting her little body in the ground. Jake sat in a chair in the living room, consumed with grief, mad with grief. The doorbell rang, but he didn't answer it. There was nobody he wanted to see or talk to. It kept ringing, insistent.

Finally he dragged himself from the chair and stumbled to the door. He opened it in time to see the bakery truck pulling away. A white cake box stood on the porch table. Lizzy's cake. He'd forgotten to cancel Lizzy's cake. He approached the cake slowly, like a man walking toward the deadly strike of a rattler. It was a sheet cake in a sturdy box with clear plastic stretched over the top. It was a beautiful cake, with fluffy white frosting, four pink candles, "Happy birthday, princess" written across the top, and a picture of Wendy's tree decorating the center. The tree was drawn with gel frosting and food coloring, and a tiny Wendy figure perched on the wide branch. Lizzy would have loved the cake.

A boiling rage held in check, taut as a guitar string, snapped. Jake shouted his rage to God and the world, frantically ripping the wrapping from the cake, gouging out handfuls and throwing them at the heavens. "Why? Why? Why?" He shouted the question with each handful of cake he flung at the God that had taken Lizzy from him.

When the cake was gone and his emotions exhausted, he carried the empty box to the fireplace and burned it.

"Cake, Jake?" Jenna approached him with a piece of cake on a colorful paper plate. Mutely he shook his head, backing away. Then he turned and walked swiftly to the closest bathroom. He barely made it, just lifting the seat and getting his face over the bowl before he started to throw up. He heaved until his stomach was empty, his sides ached, and his throat burned.

Then he pushed himself to his feet and began to rinse his mouth at the sink. "If I can get through this, I can stand anything," he thought. "Just let me get through this."

He waited until he was composed before he left the bathroom. His first instinct had been to run, run home and hide in the comfort of his solitude, in the familiar comfort of his grief. He'd fought the urge. He would not give in to his grief. It had dictated his life for two years, and now he was taking his life back. It was war, and it was a war he did not intend to lose.

When he finally emerged from the bathroom, the party was over, the guests were gone. Jenna was clearing up the balloon scraps and paper plates. Claire was on a chair pulling down crepe paper streamers. Carlee had taken Buster outside.

"Are you okay, Jake?" Jenna asked, quickly shoving dirty plates and cups into a trash bag and walking up to him. She laid a hand on his arm, looking at him with concern.

"Yeah." He nodded, even managed a weak grin. "What can I do to help?"

Without waiting for instructions, he began stuffing the torn wrapping paper from Carlee's gifts into a trash bag while Jenna finished clearing the table.

When Claire muttered an oath, Jake and Jenna both turned to see what was wrong. Claire was standing on a chair on tiptoe, reaching for a piece of tape dangling from the end of a curtain rod.

Jenna's "Be careful!" and Jake's "Let me help you there, Claire," were both too late. The chair tipped, Claire grabbed the rod, and Claire, chair and curtain rod went crashing to the floor.

Jenna and Jake rushed to Claire's aid.

"Are you all right?" Jenna asked as Claire untangled herself and sat up.

"I-I think so." Claire started to stand, then quickly dropped back to the floor. "My ankle," she moaned.

Jenna lifted Claire's pants so she could see the ankle. It didn't look too bad. She glanced up at Jake. "I can't tell."

Jake knelt beside Claire. "Wrap those beautiful arms around me. I'm taking you to the nearest couch, lady." He waggled his eyebrows roguishly.

"That's an offer I can't refuse," Claire said.

While Jake settled Claire on the sofa, Jenna went to the kitchen for an ice pack. When she returned, she inspected Claire's foot a little closer.

"It's not broken. See, I can wiggle my toes," Claire said.

"This is no time to play hero, mom," Jenna said. "I think you should get it x-rayed."

"Hours in the waiting room, then some fool jerking my foot around, just so a doctor can give an x-ray thirty seconds of his precious golf time and bill me $500," Claire grumbled.

"Oh, stop," Jenna scolded. "You've got insurance."

"That's not the point," Claire said. But when she tried to put weight on her foot and gasped in pain, she grudgingly nodded her head. "I guess I don't have much choice, do I?"

"Damn straight." Jenna stood up. "I'll get Carlee."

She glanced at Jake doubtfully. He still looked green around the edges. "Will you be okay? Maybe you should stay here until we get back."

"No, I'm fine," Jake said, smiling to reassure her. "I want to go home and work on my book. Why not let Carlee come with me. She can play with Buster while I write."

"She'd like that better than sitting around in a waiting room," Jenna conceded.

"For hours," Claire grumbled.

"But, Jake, are you sure that—"

"I'm fine. You take care of the older generation." He winked at Claire. "I'll take care of the younger."

"The older generation is aging rapidly while you two argue it out," Claire said.

After they had Claire settled in the van with Jenna at the wheel, Jake and

Carlee waved them on their way. Minutes later, Jake watched Carlee skipping ahead of him with Buster as they trod the path to his house. He hoped he hadn't made a mistake, offering to watch her. What demons would haunt him as Carlee ran through his house, stepping on the same rugs Lizzy had stepped on, touching the same things Lizzy had touched? Would he be able to withstand the pain of seeing this little girl filling the spaces where Lizzy should have been? Yes, by god, he vowed. This is just one more battle in a war he was going to win.

But the memory of his shock when he saw the birthday cake, the pain that had slammed him in the stomach, the nausea…He couldn't discount that reaction. His sides still ached, his throat still burned, he still tasted bile.

Was he ready to fight another battle so soon?

CHAPTER FOURTEEN

Jake heard the soft patter of little feet traipsing down the hallway. Carlee had asked to use the bathroom and he'd pointed her in the right direction. Now she was coming back. For a minute he closed his eyes and listened to the light footfall so like Lizzy's. For a minute he imagined it *was* Lizzy's little feet tripping along, Lizzy's little arms pumping at her sides, Lizzy's blond head bobbing.

Two years. She's been gone for two years, he thought. She would have just finished kindergarten, would be going into the first grade in the fall.

He shut out the thoughts and turned to his laptop and Wendy. If he immersed himself in the challenges of finishing the final few pages, maybe he could ignore the leap of his heart every time he heard Carlee's step, every time he caught a glimpse of her from the corner of his eye, every time, for a split second, anticipation flared before cold logic doused the flame.

Wendy tried to flap her wings, but they were still too wet. If only the sun would come out and dry them, but the golden ball was still sleeping behind a large dark rain cloud.

"I have to get across the stream," she told Arthur Armadillo. "I have to get to the bee swarm before those men cut down our trees. But I can't fly. Will you carry me across the water, Arthur?"

The little armadillo was so proud to be

asked that his chest swelled up to twice its normal size.

"It would be my great honor to carry Wendy the Wood Nymph across the water," he said. He swallowed air until his belly puffed up like a balloon and he could float on the water. That's the way of armadillos. Then he motioned Wendy to jump on.

He wished all the woodland creatures could see him now—the squirrels who always called him donkey ears, and the raccoons who called him pig eyes, the snakes who called him turtle tank, and the beavers who called him rat tail, but especially the wild turkeys who called him bubble belly. It's a good thing he had a bubble belly, Arthur thought, or he wouldn't be able to carry Wendy across the water. Then Wendy wouldn't be able to ask the bees to help. And they wouldn't be able to stop the men from cutting down the trees.

The beavers and their dam had failed to stop the men. The squirrels with their slingshots and nuts had failed. The snakes failed without even trying, because they were afraid to get close to the men, afraid of the men's sharp axes. The bees were their last hope. And he, Arthur Armadillo, was going to carry Wendy across the water to the bees. He was not going to fail.

"I'm going to be a hero," Arthur thought. "Then they'll be sorry they made fun of me."

"Jake—" Carlee's small voice interrupted the flow of his creative juices.
"Hmmm?"
"Can I take Buster outside to play?"
Jake glanced out the window. Storm clouds were moving in, but it hadn't started raining yet. "Sure. Just play right outside the window here where I can see you, okay?"

"Okay," Carlee said, already turning away. "Come on, Buster."

"Oh," she said, suddenly stopping, "she's pretty." She was looking at a framed photo standing on a shelf of Jake's floor-to-ceiling bookcase. The photo was of a little girl about Carlee's age sitting on the flat branch of Wendy's tree, with waist-length blond hair blowing in the breeze, a funny little smile on her heart-shaped face, her huge eyes blue as the June sky above her. "Is this Lizzy?"

"Yes," Jake said softly, remembering the day he'd taken that picture. He'd convinced Lizzy that it was better to capture her little insect friends on camera rather than in her fist. They'd taken the camera along on their hike to the tree and he'd caught that perfect pose on film.

"Now I know what her spirit looks like," Carlee said, tracing a finger around Lizzy's face.

"You'd better run along and play," Jake suggested gruffly. "Before it rains."

After Carlee and Buster left, Jake's gaze remained fixed on the photo of Lizzy. Every day. He missed her every day.

Resolutely he turned back to the manuscript.

```
The water was rough, blown about by the
strong wind. Waves rushed at Arthur and
Wendy. In a few minutes it would be storming,
and they might not make it across the stream.
The little wood nymph wrapped her arms around
Arthur's neck and clung tightly.
```

Jake lost himself in the story, winding it up with a few fast-paced paragraphs. Wendy with her sharp eyes guiding the armadillo through the blinding storm, across the rough waters. The swarm of bees carrying Wendy as she led them to the woodcutters. Woodcutters with axes and saws pressed against Wendy's tree, greed mixed with anxiety, as they hurried to finish their illegal operation before they were discovered. Attack and rescue. Wendy wet, tired, triumphant, safely reunited with the ancient live oak.

He was typing, "You are my tree and I am—" when a sudden brilliant streak of lightning was followed almost immediately by a loud clap of thunder. Jake looked out the window to a sky dark with menace.

He whistled. "That sure moved in fast," he said to the empty room. He quickly typed in the last few words, hit the save button, then began printing the story. While it was printing, he went to the door to call Carlee inside. He was two steps from the door when it burst open and Carlee ran into the room, Buster at her heels. Her eyes were wide with terror.

"What is it?" Jake asked.

Carlee ran to him and huddled against his legs, drawing security from his tall frame. "I'm scared."

Jake looked down at the wide eyes, the small body. He scooped her up in his arms. "Scared of the thunder, are you?"

She nodded as one little arm curled naturally around his neck. "It's loud. It sounds mad. Like," Carlee got real close to Jake and whispered in his ear. "Like my daddy."

Jake tightened his hold protectively around Carlee, wishing he had her dad in reach of his fist. He and Jenna had never discussed her divorce. One of these days he'd have to keep his lips off her long enough to exchange a few words. Yet, despite the hormones that took over whenever they were within arms' reach of each other, he felt he knew her pretty well. He'd seen her at work, at play, interacting with family and friends, and he sensed beneath her joking exterior a serious, level-headed, loyal woman. He couldn't imagine her disrupting her family for any but the most irreparable differences. Her ex had to be guilty of some serious misconduct or character fault that Jenna couldn't find it in her mind to understand or heart to forgive. He had a pretty strong notion that the relationship between Carlee and her father had a lot to do with Jenna's decision to walk away from the marriage. Jenna wouldn't stay with a man who was a threat to Carlee's well-being.

He carried Carlee into the office and to the window where they could watch the flashes of lightning. Another bright flash and another clap of thunder were followed by a cloudburst as the heavens opened up and pelted the earth with sheets of rain.

This is the way it was that night, Jake thought. The rain coming in sheets, blinding drivers, the roads slick with water, a car hydroplaning, a tree looming in the glare of headlights—He stopped the memories. They were the stuff of nightmares.

What could he tell this little girl shivering in his arms that would make her less afraid?

The storm, which must be right overhead, was creating a cacophony of sound in the room. Streak after streak of lightning flashes were almost immediately followed by loud rumbling crashes of thunder that shook the house in their ferocity. Carlee buried her face in Jake's shoulder; her arms tightened convulsively around his neck. Even Buster scooted under the desk to hide.

Jake sank down in his desk chair and let Carlee get comfortable on his lap. "Ol' Mother Nature is just trying to dazzle us with bright smiles," he said. "And because she's so happy, she claps her great mountain-sized hands and stomps her great mountain-sized feet. And when she's in a really playful mood, like now, she jumps on one of those big, fluffy clouds like it's a giant water balloon and showers us with rain."

Carlee gazed at Jake. Her eyes were wide, but behind the fear, Jake could see the wheels turning in her active little brain. She seemed intrigued with the metaphor. She looked out the window at the rain beating against the glass. Then she looked back at Jake, pressing closer. "I don't think Mother Nature is very happy right now," she said.

Jake chucked her gently on the chin, determined to wipe the fear from her face, to make her laugh. "Of course she is. Mother Nature doesn't have a face like we lowly humans do," he said, continuing the metaphor. "Oh, no. That big sky up there that stretches from here to China and back, that's her face. So her smiles are a little different from yours and mine." He thought of Jenna's smile, sometimes mischievous when a wisecrack was about to trip off her tongue, sometimes delighted over something as simple as an orchid bud, sometimes gentle like a butterfly kiss, but always a beacon guiding him from dark memories into the light. "But in some ways they are the same. You ever noticed how your mom's smile lights up her face?"

Carlee nodded, her eyes glowing. "Like when she gave me my birthday cake?"

The cake. Jake suppressed a groan and ignored the lurch of his stomach. "Mmm-hmm. Well, you see, when Mother Nature smiles, her face lights up the same way."

As though to prove his point, a wide, long streak of lightning dazzled outside the window, followed by a rattling clap of thunder. Carlee buried her face in Jake's shirt. "Mother Nature's scary," she said.

Jake sighed. Forget metaphors. Time to try something else. "Would you like me to read you a story?"

Carlee sat up, the storm forgotten. "Do you have Wendy and the Butterfly Queen?"

"I do. But I think we'll try a new Wendy story. It's so new, it's not even bound into a book yet." He reached over and plucked his manuscript from the printer.

Carlee crossed her legs and nestled against Jake's solid chest. As Jake began to read, Buster scrambled back to his rag rug, laid his head on his paws, and with a thump of his tail and a contented sigh, prepared to listen.

* * *

Jenna drove Claire home and helped her get comfortable before leaving to pick up Carlee. A simple fracture in one of her foot bones, the doctor had said. Jenna couldn't remember the name of the bone, although she could rattle off the genus and species names for 300 orchids. Claire was now wearing a cast to just below her knee, and she was not a happy camper.

Jenna grinned, remembering their ordeal in the hospital. Claire's aversion to all things medical, combined with her willingness to let the doctors and nurses know exactly how she felt, had sped things up. They couldn't wait to be rid of her. So from start to finish it had only been about three hours rather than the five or six she had dreaded.

As she drove back to Jake's to get Carlee she was glad to note that the rain had stopped and the sun was shining with fierce determination through several scattered clouds that refused to say die. It might rain some more, or it might blow over and be hot and humid. She'd learned that thunderstorms in this part of the country often came in twos or threes. Just about the time you put your umbrella away, another storm blew in. But for now the rain had cooled the air, and she would enjoy it.

When she got to Jake's house, she rapped lightly on the door in case Carlee was napping, as she often did in the afternoons. After a few minutes without a response, she let herself in, softly calling Jake's name. If he was immersed in his writing, she didn't want to startle him with her sudden appearance. She took a few steps into the room and heard the soft murmur of voices coming from the back of the house. She followed the sound to a door on the other side of the family room. When she reached the door, she stopped, transfixed. Carlee was sitting on Jake's lap, stretching her hand up to brush at his face, her childish voice edged with concern.

"Don't be sad. Don't cry. Wendy will save the trees."

Jake had unexpectedly stopped in the middle of reading to Carlee, the situation suddenly hitting him like a sledgehammer. Carlee on his lap, her birthday, his reading her the new Wendy book. If Lizzy were alive, this is exactly what he would be doing with her. Tears had sprung to his eyes and Carlee, looking up to see why he had stopped reading, had seen them.

Jenna couldn't take her eyes off the scene as her heart warmed with love and gratitude. The first time Jake and Carlee had come face to face, Jenna had sensed danger, and from that point on she had been watching for it, expecting it. She had believed that this man holding Carlee on his lap, this man with an imagination that delighted children, with his love for children, his gentle ways, would harm her daughter. She had feared that in a moment of unconquerable anguish he would strike out, with words certainly and possibly with blows, at the injustice that had taken his little Lizzy from him. And she had worried that Carlee, a constant reminder of Lizzy, a block of salt rubbing his raw wound, would be the catalyst that would unleash Jake's rage.

She'd been wrong. Over and over Jake had proven her wrong. He'd proven her wrong each time he brought Buster over to play with Carlee. He'd proven her wrong the day he helped Carlee through the anguish of her caterpillar's death. He'd proven her wrong today at the birthday party, and even here in this house where Lizzy had lived and loved and played. And now as he held Carlee on his lap, reading her a story, he had proven her wrong yet again.

Carlee didn't show one trace of fear or temerity as she reached her little hand up to brush Jake's wet cheek. She wasn't afraid, not even a little. *That's the way it's supposed to be.* Jenna couldn't help but compare Carlee's interaction with Jake to the distorted interaction between Carlee and Ned.

Jenna had thought Jake would harm Carlee, scare her with his anguish, but instead he had healed her. Jenna's heart sang. There was hope for a relationship between her and Jake after all.

Suddenly, Carlee spotted Jenna in the doorway. With a glad cry she slid from Jake's lap and ran to her.

"Jake's reading me a new Wendy story, momma. It's kind of sad, because the bad men are going to cut down Wendy's tree. It made Jake cry, but I didn't cry because I know Wendy will save her tree."

While Carlee rattled on in a nonstop voice, Jake rose quickly, took a tissue from the desk to wipe his eyes, and turned to face Jenna.

"Dust. Dust in the eye," he said, tossing the tissue into a wastebasket.

Jenna nodded as she moved toward him. She figured the dust was more likely a memory of Lizzy, but saw no reason to challenge his story. "Thanks for taking care of Carlee. Was she any trouble?"

"No, no trouble at all. The little rug rat can eat crackers on my carpet anytime."

"I wondered when it started to storm. She's afraid of thunder."

"We made it through the storm okay. She didn't buy my explanation of the lightning and thunder, but everything was cool. I want to hear about Claire. But first can I get you something. Coffee? Soda? Water?"

"Water, please. I'm parched," Jenna said.

"Momma, can I go outside with Buster? It's stopped raining." Carlee was looking out the window, Buster beside her.

Jenna hesitated. "I don't want you running in and out, tracking mud into Jake's living room," she said.

"She can use the back door through the garage," Jake said. "I'll open the garage door for her."

A few minutes later Buster and Carlee were romping in the yard and Jake and Jenna were sitting in the office talking about Claire's broken foot.

"She'll be in a cast for six weeks," Jenna said. "And she's already getting cabin fever. She's like a snarly grizzly that got up on the wrong side of hibernation."

Jake chuckled sympathetically, watching her kissable lips, watching her white throat move as she took a long drink of water. As he watched her, he realized there was something different about her. An openness that hadn't been there before. The wariness he'd always seen in the back of her eyes was gone. Hope leaped inside Jake.

"Well," Jenna said, growing self-conscious under his intimate stare, "did you finish your writing or was Carlee too much distraction?"

"I finished the story, but speaking of distraction—" He stood, took Jenna's hand, and pulled her to her feet. "I seem to remember we were in the middle of something earlier today when Claire so rudely interrupted us."

He took the bottle of water from her hand and set it on the desk. "That's better," he said with a sigh. "Now we can pick up where we left off this morning. Let's see, I believe your hands were here." He took both her hands and placed them around his neck. Jenna remembered that explosive kiss too and anticipation sent shivers of desire racing down her body. "I believe my hands were here." He stroked his hands down her hips, cupped them around her derriere, and pulled her against him. Desire exploded where his hard body pressed between her legs. "And I know our lips were here." He bent his head and kissed her.

They did pick up where they'd left off, their need immediate, demanding. Jenna was against the desk, carried backward by the pressure of Jake's need and her eager yielding. His feet were on the floor, but he'd moved between her legs and leaned over her as she lay back against the desktop. He slid his hands under her shirt, shoved it up to expose the lacy black bra, the soft swell of breasts.

With a low cry that conveyed a need as old as earth, as new as tomorrow's dew, he buried his face in her sweet breasts, sliding his hands behind her to unhook the bra and free the peaked nipples to his seeking mouth. Jenna's soft cries of pleasure drove him into a frenzy, while her hands laced through his hair, pressing, kneading, urging him take more. Jake pressed his body between her legs.

Through his clothes and hers he felt the sizzling heat as his hard shaft found her warm center. His hand fumbled at her jeans, with the snap, with the zipper, impatient to be rid of the confining garments. His hands slipped inside the waistband, ready to tug her clothes down.

But first he dragged his head up from the Eden of her breasts and looked at her, knowing what he would see. The desire smoldering in her green eyes, the proof that she wanted him, needed him, was his completely. The look that filled him with fierce exultation, and unstoppable lust.

She moved her arms around his neck and pulled his face down, seeking the honey of his mouth, while her hand moved to his jeans and she fumbled with the zipper.

"Not here, sweet, not here," he murmured in the only moment of sanity he'd had since the kiss had started. "The bedroom." He stood, pulling her with him, unwilling to relinquish even for a minute the glorious excitement of her body against his. The movement, the pause in their lovemaking was just enough to allow the voice of reason to intrude. He remembered the vow he'd made. *The next time I get her in my arms, I'm toting her away where there are no kids, no mothers, no stopping!*

The thought made him glance out the window, look for Carlee. He saw her—and he froze. Then he jerked out of Jenna's arms and ran for the door.

Jenna, losing her support in such an abrupt fashion, nearly toppled to the floor. Straightening, she rushed after Jake, her heart pounding. Something must have happened to Carlee. What else would have made Jake run like that? She was a few steps behind him, stumbling out the door he'd left open, when she saw Carlee.

Carlee was okay. She was riding a bike in the driveway. Weak with relief, Jenna collapsed against the house, a hand pressed to her heart to slow the beat. Fleetingly she thought, "Well, she's a little wobbly, but I'd say that's a damned good first effort." Coincident with the thought, she wondered if Jake had shown her how. While those thoughts were running through her head, she zipped her jeans, hooked her bra.

Then, in the space of a minute that seemed to move in slow motion, Jenna's worst fears were realized.

"Get off! Get off the bike!" Jake shouted.

Carlee, startled by the angry shout, looked back at Jake. The bike swerved and the inexperienced little rider couldn't bring it under control. Bike and rider wobbled toward Jenna's van and crashed against the door.

By the time Jake reached them, Carlee was standing, trying to pick up the bike. Jake pulled it from her grasp, his face white. With trembling hands he straightened the huge pink bow dangling from the handlebars.

"You had no right," Jake said, in a voice low and ragged with emotion—rage or pain or both.

Carlee shrank against the car, tears welling, eyes filled with fear.

"I thought it was a birthday p-present," she said, starting to sob.

"It is," Jake said in a deadly quiet voice. "Lizzy's birthday bike."

Carlee's little hand pressed against her mouth. Her eyes got big. A strangled "Oh," escaped her lips.

By now Jenna had recovered her shock and run to Carlee's side, overhearing the exchange of words. The sight of her daughter's tear-streaked, scared face and her trembling body pressed against the car aroused every protective instinct in Jenna. She whirled on Jake, ready to do battle. But the sight of his pale anguished face, his shaking body, stopped her. He had his own demons to battle. She wouldn't add hers to the fray.

She turned to Carlee, picked her up, hugged her, kissed her, and spoke soothing words as she opened the van door and settled her inside.

Then she turned back to Jake. She sucked in a long breath to steady herself and swallow her anger, her disappointment, her aching heart. She should have trusted her first instincts. They'd tried to warn her this wouldn't work, couldn't work. "I understand what you're going through," she said, and despite her best efforts, her voice trembled. "At least, I think I do. And I hope," she swallowed a sob, "I hope you find peace." She paused to collect herself, glancing back at Carlee's tear-stained face watching them through the van window. She turned again to Jake. "But not at Carlee's expense. This is good-bye, Jake. I don't want to see you anymore, I don't want you to call me," she swallowed again, blinking back tears. "I don't want you to bring Buster over to play with Carlee."

Jake balanced the bike in one hand and stared at Jenna, stared at the green eyes, not smoldering now but burning with a steady, determined flame. Slowly her words penetrated the fog of his pain. But before he could comprehend the full import of them, she had climbed in her van and shut the door.

He couldn't move. A weight heavier than swampland was pressing against him, seeping through his body, slogging through his blood. He wanted to cry out, to stop Jenna, but all he could see were those green eyes. Green as emeralds, deep as emeralds. Eyes that said good-bye. Words clogged in his throat, crushed under the weight dragging him into the dark.

When Jenna started the van and turned it around, Carlee's tear-streaked face peered out as she feverishly rolled down her window.

"I'm s-s-sorry," she sobbed, digging the heels of her hands into her eyes. "Tell Lizzy I'm s-s-sorry."

He stood there unable to speak, unable to move, holding the bike, and watched his one chance for happiness drive away.

CHAPTER FIFTEEN

When Jenna reached the house she helped Carlee out of the van, then stormed inside. How could she have let this happen? Jake's loss of control had probably reinforced Carlee's fear of men tenfold. And it was all her fault. She'd known Jake was wrong for them the first time they'd met, from the moment he'd turned his back and walked away from Carlee. But she'd let his gentle handling of Carlee blind her judgment. Never again! Never again!

Jenna closed the door and leaned against it for a minute, appreciating the solid wood that shut out the outside world. That shut out Jake.

Was that hot rhubarb pie she smelled? Had to be. Claire always baked rhubarb pie when she was out of sorts. She said the tartness complemented her mood. They'd probably be having rhubarb pie for the next six weeks, until Claire was walking normally again.

Jenna took a few deep breaths and looked around at the familiar sight of pale yellow walls and white appliances, her small, fragrant herb garden on the window ledge, an orchid plant in a crystal vase on the table. And she began to calm down.

She lifted Carlee and perched her on the counter beside the sink, then wiped her tears away with a damp paper towel.

"You okay, honey?" she asked

Carlee nodded, but her eyes watered with fresh tears.

Claire rolled into the kitchen on an office chair. She was riding the chair like a scooter, one knee on the seat with the cast sticking out behind her, the other leg propelling her along, while she steered with the back of the chair.

"Is that your batmobile?" Jenna asked, striving to make her voice sound normal. She felt like she was falling to pieces.

"It's more comfortable than crutches," Claire said "And it keeps my hands free to do things. It also gives me a place to carry stuff." Then, seeing Jenna's anguished eyes and the tears pooling in Carlee's eyes, she asked, "What's wrong?"

"Jake's m-mad at me," Carlee said, starting to sob again.

Claire looked inquiringly at Jenna.

"I'll tell you later," Jenna said. "Right now I want to get Carlee cleaned up. She needs a bath."

A few minutes later, having left Carlee looking at her Wendy book while the tub slowly filled with water, Jenna joined her mother in the kitchen. It would take about ten minutes for the tub to fill, so over wedges of pie, tart enough to make her taste buds curl into the fetal position, Jenna told Claire the whole sad story.

"So I told him I don't want to see him any more," she finished.

Claire was silent for several seconds, slowly chewing her last bite of pie. When she had swallowed and unpuckered her mouth with a sip coffee heavily laced with cream, she said, "Because…?"

Jenna stared at her mother like she'd lost her wits. "Because?! Because he yelled at her, he terrified her. I thought she was all over being scared of men. Now she'll probably be worse than ever. He's not good for her."

"Ah. I see." Claire leaned down to put her hands under her cast and lift her leg on to a chair. "That's better," she said with a sigh.

"That's better," Jake said with a sigh. "Now let's see. I believe your hands were here…"

Jenna dragged her mind back to Claire. The cast already had a few colorful cartoons decorating it, she noticed.

"I left the rest for Carlee to color," Claire said, motioning to it.

Jenna stirred impatiently. "So, don't you think I did the right thing? I mean, I have to put Carlee's welfare first."

"Well," Claire said slowly, "maybe you should wait and see just how seriously that little altercation actually affected Carlee before you make any sweeping proclamations."

"Little altercation? That was no little altercation. Jake was shaking with fury—or something—and Carlee was trembling with fright."

"Yes, it does sort of run in the family," Claire mused as though to herself.

"What's that supposed to mean?"

"Oh, I just remember how terrified I was when my dad got out the strap. They used a strap in those days, you know. He only used it on me a couple of times in my whole childhood, and in retrospect, I'm sure I deserved it. I was a terror."

Jenna knew. She'd heard a few tales of Claire's childhood.

"I realize now he didn't even hit me hard. But I sure was terrified when he got out that strap. It didn't turn me into a sniveling coward though. I knew he loved me and I felt secure in that love. I never doubted his love, not for a minute."

"That was different," Jenna said, a little doubtfully.

"No, honey," Claire said. "That was normal. Ned was different."

"And Jake is different," Jenna insisted, her chin lifted in a stubborn gesture. "Carlee has suffered enough at the hands of a man. I'm not going to let it happen again."

Jenna stood, not willing to listen to Claire's arguments. Claire had been partial to Jake ever since the first day she'd laid eyes on him tangled up with Jenna under the red hibiscus. Claire was too persuasive, and Jenna didn't trust herself to not let Claire persuade her.

"I'm going to get Carlee into the tub," she said. "She'll need help washing her hair."

"Oh, by the way," Claire said as Jenna started for the stairs, "the phone's not working. I tried to call Phil to let him know about my foot—figured if I played on his sympathy it would be worth a few dinners out—but the line was dead. Guess the lightning hit a box somewhere. Just thought I'd let you know in case you were expecting a call. So you wouldn't be upset at not getting one."

"Don't start, Claire," Jenna said, escaping up the stairs.

Carlee's bath did not take long; she was still too upset to linger in the tub with her toys. Once dressed, she climbed up on Jenna's bed. While Jenna worked a comb through her wet curls, Carlee asked in a tiny, worried voice, "Will Jake let Buster play with me now?"

Jenna didn't know how to answer. If she told the truth, that she'd forbidden Jake to bring Buster over, it would make her sound like a villain. That didn't appeal to her. On the other hand, she couldn't deliberately lie and make Jake the villain, though he was more deserving of the title than she was, Jenna reasoned.

"I don't think Jake will be bringing Buster over for a while," she said. There wasn't any chance that Carlee would forget about Buster, and she could already hear those pleas plaguing her all day, every day. "So," she added brightly, "I guess it's about time we got you your very own dog."

Carlee pulled away from Jenna and gave her a reproachful look. "Buster's my best friend. I don't want another dog. It would make Buster sad. He'd think he's not my best friend anymore." She glared resolutely at her mother, then added, "If Jake wasn't mad at me, I bet he'd bring Buster over."

"Well," Jenna said helplessly, searching for a good response, wishing she had Jake's imagination, "well, we'll talk about it tomorrow." Good grief, just like Scarlet O'Hara. "Right now I need to cook dinner. You know grandma's got her leg in a cast. Which reminds me, she wants you to help her color it."

"I don't want to," Carlee said ungraciously.

Jenna sighed. "Well, at least trot outside and check your butterfly garden while I'm cooking. There will probably be some broken branches and things to clean up after that storm we just had." The butterfly garden usually kept Carlee busy and happy. This time Carlee didn't look too happy, but she mumbled okay.

Jenna felt a pang as she watched the dejected little figure descend the stairs.

* * *

Jake couldn't erase the image of Jenna's eyes. The good-bye he'd seen there, the finality. He carried the bike back into the garage, to its usual place, where he'd originally put it before Lizzy's birthday. He'd never touched it after her death. Once it was in its rightful place, he stared at it. Waiting for some semblance of peace to return. None came. He stood there looking down at the bike, trying to analyze his feelings.

What was so important about the bike? What was so important about the bike that because of it he had scared poor little Carlee half to death and chased Jenna out of his life? It was just a bike, after all. It didn't change anything. It could be sitting in this garage, it could be leading the Disney Electrical Parade down Main Street, it could be dumped in the Gulf. It didn't change anything. Lizzy was dead.

I've been in denial. The thought was illuminating, but somehow it didn't surprise him. As long as Lizzy's bike was sitting here, all beribboned for her birthday, he could still believe. Still believe he'd wake up one morning and find everything had been a bad dream. He'd give Lizzy the bike and teach her how to ride. When she wobbled, he'd catch her, he wouldn't let her fall. They'd laugh about it, it would all be so funny, her wobbly attempts. Then they'd go for ice cream to celebrate what a quick learner she was. She'd have two scoops of strawberry with chocolate syrup and whipped cream. She'd ask for extra cherries and the waitress would add a spoonful.

A chokinging sob climbed up Jake's chest, followed by another and another. He fell to his knees, dropping his head in his hands. "You're dead, Lizzy. I know that. But I miss you so much, princess. I miss you so much." The sobs continued, great, heaving sobs of anguish, spewing forth all the grief he'd kept bottled up for two long painful years.

It was many minutes, closer to an hour, before the sobs lessened and finally stopped. Jake sat on the garage floor, spent, empty. So empty. He looked around, surprised to see it was still daylight. He glanced at his watch. Only eight o'clock. He felt like he'd been there for hours, days. He felt totally bereft, but also more at peace than he'd felt since Lizzy's death.

He had finally let Lizzy go.

Buster was lying at Jake's feet, his head resting on Jake's knee, watching his master with worried eyes. Jake scratched behind his ears, then stood up. He went inside, splashed cold water on his face and cleaned up. When he was presentable, he went back to the garage and started to wheel the bike outside, Buster prancing at his heels.

Jake spoke to the dog, though it was himself he was trying to convince. "Lizzy can't ride this bike, but I know a little girl who can. And I know if Lizzy could talk to me, she'd tell me to give this bike to Carlee."

At mention of Carlee's name, Buster barked excitedly.

Jake laid the bike in the back of his Land Rover.

This is good-bye, Jake. I don't want to see you anymore, I don't want you to call me. I don't want you to bring Buster over to play with Carlee.

Well, she hadn't said anything about a bike. And he had to square things with Carlee, apologize to her, make her understand she hadn't done anything wrong.

Buster was whining anxiously, trotting back and forth.

"Sorry, boy," Jake said, grasping him firmly by the collar and hooking him to the chain. "Not this time. I'm in enough trouble without any help from you."

Buster objected vehemently to being left behind, barking frenziedly and pulling at his chain. Jake had never seen the dog so worked up, but he knew taking Buster along would compound the difficulty of explaining and apologizing to a certain neighbor who was in no mood to listen to anything he had to say. She had already said her final good-bye. With her words. With her eyes.

When he got to Jenna's he took the bike from his vehicle and was wheeling it toward the patio when Jenna came out the back door.

She stopped short when she saw him, her first, involuntary look of gladness replaced immediately by a frown.

"What are you doing here?"

"I came to apologize to Carlee, and to bring her the bike. I'd like her to have it."

"I told you," Jenna began in a fierce, determined voice, "that I don't want—"

Jake held up a hand to silence her. "I know. I know. But I want to square things with Carlee. Please, Jenna. I have to make her understand it wasn't her fault."

Jenna hesitated. Would it do more good or more harm to let Jake apologize to Carlee, she wondered. She thought about the dejected little figure walking down the stairs. Surely it would be beneficial if Jake explained that she hadn't done anything wrong.

Jake watched her, knowing she was weighing the pros and cons. And knowing if she gave in, it would be for Carlee's sake, not his. There was no welcome in her green eyes.

"I'll just apologize to Carlee and then be on my way," Jake said, swallowing the lump he felt forming in his throat.

"Okay," Jenna finally agreed. "She's in the butterfly garden. I was just going there myself."

Jake parked the bike beside the patio and they walked side-by-side toward the butterfly garden. Side by side, not touching, not talking.

But Carlee wasn't in the butterfly garden.

"She must have gone back inside," Jenna said, a little puzzled.

They walked back to the house. Side by side, not touching, not talking. Jake followed Jenna inside, through the kitchen and living room into the office.

"Have you seen Carlee?" she asked Claire, who was at the computer.

Claire turned, registering some surprise, followed by a delighted smile, when she saw Jake. "No. I thought she was out in her butterfly garden."

"She must be upstairs," Jenna said, heading for the stairs.

Jake lingered to talk to Claire. "How's the foot?"

"About like you'd expect any appendage that's been locked into position and wrapped in concrete," she grumbled. "I understand you're on Jenna's hit list."

"Yeah, I made an ass of myself."

"Ah, she'll forgive you. That's what women are best at."

"Maybe," Jake said. *He couldn't forget her eyes.*

Jenna hurried back into the room. "She's not upstairs. Where could she be?" Her voice held a note of panic.

"She must be outside," Jake said. "We probably just missed her the first time."

He headed outside, Jenna at his heels. A thorough search outside, and another search inside, convinced them that Carlee was nowhere to be found. She had disappeared.

Jenna was frantic, and she wasn't alone. Jake and Claire felt the same panic. Thunderclouds were rolling in again, and it would be dark within the hour.

"Where could she be?" Jenna cried. "There's no place to go except the woods. Do you think she went back to your house, Jake?" she asked, hope lighting her face.

"I'll check," he said, running toward his Land Rover as he spoke.

Jenna and Claire waited frantically for him to return. He was back within minutes, shaking his head as they queried him with anxious looks.

"I was going to bring Buster to help us look, but the stupid dog managed to pull the anchor free and was gone." He couldn't believe Buster had managed to pull the hurricane anchor out of the cement. He must be dragging the whole fifteen feet of chain along behind him. Jake shook his head. He didn't have time to worry about that now.

"We have to find her," Jenna said. "Mom, call 911. Get some help."

Claire snatched up the phone, listened, and replaced it slowly. "The line's still dead." Her lips started to tremble.

"I think," Jake said slowly, "I know where she might have gone."

Both women looked at him hopefully.

"Where?"

"Wendy's tree," he said.

"But—why would she go there?" Jenna asked.

"Because—because she wanted to tell Lizzy she was sorry. Sorry she rode her bike." Jake felt a cold fear clutch at him as he realized just how much his outburst must have affected Carlee. Because his gut instinct told him that was exactly where Carlee had gone. Where they would find her—if she knew the way, if she didn't get lost, if she reached it before dark, before the storm hit.

He didn't waste any more time speculating. He hurried out the door and into the darkening gloom, the first drops of rain splashing across his face as he went. Jenna was right beside him as he raced along the edge of the woods toward the twisting path leading to Wendy's tree. They didn't talk this time because they were running too fast to exchange words. Every few minutes one of them would call out Carlee's name.

This is my fault. If anything happened to Carlee—Jake tried to keep his thoughts on the positive side, but horrific images kept intruding. Had she even entered the woods or was she lying hurt somewhere? And if she were in the woods, was she lost? How would they find her if she wasn't at the tree? Rain was beating in their eyes now, wet sheets of rain driving through the trees, puddling below their feet.

A streak of lightning, sharp and white, speared into the woods, followed instantly by a rending crack of wood, and a deafening clap of thunder. Would Carlee be standing under a tree during the lightning storm, he wondered. Did she know that was dangerous? And he knew that you didn't even have to be standing where the lightning struck. It could travel underground and strike you from the feet up.

Terror urged him faster, faster, like the night Lizzy had died, with the storm blinding him, his car skidding, forcing him to slow down. He felt like he was reliving that nightmare. But this time, this time he couldn't be too late. Please God, please God, he prayed.

He thought of Carlee's little arms curling around his neck, the way she frowned and concentrated when her inquisitive little brain was trying to figure something out, her girlish laughter that lifted his heart. He wanted to watch Carlee grow up. Wanted to teach her things, like how to roller skate and dance. He wanted a future that included her. Please God, please God. Let her be okay. Give me this chance. And Jake realized that he wanted that chance more than anything else in this world. Wanted a future with Jenna and Carlee. Claire had been right when she'd talked about love. He still loved Lizzy, would always love Lizzy, with all his heart. But now he also loved Carlee with all his heart and Jenna too. The mysterious circle of love. Why had it taken him so long to find that out? Don't take her away from me, God, please God.

This was her fault, Jenna thought as she raced behind Jake, gasping for breath, holding the sharp pain in her side, but refusing to stop. Her fault. Carlee had just wanted to play with Buster, but would she let her? Oh, no, she couldn't do that. Carlee thought Jake was mad at her, that he wouldn't let her play with Buster because he was mad. But did Jenna tell her the truth? Oh, no, she didn't want to do that. She's got to be all right, she's got to be, Jenna thought, willing herself to believe it.

As soon as Jake had mentioned Wendy's tree, Jenna knew that's where Carlee had gone. She knew Carlee talked to Lizzy when Jake took her there to play with Buster and eat lunch in Wendy's tree. Sometimes Carlee told her about the imaginary conversations she carried on with Jake's little "princess."

She, too, remembered Carlee's anguished cry as she was driving away from Jake's house. "Tell Lizzy I'm s-s-sorry." Yes, it would be just like Carlee to decide to come and tell Lizzy herself. She must have figured that if she apologized to Lizzy, Jake wouldn't be mad at her anymore.

I should have told her, Jenna agonized. I should have told her Jake wasn't mad at her, that she hadn't done anything wrong, that she could play with Buster. I should have told her. If only she's okay, she can play with Buster every day, eat with him, sleep with him. Just let her be okay.

Another shaft of lightning struck close by, followed by a clap of thunder. She's so scared of thunder, Jenna thought. Please God, please God, keep her safe. Don't let her be too afraid.

As abruptly as the storm had blown in, it passed on, carrying its wind and rain inland. By the time Jake and Jenna reached the clearing around Wendy's tree, the last of the clouds were fading in the distance. Frantically, their eyes searched through the darkening gloom—settling on a small figure huddled on the ground against the base of the great tree, Buster sitting beside her.

"Carlee!" Jenna cried, tears of relief and joy stinging her eyes. She ran to Carlee, Jake beside her. As Jenna drew closer, she saw Carlee's arms wrapped tightly around the dog's neck, and Buster with one paw resting protectively on her leg.

Carlee heard Jenna's call and scrambled to her feet. She ran toward them, not into Jenna's waiting arms, not even seeing Jenna's waiting arms. It was Jake she made a beeline for, Jake's arms she hurdled herself into, practically climbing his body until she could wrap her arms around his neck and cling tightly.

"I'm sorry Jake. I'm so sorry. Please don't be mad at me."

Jake was laughing and crying and kissing Carlee's face all over, reaching out to pull Jenna into the embrace.

"Oh, Carlee," he said. "I'm not mad at you. I never was. It was wrong of me to yell at you. And I love you, sweetheart. I love you."

Carlee's face broke into the smile he loved to see. "I love you too," she said shyly, burying her face in his shoulder.

"You scared us, darling," Jenna said, hugging Carlee, patting her, touching her, kissing her. "We were so scared."

"I wanted to tell Lizzy I'm sorry for riding her bike," Carlee said. "But then it started to thunder, and I got scared so I hid under the tree. I was glad when Buster came to stay with me."

Reminded of Buster, Jake looked down at the dog. Sure enough, all fifteen feet of thick chain and the heavy hurricane anchor were still attached to his collar. He noticed blood around Buster's neck where the collar must have chaffed it raw while Buster was trying to break loose. Jake thought about how agitated the dog had been when he'd chained him up.

"His instincts must have told him Carlee was in danger," he said.

"Yes," Jenna agreed, reaching up to stroke his cheek, "just as Carlee's instincts told her you're a good man, Jake Corbin." Just as Carlee's instincts had told her Ned was not such a good man. Jenna could not remember any time in Carlee's young life ever seeing her rush into Ned's arms. Or even walk into them impulsively.

Surprised, Jake looked at her. "How can you say that after what I did?"

"Because it's true." Jenna laughed, relief and happiness flooding over her. She was drenched to the skin and the stitch in her side felt like a knife wound, but she didn't feel anything but love. In that instant, Jenna knew without a doubt that she loved Jake Corbin. And she was pretty sure he felt the same way too. She laughed again. She couldn't seem to stop laughing. She was in Jake's arms and Carlee was safe. Life couldn't get better than this.

Jake was laughing too, his relief and joy as great as hers. They clung to each other while the laughter bubbled and finally died away, and his blue, blue eyes raked across her face, fastened on her lips, darkened to midnight. She felt the wanting flood through her and leaned into him. The arm encircling her waist tightened, and his hand slipped lower, caressing her thigh. Oh yes, she thought. Oh yes, it can get better.

Jake lowered his head around Carlee and Jenna stretched into his kiss.

"Much, much better," she murmured.

"Momma, Jake," Carlee piped. "Let's go. I'm hungry."

Jake raised his head and slid his mouth to Jenna's ear. "The next time I get you in my arms," he whispered, "I'm going to tote you…"

He broke off as Carlee tugged impatiently at his shirt.

"You were saying?" Jenna prompted.

"Never mind," Jake said with a rueful grin. "It was just one of those impossible ideas writers of fiction are so fond of."

They started walking out of the clearing. One of Jake's arms cradled Carlee against his chest. The other arm was wrapped firmly around Jenna.

Behind them Wendy's tree sighed in the evening breeze and dipped its branches as though nodding approval.

EPILOGUE

Jenna stood next to her orchid display, nervously drumming her fingers against her thighs. The judges had been deliberating the scores for over an hour.

"Momma, what's taking so long?" Carlee said, tugging on Jenna's shirt. "When can I name the orchid?"

"I don't know how much longer, Carlee. Carlee Beauty," Jenna added with a grin, giving Carlee's ear a playful tug. She already thought of the orchid as Carlee's Beauty. It had better win. She strained her neck trying to get a glimpse of the judges sitting around the table at the far end of the room. It was no use; there were too many people milling about. "And remember, we might not earn a First Class Certificate," she cautioned. Her hopes were as high as Carlee's, probably higher, but she felt she had to prepare her daughter for the possibility of the unthinkable happening. *I really want this. I really, really want this.*

Jake held out a hand to Carlee. "Come on, wood nymph, let's go find some drinks. All this waiting works up a thirst."

Jenna gave Jake a grateful smile and he responded with a mischievous wink. Carlee had behaved remarkably well all evening, but as time wore on, she was becoming more and more restless. It was an hour past her normal bedtime and Jenna was facing the possibility of having to leave before the judges rated Carlee's Beauty.

"Can we get either of you two ladies a drink?" Jake asked, looking from Jenna to Claire, who was sitting on a stool with her cast propped on the rail of Jenna's display booth.

"No thanks, I'm fine," Jenna said distractedly, her attention already back on the opposite end of the room.

"Well, I'd love a bottle of water, cold and wet," piped in Claire. "But what I really need is something to slide inside my cast and scratch until my eyes cross."

"I can do that for you," said Phil Averies, from behind Claire.

"Phil!" Claire gasped in surprise, turning toward him. He was flexing his fingers and grinning roguishly. She batted at them as he wriggled them toward her leg. "What are you doing here?"

"I just knocked off for the night. I called your house to see how Jenna did. When I didn't get an answer, I figured you were still here."

He twitched his fingers. "So how about...?"

She swatted at them again, uttering a laugh. A laugh that sounded almost like a giggle.

A giggle? Jenna exchanged an amused glance with Jake, who grinned and winked.

As Jake walked away with Carlee, Jenna's thoughts of Carlee's Beauty were overridden for a moment by thoughts of Jake. Perhaps some day Jake would feel comfortable enough with the thought of marriage to try it again. She wouldn't push him. But she had thought about it. And when she did, it always brought up another question. What about Claire?

Her eyes slid to Claire and Phil. Phil had found a chair and placed it close to Claire. He was sitting with one arm across the back of Claire's chair, his head close to hers as he spoke into her ear, shutting out the noise and hubbub around them. Jenna pretended to be rearranging an orchid as she watched them from the corner of her eye. It looked like—yes, no question—Phil was not just murmuring into Claire's ear. He was nibbling it.

How funny, Jenna thought. Her irascible mother sitting in the middle of a crowded convention hall, having her ear nibbled by a handsome, white-haired lawyer. And enjoying it. It was kind of—neat, kind of—poignant. But extraordinarily funny.

A sudden rise in noise around the judging table brought Jenna's attention back to the business at hand. As she craned her neck to see what was going on, she noticed a clerk walking away from the judging table, a gorgeous yellow and orange orchid cradled in his arms. Behind him, several people who appeared to be from the media got their cameras and notebooks ready. Had that orchid won some kind of award? She followed the clerk with her eyes until he passed out of sight before once again returning her gaze to the judging table. A few minutes later another clerk walked off carrying a brilliant purple orchid.

"Oh, this is so nerve-wracking," she said to Claire.

"Calm down, Jenna," Claire admonished. "It won't be the end of the world if you don't get a certificate."

"Easy for you to say," Jenna groaned. "My orchids are my world."

"Right," Claire replied in a voice that said "wrong." As though to emphasize her comment, she looked pointedly at Jake and Carlee, returning with their drinks.

Jake handed Claire a bottle of water. "Sorry, they didn't have any rulers with groping fingers."

Before Claire could come back with a witticism, he turned to Jenna and offered her a bottle. "Just in case you changed your mind."

She took it gratefully and rubbed it against her forehead. "Mmm, feels good. Thanks."

"Anytime." Eyes gleaming, he used his thumbs to wipe at the moisture beading on Jenna's face where the bottle sweated. "Anytime," he repeated softly. He wasn't talking about water, and they both knew it.

"Momma. Momma…" Carlee tugged at Jenna's arm, trying to turn her around. "That man has our orchid." She pointed toward a clerk walking Jenna's way with an orchid held aloft. It was hers all right. Each of the dozen blooms was large and dazzling white with vibrant magenta spots and a splendid, brilliant amethyst lip. "Now can I name it?"

"Let's wait and see, honey." Jenna took a deep, steadying breath. Had Carlee's Beauty won an award? Or was the clerk just bringing it back because the judges were finished rating it? She felt Jake's hand grasp hers and squeeze encouragingly.

Carlee was fairly dancing with impatience. Claire and Phil watched hopefully.

When the clerk was finally close enough to hear her, Carlee started jumping up and down. "Did we win? Do I get to name the flower?"

Claire reached over and put a restraining hand on Carlee's shoulder, but it was little help against Carlee's exuberance.

"Jenna Kincaid?" the clerk asked.

"Yes," Jenna said, swallowing nervously.

"Congratulations!" The clerk beamed at Jenna. "Your orchid has won the highest rating so far today. It scored 94 points out of 100! I just need to know the orchid's new name and we can issue you a first class certificate."

Jenna felt the air rush out of her lungs in one quick whoosh. Tears of happiness stung her eyes. She stooped and scooped Carlee into a hug. "We did it, honey, we did it."

Wiping tears away, she stood shakily and leaned into Jake's solid strength. "Okay, my daughter is going to name it. Carlee," she said, with a wide grin she couldn't have wiped off her face with a dust mop, "tell the man the name you've chosen for this soon-to-be-famous-the-world-over orchid."

Carlee looked at the orchid, then up at Jenna, then up at Jake.

"The clerk's waiting," Jenna urged gently.

Carlee took a deep breath. "The orchid's name—" she swallowed and looked up at Jake again. "The orchid's name is Princess Lizzy," she announced in a clear voice.

The clerk began to write. "Is that Lizzy with two zees?" he asked, glancing up.

Jenna stared at Carlee, too astounded to say a word. Her mother and Jake and Phil all seemed to be in an equal state of astonishment.

Carlee didn't answer the clerk. She was looking at Jake, suddenly looking uncertain. She swallowed. "Now Lizzy will be in orchid gardens all over the world," she said in a small voice. "I thought—"

Jake stooped to pull her into his arms. "You thought right. It's a beautiful name. Thank you," he said, brushing curls away from her face and kissing her cheek. He brushed at his eyes and pulled Carlee into a bear hug. "Thank you," he whispered again.

"Yes, that's with two zees," Jenna told the clerk, feeling a smile stretching across her face.

Jake was still stooping beside Carlee when the clerk walked away. He slipped to one knee and looked up at Jenna. "I was going to wait until later, but it's a shame to lose an opportunity when I'm kneeling in front of you anyway," he said, pulling a small box from his pocket. "I love you, Jenna Kincaid. Would you do this moody, sex-crazed, struggling fiction writer the honor of being his wife?"

Jenna's smile faltered as tears filled her eyes. She pressed a hand to her mouth to stop the trembling. All she could do was nod through her tears.

Jake flipped open the box as he stood up. From inside, he removed a sparkling diamond set between two small emeralds in a gleaming band of gold.

"I had them add the emeralds because they remind me of your eyes," he said softly, slipping the ring onto Jenna's finger. "I hope you like it."

"Oh, Jake," she said, sniffing back sobs, "I love it. And I love you."

Through her tears she noticed another ring lying in the box. Jake saw her look of confusion and picked it up. It was a small silver and turquoise friendship ring. "I know when you marry, you also marry the family," he said, turning to Carlee. "So, little wood nymph, will you let me be your daddy?"

She giggled, then rested her chin on her hand while she gave it some serious thought. Jake held his breath, wondering what was going on in that little head. "Does that mean Buster will get to live with us?" she asked.

"Well, yes, I suppose it does. It's a package deal. Where I go, he goes."

"Okay," she shouted, holding out her finger, just as she'd seen Jenna do. Jake slipped the ring on the small hand, then kissed her on the cheek. "I love you, little wood nymph."

Carlee wrapped her arms around Jake's neck. "I love you too," she whispered shyly.

Claire made a loud hmph sound. "I don't see a ring in that box for me."

"The only person giving you a ring is going to be me," Phil said gruffly.

Claire stared at him, for once in her life too flustered to speak.

Jenna, so often the brunt of Claire's wisecracks, was delighted at such a rare moment of silence in her mother's life, but she was too busy to fully appreciate it. She was wrapped in Jake's arms, lost in his kiss, anticipating a rare moment in her own life—some time alone with her fiancé.

THE END

Printed in the United States
45333LVS00005B/250-291